A Santa Cruz Love Story

Jai Lev

Originally published in paperback by Sunrise Publications, September 2013
3070 Prather Lane, Santa Cruz, CA 95065

Edited by: Iona Singleton
Art Direction, Design and layout: Jerad MacLean (CanyonGraphicArts.com)

Printed in the United States of America

Is this a true story? Who can say? And anyhow, what is the truth? Most of what we remember never happened the way we remember it. What is true, is this is my story. With the exception of recognized spiritual leaders, names have been changed to maintain peoples' privacy.

To my gracious editor, Iona Singleton, and to all those friends and family who held me up when I was falling down, I offer my gratitude and dedication of this book.

"There are three ascending levels of how one mourns. With tears—that is the lowest. With silence—that is higher. And with a song—that is the highest."

— Abraham Joshua Heschel, <u>I Asked for Wonder</u>

Days before Eileen crossed, three musicians came to the back porch to lead *kirtan*. They came with tabla and harmonium. Eileen's bedroom window was open so she could hear melodies sweet to her heart. Thirty of us sat in lawn chairs singing *bhajans*. A friend held my hand as I struggled to sing. She turned to me and said, "You are losing your beloved, Jay, and Santa Cruz is losing its Queen."

Red Tulips

1983

I met her at a post Christmas toy swap party. My kids were the charity case because I'm Jewish and the only gifts Natasha and Gabriel each receive for Chanukah are a pair of wool socks.

The four mothers and I were playing a board game and every time Eileen rolled a winning number, she laughed. It was the sound of angels playing tag.

She lived in the countryside, had a daughter eight years old and a son three years younger. She owned a tofu factory and created a popular once-a-month women's gathering named The Women's Cooking and Terrorist Society.

I owned a five acre farm, drove a pick-up truck with a busted window crank, smoked a lot of cannabis and my hair looked like Harpo meets Einstein. I didn't even stand out in the hippy hierarchy. I didn't play guitar, never went to India and had no family trust.

I was a house husband with two kids and a wife. Natasha was ten. She rode unicorns in her dream time. Gabriel was seven. He sailed on a raft with Thor Heyerdahl in his bunk bed at night.

Debbie and I decided to make the role reversal after she completed her doctorate. She wanted to be a professional. I wanted to be lazy. Of course I had no idea what being a housewife entailed or I would have never agreed to the switch.

Debbie was genuinely friendly, warm and happy. In keeping with the fashion of the 1960s she had straight brown hair reaching to her waist. Not tall enough to dance in a chorus line, nevertheless she had calves the size of biceps from folk dancing four nights a week. She was sweet, thoughtful and kind. My grandmother liked her.

I was neurotic and my mood swings could keep pace with a hectic game of tether ball. Debbie's mother thought her daughter should have continued dating the accountant.

Debbie was offered an attractive job in Eugene. It's a major career move and she's ecstatic. I didn't imagine the role reversal might include relocating to an urban environment at a time when I wanted to move further into the mountains.

She starts work in two weeks. Until we find a place to rent, she'll stay with a friend down there while I pack our belongings.

Whatever couldn't be packed in a box wasn't going to fit in Eugene. If it was kept inside a barn, it wasn't likely to find a place in a three bedroom house on a cul de sac.

Natasha's pony was adopted by a neighbor. The rabbits were freed from their cages and new homes were found for the kittens. What to do with the ninety pounds of soybeans, filling a small barrel in a corner of the barn, was a more serious challenge.

I purchased the soybeans as insurance against apocalyptic famine and because Mother Earth News advised self sufficiency. Looking at them I was reminded of the fact that Eileen owned a tofu factory. A friend at the food co-op gave me Eileen's phone number and I called to see if she was interested in the soybeans.

It's been a damp and dreary month, but today the sky was clear blue. I've never known anyone like her. When she laughs the sunflowers turn to face her. She's six years younger than me, has thick milk chocolate shoulder-length wavy hair, dimpled cheeks, a mischievous smile and curves.

Some hippy women wear two skirts as a fashion statement. I've nicknamed her "Three Skirts." She has a giant floor loom in the living room where she is weaving a Navajo rug. A spinning wheel stands in a corner. She has vegetable starts on every windowsill and art books line the shelves alongside a stand-up easel. She keeps a collection of Indian arrowheads she found on the banks of the

Columbia River when she was a kid.

She was chosen Homecoming Queen by the football team in high school and I wondered what the heck I was doing socializing with her. Where I grew up we did not have homecoming queens. We did not have football teams. We had knife fights.

She spent high school playing varsity basketball and necking in the park overlooking the river. I spent high school smoking Camels behind a fence. Being with her is like being in a soap commercial.

We spent the day talking and I was late picking up the kids from school. I'm going back to visit her tomorrow. I was thinking about a Leonard Cohen song in which the woman peels the man oranges, all the way from China. I didn't make any progress in packing today and we're moving next weekend.

The soybeans were old and there was no sense bringing all of them unless they were still usable, so I only brought a sample. Before getting in the truck I snipped a half dozen red tulips from my garden to bring as well. Her house was a white frame building in the center of the next hobbitville east of town. Obviously, the tofu factory was located elsewhere.

"Here are the soybeans," I said, handing them to her.

She looked bewildered. "Are these all that you brought?"

"They're just a sample."

"Come in. Would you like a cup of fresh mint tea?"

"Okay, but I have to be honest with you. I don't really care about the soybeans. I'm moving to Eugene next week and after meeting you at Camille's house last month, I wanted to know who you are. By the way, where's your factory?"

"I sold it two months ago."

We visited throughout the week. We spent an afternoon in the dark recess of a tavern sharing one beer. Another day we ventured to a mountain waterfall and I nearly went swimming until the snow melt touched my toes. I studied her art work like a curator for the Metropolitan Museum of Art and her vegetable starts like Mr. Burpee.

It was a cultural exchange program. I showed her how to make a whistle by blowing into a tire valve cap. She showed me how to do it with a blade of grass. I showed her how to shuffle. She showed me how to glide.

She thought I was funny. I thought she was a rainbow. She liked the way my mind worked. I liked the way her soul danced. She was light and easy during a week when I could have been ashes in yesterday's fire. When we said goodbye on Friday, I was saying goodbye to someone I'd known all my life. I was also aware that packing the house had become a secondary interest and the kids had filed a missing person's report on me with the police.

The neighbors who helped pack the U-Haul promised to visit. The last to leave was Grandpa.

Grandpa Sorensen was a retired farmer who lived on the other side of the road. At age fifteen, he traveled alone from Norway to Wyoming to live with a family that came from his native village. Eventually he made it to Oregon where he married, raised a family and grew strawberries which frequently won first prize at the County Fair.

Long hours in the fields prevented him from spending a lot of time with his own children when they were young, so when Natasha was born he seized the opportunity to become an honorary Grandpa. As the years went by, he and I became more like a father and son and no matter how poorly my garden grew, he was always proud of me.

Farm people are often stoic about life and Grandpa was no exception. In the course of his life, he had stacked up his share of grief and sorrow and I had never known him to show any of it. But we stood there holding each other and we couldn't pull ourselves away.

Eugene's grey skies mirrored my mood. Debbie had an immediate friendship circle at her office, but I spent most days alone and couldn't sleep at night. Lying in bed I could hear an occasional car moving down the street and the constant low hum of a street lamp but the world was mostly silent.

The casual chatter of crickets spreading gossip was gone. The bullfrogs' loud boasting was absent. The senseless snorting of a neighbor's horse had disappeared. The birds had stopped singing and I was in the mind of Edgar Allen Poe without his laudanum.

In our farm town I had been an active member of the community. I wrote a column for the local paper and founded a theatre company. I could list every store that gave away free coffee and I had the movie schedule taped to the refrigerator for the upcoming three months. When I walked down the street, people waved to me.

In Eugene, even the dentist didn't recognize me without first looking at my x-rays. I took to wearing a name badge to sleep at night so I'd be sure to be me in the morning. My ankles swelled. I could barely walk. On the farm I spent the majority of time walking on dirt. In Eugene I spent all day standing on concrete.

One morning when I was playing solitaire and cheating, I noticed a vague, gauzy image of an emaciated old man in dirty undershirt and boxer shorts on the living room paneling. I had never seen a ghost, but this apparition definitely fit the description.

"You need a shave," I said with bravado, to hide my fear.

The ghost didn't answer and his image eventually evaporated.

He returned often. He never moved from his reclining position and he never spoke to me. If Gabriel hadn't desperately needed me, the ghost and I might have wound up as matching gargoyles for the atrium at a loony bin.

Gabriel is likely to be held back a year in school because he isn't able to read on par with the other kids. This past year he's bounced between two alternative free schools and home schooling where he mostly idled away his time. This has to change. Who the heck fails second grade?

It was two months before school ended and if Gabriel couldn't read on grade level, he was going to repeat second grade. We had already held him back a year from starting school because he was small for his age.

The teacher loaned me a copy of the primer and I was given a reason for being awake each afternoon at 3:00 p.m.

Effortlessly he progressed into the first reader. We conjured new conclusions to the stories, the more macabre the better. The little train that could, blew a gasket and Horton snatched a Who and ate it for dinner.

By the time his classmates were ready for graduation, Gabriel was in the advanced reading group.

Eileen was in town attending a conference. We met for tea. Debbie was not pleased that I was going without her to meet another woman.

While I was mal-adjusting to Eugene, Eileen was making plans to wander. The tofu business was finished and her marriage collapsed. In its wake, she and her best friend, Sita, had taken their kids on an extended road trip that included ceremonies with Native American elders and travel with Yogi Bhajan.

She and Sita are currently living in the Santa Cruz mountains. One minute she reminds me of dandelion snow, the next moment she's alpine paintbrush. I forgot how much I enjoyed her company.

Meanwhile, Natasha is insistent on attending Hebrew School and having a Bat Mitzvah. I am ambivalent about the idea, probably because I'm ambivalent about my relationship to Judaism, but she has convinced me of her sincerity.

Walking to temple became a Saturday morning ritual. Natasha bought gum at the 7-11 while I lit a joint. She waved to people she recognized. I waved my hands in front of me.

"How come you keep waving to people you don't know, Daddy?"

"What makes you think I'm waving at anybody? I'm making sure I don't walk into a lamp post."

There were twenty people who attended services. The majority were in their thirties and forties, half of them were women. Natasha and I took seats in the back row. When we sat, we concentrated on following the prayers being read out loud. When the congregation rose for prayer, I rocked back and forth with the best of them. Until people got to know me better, they all assumed I was pious.

Natasha enjoyed the strong women, those who sang the prayers with voices like caramel and who tapped out rhythms on their prayer books like court dancers in King David's courtyard.

I liked the three older men who were hard of hearing. They spent most of the morning talking out loud to each other.

Sometimes when their voices drowned out the rabbi, he would stop the service and say, "Can we please have a little quiet?"

"What did he say?" one of the men would ask.

Natasha would lean over, hug him and tell him "ssshhh."

He would pinch her cheek and say, "Such a beautiful *maidelah*."

Those words were an echo from the East European *shtels* and a form of prayer on the lips of one old man.

The director of Disaster Services in Portland asked if I want to assist flood victims in Arizona. My heart's pounding. I have plane reservations for tomorrow morning.

When Mount St. Helens erupted, I became a Red Cross volunteer and enjoyed the work. This was my chance to assist at other national calamities.

Adrenalin surged through my body. I didn't know what I

should do first? Pack my clothes? Find my boy scout snake bite kit? Review the forms for disaster relief? Write a note to Debbie and the kids? I decided on writing a note.

Dear Debbie, Natasha and Gabriel,
Have gone to Arizona.
Love,
Daddy

By the time I finished doing a laundry the kids returned home from school, Debbie came home from work, and I found the snake bite kit. The razor blade in the kit was so rusty and potentially blood poisoning, that it made dying of snake bite venom look like an underdog in a race to my heart.

"Are you going to be home for supper tomorrow night?" Gabriel asked nervously.

"I'll be home in a couple of weeks."

"I think it's a sneaky way to get out of your responsibilities here at home," Debbie said, "but if it makes you this happy, enjoy yourself. Everything will still be here when you get back." She kissed me on the cheek.

"Will you bring me home a scorpion, Daddy?" Gabriel asked.

"Will you write me letters?" Natasha asked.

I gave them each a nod. After dinner I continued reading to them from our latest book, <u>Dune</u>, by Frank Herbert. Afterward they all promised not to read ahead without me.

The disaster operation was everything I hoped it might be. For thirty days I worked hard, played hard, ate three meals a day in restaurants, regained self confidence, made new friends and earned the respect of my colleagues.

Back in Eugene there was a crowd of three waving banners

in the airport waiting room. It fell good to be home and when I walked through the door, I didn't pay attention to the spook on the wall.

Within a week I made an offer on a nine- hundred- square foot older house with a big back yard. The previous tenants were gone and as Debbie and I viewed the property I was extra vigilant to see if there were any resident ghosts. I used my teacher's retirement fund for the down payment.

For the past two years I've been selling my self-published book of children's stories, Tales for a Child's Heart, at the Portland Saturday Market, but the week before Christmas, the craft fair is open every day and I cannot possibly drive a hundred miles in each direction, leaving at four in the morning and returning home at nine at night. Instead I plan to stay at Abbie and Damon's house near where we had the farm.

An open air crafts market in Portland, Oregon is idyllic during June and July when a breeze blows off the Williamette River. On those clear, hot days, snow crowned Mt. Hood looms over the city like an invitation to an ice cream sundae with whipped cream topping.

An open air crafts market in Portland the week before Christmas is really stupid. The same wind that blows across the river now tastes of Freon. The mountain is buried under a hundred feet of snow and Bigfoot is standing in line for a cup of iced tea.

When I left home on December 18th I was looking forward to the event regardless of the Fahrenheit. On an average Saturday I sold ten or fifteen copies of my book but during the Christmas buying frenzy I could easily sell twice that number every day.

By 7:00 p.m. when I finished packing the pick- up truck, the only people still on the streets were derelicts cradling bottles of Thunderbird.

I saw two Sisters of Mercy delivering coffee to the street people and I stood in line with the other men. In moments I had a steaming cup in my hands.

"Would you like a donut?" the nun asked.

"Thank you Sister, I think I prefer just holding this hot cup."

Once on the road, the heater warmed the cab and my body thawed.

Abbie and Damon lived alongside a mountain creek. When I arrived, food was on the stove, their four kids were busy fighting tigers, the Christmas tree was brightly lit, and I felt the peace of the holiday season.

After everyone went to sleep I went for a walk along the creek. The moon lit the sky and the air crackled as I walked beyond the pale of light cast by the lamp in their living room window.

Few people lived this far up the mountain but Sita lived about a half mile further along a narrow dirt path. Her cabin, without plumbing or electricity, was built alongside the creek and what it lacked in modern day conveniences, it made up for in charm. If Sita was still awake, I'd pass along my Christmas greetings to Eileen.

I saw a child coming out of an outhouse. I wasn't sure what Sita's daughter looked like, but I called to her anyway.

"Hi. Is Sita home?"

"No, she's at work."

"Where's she working?"

"I don't know."

I thought to myself, this is not a very bright child. "Can you remember to wish her a merry Christmas from Jay?"

"Okay. She'll be here in the morning."

I retraced my steps to Abbie and Damon's home. I was in front of the stove long enough for the steam rising from my socks to fog the bay window when I heard a knock.

Eileen was standing in the doorway.

We whispered to avoid waking a houseful of people.

"I thought you were living in California?"

"I do. I live in the redwoods outside of Santa Cruz. How do you like living in Eugene?"

I shrugged. "How did you know I was here?"

"When Eden came back from the bathroom, she told me she met a man named Jay who was looking for Sita. You're the only Jay I know, and I remembered you were a friend of Abbie and Damon so I took a chance and came down here to see if it was you."

"Is your son with you too?"

"They're both up at the house asleep. I should be going. I don't really want to leave them alone for too long."

"I'll walk you back."

"It's a long walk."

I grabbed my coat.

We sat on a tattered couch in front of a wood stove. The creek, swollen with winter rains, tumbled over rocks a few feet from the house. Even with the door closed the creek was able to serenade us.

I felt indebted to Eden. She could have mentioned me to Eileen in the morning and I would not now be sharing this sweet trance.

We stayed that way throughout the night. When the darkness began to lift, it was time to leave for the craft fair. Wrapped up in my coat for the walk down the road, I turned to Eileen and said, "I have a problem. I think I'm in love with you and I don't know what to do."

"You should probably kiss me."

I hugged her instead.

As I turned to leave I asked if she'd join me for dinner.

"I can't. I have a lot of business to take care of today. But I'm dropping the kids off at their father's house in Portland late tonight. I can meet you for breakfast tomorrow."

"I'd like that."

"How will I find you?"

"I'll be under the Burnside Bridge at the Saturday Market. Each booth space is numbered. I'm in booth number seventeen. I'll meet you there."

"Tomorrow morning," she said kissing me on the cheek.

A wind storm arose during the day. A craft booth, roofed with a blue tarp, strapped down with bungee cords, is a terrible design when the wind blows strong. First the wind gets up under the tarp. It billows the tarp out like an aorta pumping blood into the heart, and then with a final thrust it lifts the entire booth off the ground like a box kite. The pottery crashes, the vendor goes into panic and the other vendors shudder.

When the wind abated, snow began to fall. Fat wet flakes descended on rooftops, streets and hat brims. It gathered in drifts, covering fire hydrants and transformed our booths into igloos.

Offices closed early. Buses were re-routed to avoid steep hills and the Salvation Army bell ringer's pot filled with snow.

When several potential customers whizzed by on cross country skis, it was time to make a decision. If I delayed it might be impossible to navigate the one hundred miles back to Eugene and Eileen certainly wasn't meeting me for breakfast the next day. The market wouldn't be open and if it was, a person would need a dog sled to get there.

This was no time to carefully arrange gear in the truck. I felt like a member of the Donner Party; either get over the pass before it closes or face the consequences.

Only one lane of the freeway was open and the shoulders were littered with vehicles that skidded off the road. The drive took four hours.

In the morning I made chocolate chip pancakes and distributed an array of household sleds. We played until we were numb and thirsty for hot chocolate. There was joy to the world in the air and Frosty the Snowman was doing a jig. I wished I were sharing these moments with Eileen.

The next day was Friday, the last day before Christmas. The snow was cleared off the roads and the freeway was passable. I was determined to finish the Saturday Market Christmas Week Endurance Test.

There were a handful of vendors waiting to sign in as I approached the registration booth. Only half the spaces were filled, but I was glad to be among the stalwart. I walked over to my booth to survey the damage done by the storm.

A note was wedged behind a wooden sign indicating my booth space.

Dear Jay,

I'm sorry you're not here. I arrived at eight, but there's only a couple of people hanging around. I'll wait a few more minutes and leave this note with someone in case you come later. Happy New Year. Eileen.

1984

I wanted to own a home with a white picket fence, a collie, a wife with an apron and two darling children. It just hasn't worked out that way. Instead we have created a violent co-dependent paradigm that is damaging each of us. Debbie and I can't agree on how to discipline the kids and wind up triangulated whenever Natasha and Gabriel start fighting.

"Stop it! Stop hitting each other," Debbie yelled.

"She's hitting me. I'm not hitting her."

"Mother! Make him stop!"

"Both of you stop it! Stop hitting each other," I demanded, wrenching Gabriel's arm.

"You're hurting him," Debbie screamed.

"I'm out of here," I said, slamming the door behind me.

Grandpa is dying. I sat on the edge of his hospital bed and told him stories about growing up in the Bronx and he told me stories about his hamlet in Norway. We didn't cry when I got up to leave and he promised wherever he was, he'd keep in touch.

I needed a place of solitude where I could surrender my pain. I wasn't far from the cabin where I sat all night with Eileen and the memory of her kept me company as I drove up the mountain.

I parked my car where the road became a narrow muddy washboard. A quarter mile up the path I saw Brad standing by his mailbox, reading a letter.

Brad worked for Eileen when she had the tofu factory. They met while Eileen was sweeping leaves from her front porch. She gave him a job and a family. When Eileen closed the business, he moved to the mountain.

"This letter is for you. It arrived this morning," Brad said.

The letter was from Eileen, addressed to Brad.

Eileen was struggling in Santa Cruz. She was cleaning houses and providing respite care. She had no money. She was moving from place to place and attending school to obtain a license to do massage. At the end of the letter she asked Brad, if he chanced to see me, to say hello.

"When I saw you coming up the road, I knew I was being asked to be a mailman." Brad looked at me quizzically. "Are you in love with her?"

I nodded.

"Does she know?"

I shrugged my shoulders. "What good does it do?"

Schools provide child care for nine months a year. During the summer months there are sleep- away camps, day camps and Prozac. In July, while Gabriel's at the YMCA, I'm taking Natasha hiking on the Pacific Crest Trail for a week and in August, when Natasha is at Camp B'nai B'rith, Gabriel and I are going on a bike tour of the San Juan Islands. In September I am going to a rest home.

Natasha and I have gone hiking every summer since she was seven. On our first trek she was short and carrying a large North Face back-pack. Seen from the rear, the pack looked like it had grown legs and was bouncing along the trail on its own power.

She was my favorite hiking buddy. The three of us, me, her and Snoopy doll had trekked more than a hundred and fifty miles since that first summer and I always looked forward to our adventures; but this was the first time I was taking Gabriel out on an excursion and I was nervous.

If I ever meet the liar who said the San Juan Islands are a place to bicycle, I'm going to give him a piece of my mind. There are mountains there that look like they're auditioning to become the Swiss Alps. I saw a whole herd of deer gasping for breath trying to get up San Juan Hill. As for bicycling, there are no bike lanes, no rest stops, and no hospitals.

"I think we're out of our league, Gabriel," I said indicating the Grand Prix finalists who were strapping their feet onto bike pedals like hockey players lacing up their ice skates.

"Don't worry, Dad. If you wear an extra large sweatshirt no one will be able to tell you're out of shape."

I've been hired by FEMA as an on call disaster relief specialist. I was afraid I wouldn't get security clearance because of being arrested at anti-war rallies when I was in college, but I worried needlessly. The deal is I automatically agree to go wherever they send me within one day of notification.

I'm on a ten member FEMA team out of Seattle, supervised by Hitchcock, who when not on assignment for FEMA, lives in a teepee perched over a hot springs in Northern Washington. In a makeshift office overlooking the white sands of Sarasota Florida, he gave us our assignments. One worker was tasked with finding the best place to stay as far away as possible from the other disaster workers lodged at The Hilton. As the new guy on the team I was given the plush job of finding the best night clubs, but only after working twelve to sixteen hours a day conducting home inspections. What do I know from night clubs?

1985

The on-call work for FEMA is wonderful but I need a regular pay check. There's a job advertised for a program director at the YMCA. If I'm hired, Gabriel can attend the after- school and summer day camp for free, which is a huge burden off my shoulders, and the men's shower room comes with free soap and cologne. It's even possible that I will be allowed to take personal leave whenever I get a disaster assignment.

Ronald Reagan was busy running the country into the ground and slashing social service programs like a sushi chef with an attitude. In place of government funding, he created two hundred teen volunteer programs across the country. I applied to run one of these programs.

"The job pays minimum wage," Doris said.

"I'll take it."

"The grant is only for two years."

I nodded.

"There's no chance of the grant being renewed and there's no room for advancement. It's a dead end job. This is re-entry work for women who graduated college with degrees in social sciences. I wasn't expecting to hire a man. Just how badly do you want this job?"

"I'll make you coffee every morning."

"In that case let me show you the office."

There was an empty desk facing a window. In the file drawer

I found a small flower vase and a plastic cube in which to place photographs of my children or the dog.

"Doris, does my job come with health benefits?"

"That's what husbands are for, Jay."

"What about sick leave and vacation?"

"If you don't report to work, we consider it leave without pay. But if you need to stay home with a sick kid, I'll do my best to look the other way."

"Is there anything good about this job?"

"There's a meeting of all the directors in San Francisco this year, if you like to travel."

Our household is out of control and I'm a large contributor to the chaos.

"I'm talking to you, put the Atari away now," I demanded.

"You're not talking. You're yelling," Gabriel said with his back to me.

"If you don't pick it up off the floor, I swear I'm going to break it."

"I don't care, you broke it once before."

"Whose turn is it to do the dishes?" Debbie asked.

"It's not my turn. I did them yesterday," said Natasha.

"Gabriel, get in there and wash these supper dishes," I commanded.

"I'll do them later."

I'd like to take Natasha to Israel as a Bat Mitzvah gift. It would give Debbie and me some breathing room to sort out our marriage.

Debbie wasn't going along with the plan.

"You'd like to go on vacation with Natasha and leave me alone with Gabriel and all the household problems? No thank you. Why don't you take Gabriel with you instead and leave Natasha with me."

"Gabriel doesn't want to go to Israel. He has no interest in Judaism. Natasha will be *Bat Mitzvah* in a couple of months and is eager to visit. It makes more sense to take her."

"No."

"Why are you being so obstinate?"

"I'm protecting my sanity."

"Wouldn't you like to spend some quality time alone with Gabriel?"

"The truth is I'm tired of all the men in this house. When it's just Natasha and me, we have a fine time. There's never any fighting and it's fun. I agree that it's time for you to leave, but when you go, I want you to take Gabriel with you."

"To Israel?"

"To Israel or to the moon. Just so long as I get some peace and quiet in my life. Listen. Find an apartment near here to rent where you and Gabriel can live. Maybe once we separate we can find a way to heal this mess."

It's a two- bedroom condo. The windows in the back bedroom and the kitchen face a wooded area where deer wander through the trees. There's a small community swimming pool and a billiards table that Gabriel and I use after he finishes his homework. He has a bed in his room and I have a mattress on the floor in the master suite. The living room is furnished with an old couch that had been in the garden. Traces of slug trails are still apparent on the sofa no matter how often I try cleaning it. The only lights in the condo are overheads in the bathroom and kitchen.

The apartment has wall to wall carpeting. I don't own a vacuum cleaner so instead of meditating, I spend twenty minutes a day on my hands and knees picking up particles, one square foot at a time. I call it zen carpet cleaning.

Poverty sucks. If I ever climb out of this hole I am going to have a car with working windows, a six pack of beer that have gold or silver foil around their bottle necks and two pair of heavy grey wool winter socks.

"Damn it!" I said aloud, stubbing my toe on the leg of the dresser. "I'm coming. Quit ringing the doorbell." From the moonlight streaming onto his bed I could see Gabriel was awake as well.

"What's happening, Daddy?"

'I don't know. Somebody's thumb is frozen to the doorbell."

I slowly navigated the living room in the dark, hoping I remembered where the furniture stood.

"What's up?" I said, throwing open the door. My neighbor was standing there looking disheveled and holding a Siamese kitten.

"Your cat has been keeping me up all night. She keeps scratching the railing and crying."

"That's not my cat."

"Are you sure?"

"I don't own a cat. But I'll bring her in my house for the night and try to find her owner tomorrow. That way we can both get some sleep."

"Gee, I'm sorry I bothered you. I just figured since she was sitting on the landing she must be yours."

"It's okay. You reminded me it's time to buy a couple of lamps. I'm finished with living in the dark.

Natasha's Bat Mitzvah is nearly here.

On Saturday morning when Natasha stepped onto the *bimah*

she was draped in a woven prayer shawl personally designed for her in colors of the rainbow. When she chanted Torah, the room went silent. An hour passed as Natasha led the congregation in prayer, at times in solo praise to God, at other times blending her voice with many others.

When she finished, everyone took a breath and in a whoosh, keeping with tradition, threw candies toward the *bimah* for the little children to scamper and collect.

The party went on far into the night. When everyone had gone and my parents and sister were on planes flying East, I sat with Natasha in her bedroom recounting the day's triumphs and glories. As I turned off her light she said to me, "Daddy, I don't know if you'll be here in the morning, so I want to tell you something. You talked today about how I spent the last two years building a Jewish home for myself. I want you to know you are always welcome in whatever home I build."

"You're also always welcome anywhere I go, Natasha. Good night."

I turned off the light and joined Debbie in the living room.

"Would you like to stay here awhile, Jay? We could try living together for a couple of weeks. Maybe see if we've learned to appreciate each other more."

We both wanted that. We tried. We failed. Gabriel and I returned to the condo.

I have a scholarship to attend a Red Cross Disaster Institute in Sacramento next month, the week of my birthday. Sacramento is only two hours from Santa Cruz. I can't imagine giving myself a nicer birthday present than seeing Eileen.

Driving to Sacramento for the disaster institute, with my fedora brim pulled down to my eyelashes, I felt like Humphrey Bogart on his way to a meeting with the French Resistance. Sacramento isn't as exotic as Algiers, nor a college campus as apt to attract Lauren Bacall, but when I pulled into a gas station to top off the tank, I saw Peter Lorre making change.

The classes were interesting and the days whizzed by but I couldn't find the courage to phone Eileen. It was two days before my birthday when I wandered away from a workshop and located a public phone with a door.

She answered on the thirty-seventh ring.

"Hi, Eileen. This is Jay."

"Jay? Where are you calling from?"

"I'm in Sacramento at a Red Cross seminar." I paused. "I miss you."

There was silence on the other end.

"I miss you too."

"Thank G-d. Tomorrow is my birthday. I'm hoping you'll spend it with me."

"I'd like that."

"How about if we meet halfway, in San Francisco, say, in front of the Wax Museum, around 7:30 p.m.?"

"That sounds like you."

"Then I'll see you tomorrow evening. Good night," I said.

"Good night."

I held the phone to my ear. I waited a moment. I spoke into the receiver. "Are you still there, Eileen?"

"Yes. I was waiting for you to hang up."

"I couldn't bear to hang up but I really have to go."

"Why?"

"Because I'm running out of quarters."

"Give me your phone number and I'll call you back."

As I walked back to campus I felt dazed. Eileen said she missed me and wanted to see me tomorrow. I was afraid she would change her mind and I had my doubts if the station wagon, which had sputtered into Sacramento, could make it over the Golden Gate.

I arrived on time and waited forever. I watched twenty-three people purchase tickets to the Wax Museum. I saw a vendor sell four cable car music boxes to visitors from Akron Ohio. I learned the melody to "I Left My Heart in San Francisco" from a street performer who moved away when I began to whimper. And then I saw her.

"Hi. Did you just get here?"

"No. I've been here about twenty minutes," she said.

"That's weird. That's how long I've been here."

"Right here in front of the Museum?"

"Uh huh. Right here. I kept looking out over the sea of heads to spot you in the crowd."

"Me, too. So what do you want to do, Jay? Go to the Wax Museum?"

"No. Let's walk."

The streets of Fisherman's Wharf were draped in lace. The lapping of water against the bulks of the small fishing fleet anchored at the pier; the single dinner plate of all the appetizers at a restaurant that looked out over the water; the carriage ride where the driver kindly never looked over his shoulder to see our first lingering kiss; the motel room we rented in the early hours of dawn at which we never slept; and the soft goodbye in a dense fog that separated us as we stood longing to remain together.

On Friday I phoned Eileen and asked if we could see each other again.

"I was hoping you were more than a one night stand," she said.

"Will you take me to a place by the water and feed me oranges all the way from China?"

"Those are lyrics from a Leonard Cohen love song."

"Yeah, they are. They always remind me of you."

"Oh. Well, in that case, I'll see what the natural food store has in stock."

It was 10:00 p.m. when I reached the steep ascent over the

Santa Cruz mountains. At the crest I turned off the main road and navigated curves, switchbacks and hair-pin turns like an Olympic luge rider. When I pulled into the driveway, Eileen was sitting on the porch juggling oranges.

Eden and Dylan were asleep in the next room and she didn't want us to wake them. "I know a beach on Monterey Bay just a few miles from here. Do you want to see it?"

"Sure."

We sat on still- warm sand, walked on a wooden pier and listened to the sound of waves.

I saw all the sights and tasted all the joys until early morning took me by the hand and set me to sleep on the living room couch, a prim and proper picture of propriety.

Breakfast was the kind they served at Alice's restaurant. Eileen prepared a tofu scramble with home fried potatoes, yogurt and salsa for condiments, accompanied by a banana smoothie and fresh ground coffee. I felt like a condemned man eating his last supper.

Dylan and Eden played outside while Eileen and I washed the dishes.

"Do you want to stay tonight? Aretha Franklin is performing and I can get us tickets."

"I can't."

Eileen turned back to the sink.

"Debbie and I are sharing the kids. I can't bring them here and I have nothing to offer you in Eugene."

With poise and dignity, Eileen said nothing more.

"Shall I follow you down the mountain, just in case you have car trouble?" she asked when the last plate had been put away.

"I'd appreciate it."

We didn't kiss when we said goodbye.

The meeting in San Francisco is coming up and I called Eileen to see if we could get together. She wasn't home but I left a message. Then I rushed out and bought a telephone answering machine.

Gabriel wants to know why I need an answering machine since no one ever calls. I didn't tell him I'm hoping Eileen will phone and I hate the anxiety I feel when I think I might miss her call.

"Why do you want to see me, Jay? What's the sense of us getting together?"

"Because I love you. Because I want to spend as much time as I can with you. It's hard with you living so far away, but I can come down a few times a year. If you could come up the same, we could see each other every month."

"Thank G-d I don't live in Eugene. You'd probably want something meaningful like leaving a toothbrush at my house. Jay, I need to think about this some more."

A friend loaned Eileen the keys to a high-rise luxury apartment and put a bottle of champagne in the refrigerator. We opened the curtains and looked out over a city. We lit candles and we talked. In the morning both of our pillows were damp with tears. The candles had burned down, the champagne sat undisturbed in the refrigerator.

I was assigned to work a disaster in Boston and was gone for three weeks. When I returned home to the condo there was a message from Debbie inviting me to the house for dinner.

Dinner was terrific. Debbie basted a turkey and the sweet potatoes tasted of melted marshmallows. I finished reading <u>Dune</u> to the family and when the kids finally went to sleep after a marathon game of Monopoly, Debbie and I sat across from each other in front of the fireplace.

"Jay, I've decided that Gabriel needs to stay here. Your life is too erratic. You come and you go on a moment's notice and for who knows how long. When your phone rings, Gabriel never knows if he should start packing his bags. I'm not saying this is forever. Just until you get settled."

"Gabriel agrees?"

"We talked it over. Gabriel agrees."

"I wish you had let me be part of the conversation."

"You weren't around."

A week later Natasha and I met for coffee at Denny's. She sat across from me shredding a napkin.

"Can I come live with you, Daddy?" she said biting her nails.

I was speechless for about a minute. "Did you talk to your mother about this?"

She shook her head.

"Don't you want to talk about it with her?"

She shook her head again. "Stop smiling like that, Daddy. You look like Alfred E. Newman."

"Okay. Let's go pack your bags."

Debbie called right after she came home from work. Her words came out in gasps, like a person drowning.

"Is it true? How long is she staying?"

"She says it's permanent, but I don't believe her. She brought her Snoopy doll but not her collection of dragons."

"She's my best friend. I don't want her to leave."

"She'll be back. She just felt hurt that she no longer had you all to herself."

"I didn't stop loving her because I also love Gabriel."

"Give it some time. She's smart. She'll figure that out."

1986

Eileen's been in Portland fighting for custody of her kids. It's awful. We met this morning in the lobby of a grand downtown hotel and drove along the Columbia River. The old highway travels across moss laden stone bridges and is misted by a half dozen waterfalls. I suggested we stop at Latourell Falls and together we ventured to a lookout.

"Will you marry me?" I asked.

"Before or after you divorce your wife?"

"Now. Wed me now. I don't know how we can make this work, but I'll find a way."

"This is where I offered vows to my first husband."

"Right here?"

"Right here."

"Will you marry me?"

"No."

"Listen, Eileen. I understand I can't give you a marriage license, but I've already given you my heart."

Eileen shook her head. "Take it back, Jay. There may be a day when I can embrace it, but for now, let's hold hands."

At the airport we stood on a line at the terminal never noticing the people who politely and quietly stepped around us to board the plane. At last the stewardess tapped me on a shoulder.

"This is the last call for flight 704 leaving for San Francisco," she said.

We separated and I stood for a long time staring out the concourse window.

I read, re-read and re-read again the note card. It is a short note. She wrote it hurt too much to keep on saying goodbye. She met a guy she likes. She asked me not to write or call and prayed I would not be deeply wounded by her decision. She ended the note with "Angels fly because they take themselves lightly. Love, Eileen."

The cover art on the card was a line drawing of angels playing on flower petals.

It was my birthday. I wanted a gift and the only gift I wanted was to hear Eileen's voice. Instead, I called Sita who has also moved to Santa Cruz.

"Hello, Sita. This is Jay from Oregon."

"Hi, Jay. Are you in California?"

"No. I'm still in Eugene."

"How are things going up there?"

"Not great. Debbie and I are separated. I'm wondering how Eileen is doing? She wrote me a note saying not to write to her. Do you know anything?"

"You heard that she lost her kids in a child custody fight with her ex?"

"No. I haven't spoken to her for a while."

"I guess it got very mean. The judge ordered her to pay alimony and only granted her limited time with the kids. In the middle of the crisis she met someone and got involved in a relationship."

"How serious do you think they are about each other?"

"She married him two weeks ago."

1987

Debbie and I are divorced. For all the strife in our marriage, we parted as friends. We lit candles from a match book saved from the Hungarian restaurant where we held our wedding reception and offered each other vows of kindness and support.

Debbie and Gabriel moved a few blocks away and in a couple of months were joined by an easy going guy. They're a good match and they recently married. Natasha and I moved back into the house.

I did more assignments with FEMA, including a typhoon in Samoa where I received a Presidential Commendation for my work but seeing no possibility of securing a full time job in disaster relief, resigned from the organization. The teen volunteer job is about to end and I'm still as poor as a church mouse. It's only because Debbie is helping out financially that I have a roof over my head. I could probably go on welfare, but I don't like standing in lines and filling out forms. I have to find a job before unemployment runs out and I'm afraid no one will hire me when they see my work history.

I haven't dated and there are weeks at a time when I literally don't touch another human being.

"I'd like to thank and congratulate all of you this morning. There were more than three hundred applicants for the seventy-five positions we have open with United Inventory Service. Each of you were considered top quality applicants who, we believe, will become dedicated, competent, inventory clerks.

"During the next five days we will practice using our inventory machines until we can enter thirty codes a minute with one hundred percent accuracy. We typically begin our shift after store hours. The time varies from store to store but since our largest customers are supermarkets, we generally begin work about ten at night and try to quit by opening time the next day. By the way, do any of you have young children at home?"

It was a trick question. No one with kids at home was going to admit it to a boss on day one.

"Good," he said when he saw no show of hands. "We do our best to keep all of you working with as little down time as possible. If a job takes us on the road for two or three weeks, we'll try to give preference to those who enjoy the extra time and per diem. Are there any questions before a ten minute cigarette break? No? Okay. I'll see you all back here at nine forty. Sharp."

Outside, I recognized the mother of one of Gabe's classmates.

She was wearing a housecoat over a pair of jeans and construction boots.

"I don't know if I can do this," I confided.

"I have no choice. I've been looking for months and this is the only thing I could find."

"I just started looking. But it's not appropriate. Natasha is living with me and I can't leave her alone every time they call me to count boxes of laundry detergent."

"Good luck. If you find something with two openings, look for me on aisle fifteen at Safeway."

"Welcome, ladies and gentlemen. Allow me to congratulate you. There were more than eighty applicants for the fifteen positions we have open with Kirby Vacuum Cleaner Company. Each of you were considered among the best applicants who, we believe, in time, can be highly paid, professional door- to -door vacuum cleaner salespeople.

"During the next five days I am going to teach you everything you need to know to earn fifty, sixty even seventy thousand dollars a year. The best part of it all is you don't have to do very much to earn that money. Once inside the door, the Kirby Vacuum Cleaner practically sells itself. By this time Friday you will be capable of getting in homes of people with German shepherds and Sonipatrol. You'll know dozens of tricks on how to close a sale, and best of all, it will be fun.

"At Kirby Vacuum Cleaner we believe in fun. Everyone loves a contest, right? Well, I'm offering round trip tickets to Las Vegas and three nights at Ceasar's Palace to the first one of you who sells ten Kirbys. One of you, probably within a week of being on the street, will win these two tickets to Las Vegas. That's what I mean, when I say we like to have fun."

On Friday afternoon I had my demonstration Kirby in the back seat of the station wagon. Christmas Eve was Saturday and a light snow was beginning to fall. The radio was playing carols.

"Hey, G–d," I said. "This isn't funny. You proved your point. I know I've been bad. But I have not been this bad. There has to be something more you want me to do with my life than sell Kirbys. Please, G–d, speak to me."

It was four thirty when I arrived home. The Kirby office didn't close until five. I hurried to the phone.

"Hi. Is Mike still around?" I said feverishly into the handset.

"This is Mike. How can I help you?"

"Mike, this is Jay. I've decided I can't sell Kirbys. I'm sorry you invested all the time and trouble in teaching me the trade, but I'm sitting here crying and I don't want to do it."

Mike was sympathetic. "Look, don't worry about it. The job's not for everyone. Me, I love it and if you change your mind over the weekend the job is still available."

"What should I do with the demonstration Kirby I took home?"

"Tomorrow is Christmas Eve. We're going to close early. Bring it in on Monday morning."

"Thanks Mike. I appreciate your understanding."

"It's nothing. Have a Merry Christmas."

"You, too." I hung up.

I was thrilled. I twirled around the living room like Fred Astaire. And then I saw this marvelous Christmas present which Santa had given me: a Kirby Vacuum Cleaner. No zen carpet cleaning for me this weekend.

"Next," the voice behind the caged window barked at the long line of people who had responded to the ad in the newspaper.

I stepped up to the window.

"Name, please," she snapped.

"Jay …" I didn't get any further.

She looked up from the application form. "I'm sorry, but I think you made a mistake. This program is for displaced homemakers. You probably want the employment office. That's on River Avenue."

"I am a displaced homemaker," I said.

"But this program is for women."

"Since when?"

"Since it was funded by Congress two years ago. If you'll step out of line for a minute, I'll get my supervisor to talk to you."

I took a seat under a poster which encouraged mothers with infants to sign up for the WIC program.

A short while later I was enrolled in a job search workshop.

Snow covered the ground on Monday morning.

"Ladies and gentlemen, congratulations."

"Oh, shit," I thought to myself. "I'm going to scream if I hear this line one more time."

"…on getting here this morning," the speaker continued. "I know it wasn't easy to make this choice. It's not easy going to work each morning either. But it's something that each of you wanted to do badly enough that you signed up for this Private Industry Council job search workshop. You didn't even use the handy excuse of a snow storm to prevent you from getting here. You were all referred to us from different agencies, some from the Veterans Administration, some from the Department of Rehab and at least one that I know of from the Displaced Homemakers. But, you all have something in common. As far as I'm concerned, each and every one of you is job ready. And it's only a small step from being job ready to being employed.

"During the next two weeks you are going to prepare yourselves for a job search. From eight until noon we will build self confidence, practice interviewing skills, write resumes and identify job prospects. In the afternoons you will begin applying for work.

"The following two weeks you will spend in our phone bank, cold calling. You'll make fifty phone calls a day and try to obtain ten job interviews. While you're on the phone, one of the job coaches will be right at your elbow, coaching you, encouraging you, and applauding your successes. Let's begin.

"When it's your turn to speak, you'll say, 'Good morning!' your name and 'I want to work.' Then be quiet and wait for the class to answer. The class will answer by saying, 'Good morning so –and- so. We're cheering for you.'

"Are you ready?"

Americans love to join clubs. There's Kiwanis, Elks, Moose, Lions, Alcoholics Anonymous, Marijuana Anonymous, Overeaters Anonymous, and here I was in a meeting of "Out of Work Anonymous." In another second, it was going to be my turn to speak and I was speechless.

"Good morning. My name is Jay and I want to work." It sounded corny.

The class responded. "Good morning, Jay. We're cheering for you." Then a funny thing happened. It didn't sound so corny anymore.

The next few days were even better.

"Good morning, class."

"Good morning, Chuck," we answered in chorus. Chuck was a heavy- set black man with a style made up of Baptist preacher and street corner hustler. We liked Chuck. He helped us find humor in our personal predicaments.

"Yesterday each of you made a list of the kinds of work you want to do. This morning we are going to change the way we introduce ourselves. When it becomes your turn to stand up, you'll say your name and add, 'I want to work as a ...' Does everyone understand? Okay, we'll start to my right."

"Good morning. My name is Cindy. I want to be a bank clerk."

"Good morning, Cindy. We're cheering for you."

"Good morning. My name is Jay. I want to work for justice."

"Good morning, Jay. We're cheering for you."

On Monday morning we received unexpected news.

"Good morning, class."

"Good morning, Chuck," we answered.

"This morning I have good and bad news to share with you. The bad news is Buddy is leaving the class. The good news is Buddy got the job he wanted. Buddy will you stand and tell the class what happened?"

Buddy was a tall, thin cowboy. He wore blue jeans and a leather vest. A long chain dangled from his belt to a billfold he kept in his back pocket, a habit he developed during the years he was a long-distance truck driver.

"Good morning. My name is Buddy and I got a job."

This time there was no routine chorus response. We hooted. We hollered. We banged on tables. One of our team had won.

"I've been telling you how I wanted to be a locksmith. Every afternoon after class I been going down to the River Avenue Safe Company and bothering the owner. I told him I was gonna keep on comin until he gave me a job. He knew I could do the work. I learned it from my pop when we lived in Nebraska. Yesterday he broke down and took me with him to replace the locks on someone's house. We worked real good together and when we was done, he agreed to give me a try. He's gonna pay me six dollars an hour to start, forty hours a week. He wanted me to start this morning, but I told him I had to come here first. I know we only been together for less than two weeks. But you been my friends. And whenever I got scared, I listened in my mind to you cheering for me. I gotta go now but I wanted to say thanks."

After a dinner of miso soup, I told Natasha I had to leave for the evening.

"Portal Medical Clinic is advertising for someone to work with homeless people. I have an interview at their office at nine tonight."

"Is this like climbing the corporate ladder, Daddy?" Natasha asked.

"Are you kidding? This is like climbing up the metal rungs bolted into the wall of a sewer."

"If you get the job does that mean we'll have enough money to go hiking in Vermont this Fall?"

"Oh, Natasha," I sighed. "Have I told you recently how beautiful Vermont is in October?"

"Tell me again."

"C'mon. Get your coat. We'll walk over to the Seven-Eleven and split an ice cream. While we walk I'll tell you about the hike we're going to take."

The director of Portal had so much hair he made Bob Marley look like he wore a crew cut. He bought Maalox in the economy size bottle and guzzled it like a wino.

Sitting next to him was Arnie, whose front teeth were spread out with enough spaces in between to play checkers. He was using both of his hands, simultaneously, to draw an intricate caricature of me.

A tall, gangly, bearded fellow was sitting in a corner. He had just returned from a ninety day silent retreat and wasn't much into speaking.

My counterpart, if I was hired, was a chain smoking, too-thin, too-tough woman who was mostly in charge of the interview.

"What makes you think you can work with homeless people?" She demanded.

"Metaphorically speaking, I've been homeless most of my life, so we have something in common. Beside that, I figure homeless people are a lot like permanent disaster victims and I've been working with that population for several years."

"How badly do you want this job?"

"I want this job enough to give up forty weeks of vacation a year."

"What do you mean by that answer?"

"I mean I could continue doing what I do, work about twelve weeks a year providing disaster relief, and earn in three months what you intend to pay for a year's work."

"Hey," the director joined in. "Nine hundred a month is the highest anyone at The Portal ever earned. We wanted to pay less but it's a federal contract and they insisted on the pay scale. Me, I'm glad it pays so high. I get the average wage of everyone who works here, so actually when we figure in these two new positions, I'll get a four dollar raise a month."

"Why do you want to work at The Portal?" someone asked.

I didn't know it at the time, but many hippies thought working at The Portal was as chic as mud bathing at Woodstock. They were anxious to learn if I was a Portal wannabee.

"I figure this is my doorway back into society. I've lived way too far outside of conventions and I want to rejoin. It's not that I've done anything very wrong or illegal, it's that I'm only sorta living a life. My goal is to become a more normal member of society and getting a job like this could be a stepping stone to a white shirt and tie."

The director mused. "Anything is possible."

Arnie handed me the drawing. It was a goofy looking pen and ink but what can a person expect from a guy who draws with both of his hands. "Welcome. Are you cold? Do you need a blanket? Do you want some Boston Baked Beans?" He dug into a pocket and pulled out a box of gooey candies.

I wasn't sure I could handle going to work every day, but I could make my own hours, 24-7. I promised I would do it for a year and rushed home to tell Natasha.

"That's great. What exactly are you going to do at the clinic?"

"I'm responsible for finding homeless people who need immediate health care and telling them that Portal's doctor will see them for free."

"Does that mean you're going to be hanging out under bridges and stuff?"

"I guess."

"Eating at the mission?"

"Probably."

"Standing in line at the plasma center?"

"For sure."

"I don't think you want to tell your parents about this job."

Natasha was right. It was a pretty sketchy job.

Arnie and I walked through downtown. He pointed out the dumpster behind the florist shop where I could find half-wilted bouquets.

Kelly and I walked the riverbanks stopping at still-smoldering camp fires to leave flyers wrapped around cigarettes.

Jeremy and I ate breakfast at the Baptist church, lunch at the Gospel Mission and dinner at the Salvation Army. It all tasted soggy.

I drank coffee at a kiosk whose proprietor took home runaway boys and gave them a roof and brief love.

Aaron and I crouched in his refrigerator box, staying out of the rain, and talked about biking across America.

Mad Maggie screamed curses at me.

At a picnic table I was offered a toke that I declined.

Kelly and I plotted a poor peoples' revolt.

In the freeze before dawn I covered shivering souls with

sleeping bags donated by mothers whose sons were gone off to college.

I attended a funeral for a hobo who didn't wake up.

I stood with them when the police arrived with billy clubs.

At a Sunday mass I told what I knew about life under bridges and inside culverts.

Long Tom gave me a tour of darkened basements under the university.

A stout walking stick and a bag of day old donuts were my pass key to get past a mangy dog protecting a ragged couple covered with sores who slept in the cemetery on the hill.

I listened to men cough with tuberculosis and watched others trundle along on feet swollen with edema.

I wondered what was happening to America.

I wondered about myself.

1988

My birthday is around the corner and as a present to myself I called Sita in Santa Cruz. I haven't heard anything about Eileen for so long; anything, other than the beating of my heart, whenever I think of her.

"I was wondering when I would get a call from you, Jay. How are you?"

"I'm all right. I'm still living in Eugene. Debbie and I divorced and Natasha is living with me."

"Did you know that Eileen is also divorced?"

"No. Since the last time you and I spoke I've been praying that she was happy and if not, that she was divorced. Do you have her phone number?"

When I got off the phone, my hands were shaking. "Thank

you, G-d," I said and then went out and splurged on a birthday cake and candles.

"Hello. Is this Eileen?" I asked, my voice quivering.

"Who is this, please?"

"This is Jay."

"This is her sister, Missy. Eileen is warming up her car. Can I give her a message?"

"I'd appreciate it if you would get her before she leaves. This is important."

"What did you say your name was?"

"Jay."

"Hang on a minute." The phone went dead, me too, nearly.

"Hello. This is Eileen. What did you say your name was?"

It was the same voice I heard in my dreams.

"This is Jay."

"Jay!" Her voice twinkled. "How did you get my telephone number?"

"I called Sita. After you wrote asking me not to contact you, I've called her few times to find out how you were doing."

"You knew I got married."

"I did."

"And you continued calling?"

"Eileen, I'd have waited forever for this moment."

"Are you still married, Jay?"

"No. We've been divorced for a while. Natasha and I are living together. Gabriel is living with Debbie."

"Listen, Jay. This isn't a good time for me to be talking to you. My boyfriend is in the car waiting for me."

"Boyfriend? Are you crazy? I can offer you a million times what your boyfriend has to give."

"Like what?"

"Like, I love you."

"You love me?" There was a mixture of anger and disbelief in her voice. "We haven't spoken in years. Lots of things have happened since the last time we met. You wouldn't even recognize me in an airport."

"I would if you laughed."

"Listen, I have to go."

" Just tell me one thing."

"What?"

"Can I call you again?"

"Yes."

Artis the Spoonman calls the Oregon Country Fair "An Essential Event." It's also called "The Hippy New Year." I've had a booth at the Fair since 1981 and it's the highlight of the summer for me and the kids. We're beginning to make our preparations.

Located on two hundred and eighty acres along the Long Tom River, the Fair is the site of hundreds of craft and food booths and a dozen stages. Alcohol is not permitted, tobacco is considered uncouth and great plumes of marijuana smoke hover over the land. Twenty five thousand people pay admission to attend the Fair but after the gates close at night, there are still four thousand people camping behind their booths.

Without electricity and in the woods, lanterns, candles and glow sticks light the booths when the sun goes down. Impromptu jug bands serenade those who promenade the figure eight and under a tree, in a darkened niche, a lone pianist plays sonatas on an old upright he has brought in on a flatbed truck. Food booths stay open around the clock and it's an easy jaunt down the lane, pass the drum tower and across the bridge to Dana's for a slice of cheesecake.

If America were to someday become a nation of peace, harmony and beauty, it would look like the Oregon Country Fair.

Natasha, Gabriel and I discussed the Fair over macaroni and cheese.

"Are you going to sell your books this year, Dad?"

"I told Portal I would help barbecue chicken at their food booth. I was hoping you and Natasha would take turns staffing my booth when I'm away."

"I'd love to," Natasha responded.

"Are we going to camp in the poison oak again this year?" Gabriel wanted to know.

Natasha sighed. "All the other booths have tree houses, lofts and walled off camping sites. All we have is a clearing with bed sheets on a clothes line to give us privacy. Can't you build something?"

"I'd be happy if you just got rid of the poison oak," Gabriel grumbled.

This job at Portal is intense and surreal.

"Give us Jefferson Middle School," I pleaded. "It's been vacant for two years. We could house whole families in each of the classrooms and keep the families more intact."

The Superintendent of Education: "No."

"Give us ten thousand dollars to put into a housing pool. Landlords demand first and last month's rent plus utilities. Poor people don't have that much money in the bank."

The Community Housing Corporation: "No."

"There are simply too many veterans from the Vietnam war living on the streets. They're way out of proportion to their numbers in the general population. They need to be recognized as having war injuries and be treated with all the kindness and appreciation we can muster."

The Veterans Administration: "Get lost."

"Church of the Southern Saints is the only black congregation in town and it is the only place a person can get a free meal without being forced to hear a sermon. And you're going to close this soup kitchen because it doesn't meet city health standards? Are you stupid or just being paid off?"

City Manager: "Lock her up, boys."

"America, I swear to G-d. There is going to be a fire on our mountain. We are going to burn."

I'm developing a phone relationship with Eileen. I'd like more, but I'm grateful to hear her voice.

I called Eileen each night. Simultaneously, we read <u>The Mists of Avalon</u>, chapter by chapter, not reading ahead of one another and talked of it for weeks. Then it was on to <u>Love in the Time of Cholera.</u>

For fifty years, nine months and four days Florentino Ariza waited to declare, once again, his undying love for Fermina. I understood the man. As we finished the book in late summer, Eileen asked, "When can you come visit?"

"I have to see how much a bus ticket costs and how many days vacation I can get from work."

"What about Labor Day weekend? I'm closing my massage practice for the three day holiday. I'll send you money for a plane ticket."

"How will I recognize you, Jay?" Eileen asked a few days before Labor Day.

"I don't look any different than I did the last time you saw me.

What about you? Do you look the same?"

"I think so. Do you remember me?"

"I do."

But we were wrong.

Stepping off the plane, I walked into a crowded waiting area. I didn't see Eileen. I was frozen with fear that I was standing in the wrong place and wouldn't find her. I moved into a sea of tourists.

"Jay?" I heard someone call out above the hubbub. I turned in that direction.

"Eileen? I didn't recognize you."

She was wearing a pair of brown corduroy pants and a loose hanging beige blouse. Her body was more full, more solid, more grounded in the earth. She looked less like a promise of early morning sunlight on a hot summer day than like the truth of Autumn. She had become a matron, forlorn of children no longer tugging at her petticoats. But her eyes still sparkled like a leprechaun and gave hope of blossoms come springtime.

"I wasn't sure it was you, either."

I stood staring at her trying to recall her image from yesterday's imagination. "You cut your hair," I said.

"Years ago." Eileen turned to a pretty young blonde. "Jay, this is my sister, Missy. You talked to her on the phone."

"Hi."

"I'm ready to go. Where to?" I asked.

"Macy's!" Eileen gleefully pronounced.

I nodded my head. "Good idea! I like riding the escalator at Macy's."

As I got in the back seat of a green Mercedes, I studied Eileen's face in the rear view mirror. I still didn't recognize her.

Eileen knew her way around the mall. With only a minor detour to look at shoes in Nordstroms, she directed us straight to the cocktail dresses. I sat in a tall leather wing back chair, the kind found in English Tudor mansions, and watched the sisters twirl in front of mirrors.

Eileen was holding up a black, 1920's flapper dress with black fringes. "What do you think of this, Missy?"

"It's pretty. Try it on. It's on sale for three hundred."

Eileen went into the changing room. I turned to her sister. "Would she really spend three hundred dollars on a dress?" I asked in bewilderment.

"If she liked it, she would."

This was not my world.

Eileen came out of the dressing room, spun around, and put the dress back on a hanger. In her laugh I heard wind chimes.

At her house, she introduced me to more of her family.

"Jay, this is my brother Owen and his wife, Haley."

"Hi. Nice to meet you both." I turned to Eileen. "You know this is a little unusual. Typically a woman waits awhile before she introduces her boyfriend to the entire family."

"I have ten sisters and brothers. It can take a while to meet them all. Anyway, this is simply a coincidence. Missy lives here and Owen and Haley visit fairly often."

"We didn't even know you were going to be here," Owen clarified. "We came to see the sand sculpture contest."

"Is everyone hungry?" Eileen asked. There were nods all around.

"Do you want to help me in the kitchen, Jay?" she asked.

"I want to do absolutely anything with you."

In the evening Eileen and I walked along a promenade on the hillside as the moon rose and draped golden ribbons across Monterey Bay. We sat on a bench overlooking the village harbor and listened to the faint sounds of a jazz piano coming from a cafe on the street below. Neon lights reflected on the waters, casting muted hues of red and green.

"Do you have a particular restaurant where you'd like to eat dinner?" I asked.

"Why don't we go down to the village and see if magic will point us in a direction."

El Toro served tamales. The aroma of blackened catfish wafted from Antoines. Fried calamari and margaritas were the specialties of the Fish Grotto. Long lines formed outside Pizza My Heart. We continued walking alongside a wide creek.

"What are those lights on the other side of the creek?" I asked.

"That's the Shadowbrook Restaurant."

"Is there any way to get there from this side of the creek?"

"We can walk back to the center of the village and cross the bridge."

A gray haired man paddled by us in a wooden canoe.

"Excuse me, would you mind ferrying us to the restaurant?" Eileen asked.

He edged the canoe to shore.

It was Naples. Eileen and I faced one another in the bow of the canoe and held hands in the dark. On the other shore we thanked him for his courtesy.

"My pleasure. It brought back memories."

The Shadowbrook was serving romance. We dined in delight.

I slept that night in a back room in a bed squeezed between a washing machine and the wall. I had slept on more comfortable cots in gymnasiums but knowing Eileen was on the other side of the wall made the room feel like a penthouse at the Fairmount.

I awoke too early to wake the household and too eager to lie in bed. In a beach town catering to tourists it would be easy to find a cup of coffee

The line at the bakery looked like a run on a bank. A woman in the back of the line was in the throes of caffeine withdrawal and continually moaned for an espresso. This bakery was a California state of mind and I was a little surprised I didn't see therapists at the cash register.

"How can I help you?" the attendant asked.

"If you were going to be really, really decadent, what would you choose?" I questioned.

He looked all around the crowded room and pointed to a shaggy blond youth sipping a latte by a window.

"What if you were limited to the pastries in the case?"

"I'd choose the double fudge chocolate cake with chocolate mousse icing."

"Done! How much is it?"

"Four-fifty."

"Wow. That's cheap for a cake."

"That's a slice. The whole cake cost twenty two dollars. Do you still want it?"

"Yeah."

"I'll put it in a box."

By the time I got back to Eileen's, everyone was astir.

"Whatcha got in the box?" Eileen asked.

"Breakfast."

She took the box from me and opening the lid slowly appraised the contents.

"Bran muffins?"

"Bran muffins?" Owen echoed. "Ugh."

"Oops. My mistake. It's chocolate cake."

"Now that's my kind of breakfast," Haley announced.

On the beach the sand sculptors worked at fever pitch. Their creations were as short lived as the turning of the tide. Within another two hours their art works would be completed, judged and washed to sea.

Like kids at a fireworks display, everyone oohed at the replica of the Kremlin and ahhed at the mermaid sitting in the lap of a fisherman.

After Haley tired of window shopping for art deco perfume bottles, we settled down at an outdoor café. I kept trying to orient myself.

I turned to Eileen. "I have the sense I've been on this beach before."

"This is where we came the night I fed you oranges."

"When I was selling my poetry at the Saturday Market I daydreamed about living in a beach town, with a hippy woman who was a potter."

Eileen smiled. "As soon as I graduated from high school, I flew to France. Practically the first day, I took a job outside of Paris at a pottery collective where a half dozen of us each lived in our own small huts, surrounding the kilns. When my high school boyfriend came looking for me and convinced me to return to the States, I enrolled at Oregon State as an Art Education major and spent four years in the pottery studio."

"What was it like returning to Oregon?"

"We arrived at Kennedy Airport with less than ten dollars in our pockets and hitch-hiked across the country with the first person who offered us a ride. Mom and Dad wouldn't let us stay in the house, so instead we got married."

It was past midnight before Owen and Haley left for home.

"I had a great day, Eileen. Especially the horse back ride."

"Sunshine's a dear, isn't she? Except when she got spooked by the log, she didn't object at all to us riding double."

"I didn't mind riding double either," I said. "I liked holding you around the waist and I liked feeling your back against my chest, especially with all the bouncing. And I cheated a little bit and got a cheap feel."

"That's gross." Eileen got up to leave.

"Don't go, Eileen. I want to ask you something."

She looked at me with hooded eyes.

"I want you to sleep with me tonight."

"Wrong. I am not sleeping with you tonight. You go to the laundry room and I go to my bedroom."

"Let's talk about it."

"There's nothing to talk about."

"I just want to go to sleep holding you. I want to know how we fit."

"No sex?"

"No sex, I promise"

"And no cheap thrills?"

"I swear it."

"Okay. Let's go to bed. I'm tired."

The next morning, the party was over.

"I have to leave today, Eileen."

"Yeah, just like you. Run in, have some fun and run on out."

"I want to see you again."

"When?"

"Tomorrow." I took a breath. "I want to see you every tomorrow that ever is. I don't want to see a tomorrow that doesn't include you."

"Jay, what are you saying?"

"I'm saying I want to make a deal. I promise to be the best thing that ever happened in your life and the moment that I no longer am, I promise I will leave quietly."

"I don't know."

"Then trust me. I've known since the first time I saw you and I have waited six years for this one moment. Just tell me one thing. Was your weekend better because I was part of it?"

"Yes."

"Then I'm going back to Eugene and arrange to take a vacation. I'll come back here as soon as I can, for as long as you'll allow me."

Eileen put a finger to my lips. "Okay, Jay. Come down soon and we'll play some more."

When I got back to Eugene, I ordered a Bird of Paradise plant sent to Eileen.

My request for a ten day paid vacation was first on the Monday night agenda. I had no way to justify the request and there was no way I could afford to leave Eugene without it.

Kelly opened the discussion by saying she would cover my responsibilities while I was gone.

Arnie leaned over to me and whispered, "Did you kissy kiss?"

I nodded my head.

"Was it sweet?"

I nodded again.

"Jay should go," Arnie declared.

I looked around the room. People were smiling. Discussion ended. I could go. Vacation with pay.

This time I drove, praying the station wagon would survive the grade outside of Ashland. It didn't get that far. It overheated on a small incline fifty miles south of Eugene. The trunk of the wagon was stacked with one gallon jugs of water for this kind of emergency. An hour later I continued driving south and arrived in the pre-dawn silence.

On that first night the tape recorder played Vivaldi's <u>Four Seasons</u>, throughout the hours and into dawn.

On the second night I tried to remember how to nestle her in my arms as the phantom of the opera cried out to heaven.

Puccini, George Winston, Pachelbel, Enya, Kitaro and Manheim Steamroller became the witnesses to our week of love.

On the ninth night we were joined by Owen and Haley for dinner in an upstairs Bistro. As we waited for our table to be cleared, Shari, a friend of Eileen, famed in Santa Cruz for doing past life readings arose from another table and came over to us.

"I see you've met your soul mate, Eileen. What's his name?"

Eileen turned to me and said, "How come both of you know something that I don't know?"

On the tenth night we agreed to be together.

When I returned to Eugene I started creating a collage. I've done a lot of them. When they're finished I can sometimes see a pattern in what I've created and can use them as a road map to help direct my footsteps.

Natasha arrived home late after a rehearsal for The Rocky Horror Picture Show. We hugged. She asked what we were having for dinner and poured herself a cup of coffee.

"Who did you say you visited in California?" she asked casually.

"Her name is Eileen."

"Eileen? That's right. When I told Mom about the trip she guessed right away it must be Eileen. Who's Eileen?"

"You probably don't remember her. You met her the last week before we moved to Eugene."

"That was five years ago. The only thing I remember is walking home from school every day that week because you kept forgetting to come get us. Sooo? Did you keep up a friendship?"

"I did. She didn't. We haven't spoken in years."

"And?"

"And what?"

"And you like her?"

"Yes."

Natasha was in a time capsule, hurtling backward to not-so-distant abandonments. Daddy gone, Mommy gone, and sometimes both of us gone.

I broke her train of thought just before it went off the tracks. "Natasha, are you okay?"

"Yeah, I'm okay. Just promise me you won't do something stupid like move down there."

"Hey, Natasha. We've only been together for a few days."

'Yeah, but you like her and you don't like so many people."

Looking around she saw the half completed collage on the living room couch. "Are you doing another collage?"

"Yeah. I thought it would help me figure things out."

"You make collages like Madame Defarge knits sweaters. Every time you make a collage, life changes. Let me look."

Natasha leaned over my shoulder. "Let's see, there's a new leather wallet, a gold key chain and King Kong over there in the corner. Oh, Daddy. King Kong?"

"Get away from me," I said trying to gather together the visual proof of my psychoses.

"One more second." Natasha was skimming the clippings. Her hand stopped moving at the lighthouse on the California shore.

Natasha sat down on a kitchen chair. "Daddy, how serious are you about Eileen?"

"Serious."

"Serious enough to leave Eugene?"

"Serious enough to leave Eugene."

"Daddy!!!!" It was the cry of a wounded cub.

"Natasha, you know you're welcome to come with me. There's always room."

"Get a life!" she shouted. "I'm not leaving Eugene. This is my home. This is where I go to school. I'm a junior. I graduate next year. This is where my friends live."

"That's why I want to go. I want to get a life, too. I already missed one chance with her. If I don't do it now, I'll live in regret the rest of my days."

"Why can't she move here?"

"We talked about it. She has a successful massage practice and makes a ton of money. She even has an Apple computer. If necessary, she can support me until I find work. On the other hand, if it wasn't for the money your mother gives me each month, I couldn't afford the mortgage on this house. I think you'll like her. She wants to come meet you."

"You said she's a masseuse? A rich masseuse? Can she cook?"

"I'm guessing she's a good cook. She taught classes all over Oregon in how to prepare tofu."

"I still don't like it, but anything is better than your cooking. When am I going to meet her?"

"She's going to Mexico to study for a month. Afterward, we can plan on all of us getting together."

Eileen is in southern Mexico, There are no phones where she's staying and I have received only one letter. She was invited to live with Guru Dev in a Mayan village. She met Guru Dev when she and Sita were traveling with Yogi Bhajan after she took the kids and left Oregon. Eileen says he's world renowned and received direct transmission from the Yogi.

She will give and teach massage to the local villagers and spend time with Guru Dev studying healing arts. Eileen tells me the Sikhs know more about the body than anybody else and that Guru Dev is the most brilliant of them all, combining yogic healing with Mayan and curandero traditions.

Guru Dev is not overjoyed about me. He wants to meet me and is going to make plans to be in the Bay Area during Thanksgiving. Eileen says his approval is essential and that the plans we've made for getting together depend on what he thinks of our union. For five years my heart has ached to be with Eileen and now when it finally seems possible, I have to pass an interview with a stranger.

I took twenty-five percent of my savings and purchased a new radiator and hoses for the Pinto and in return was assured the car wouldn't overheat. Overheating in this weather, however, was the least of my worries. It was raining so hard I would have done better to invest in an outboard motor.

There were changes in Santa Cruz. Missy had returned to her boyfriend and married him and I was relegated to the alcove by the washing machine until after we met with Guru Dev the next afternoon.

Guru Dev's presence in Santa Cruz was a major event for his Bay Area devotees and there were two dozen excited guests at Sita's home all vying for a moment of his attention. Eileen was known by nearly all of the people and it was no surprise to them that Guru Dev pointed to a chair on his right where she should sit, but there were plenty of whispers when he pointed to the chair at his left and motioned for me to take my place. Everyone there was vegetarian, but I felt like a sacrificial lamb.

Guru Dev was not impressed with me. He most certainly did not appreciate that I was poor and that I worked with homeless people.

Pointing to Eileen he said, "Deva Kar has important work to do. How are you going to support her when you can barely support yourself? And why are you doing charity work before you have made your wealth? You are doing life backwards. You do this work after you are able to provide for your family, not before."

I glanced over at Eileen and thought I saw tears forming in the corner of her eyes.

When lunch was finished, people urged Guru Dev to give a teaching but he waved them aside, asking his hostess for a room where he and Eileen could have a private conversation with me.

Guru Dev asked me to lie down on the carpet. Turning to Eileen, he said, "Together, as I have taught you, we will examine his body to find out his truth." Eileen nodded her head and they took their places on either side of me and began with my stockinged feet. When they reached my solar plexus all heck broke out.

Guiding Eileen's hands across my stomach he was speaking rapidly in broken English in an Indian accent. "Quick now. Push here. Press your palm down over there. With me, now!" I felt like I was in an emergency room with a ruptured appendix.

After a moment Guru Dev faced Eileen. "This man has no strength in his stomach. You can feel that, yes? He cannot protect you. His chi is dormant. It is very, very bad. I am so sorry." Eileen had folded her hands in her lap, defeated, but Guru Dev kept exploring.

There wasn't much more to say until he reached my breast. There he stopped. Taking Eileen's hand, he placed it over my heart. "What has happened to you?" he asked. "What happened to your heart when you were young?"

I told them the story. I was born with a hole in my heart. In the 1940s, no one knew how to close the hole and babies died within a few months. We were called blue babies because we weren't getting enough oxygen. For some unexplained reason I survived and by the time I was three years old, there were doctors who wanted to do experimental heart surgery. There weren't many candidates as old as me, so I was one of the kids chosen as a guinea pig. My first memories in life are of the anesthesia and the pain of them taking out the stitches ten days later.

Guru Dev motioned for me to lie back down and taking Eileen's fingers, brushed them across my chest. "This man has a wounded heart. It has never mended. If you can heal his heart, he will fight for you. I cannot say more. I leave it to you, Deva Kar."

That night, Eileen needed to talk. "Jay, I realized while I was in Mexico that I needed to ask you two questions."

"Go ahead."

"Do you still smoke pot? If you do, we have to stop right now and give blessings for what we've had."

"I haven't smoked in over a year. I made that decision when I decided I wanted to return to work."

"Doesn't everyone at The Portal smoke?"

"A lot of them do. I'm considered Mr. Straight at the clinic."

"That's ironic."

"Yeah. It is. What's your other question?"

"Are you a jealous man?"

"I don't know. I never have hungered for someone."

"It's important you find out right away. Because you'll never be number one, not even number two in my life. G-d is number one and my kids are number two. You have to be okay with that."

"That's fair."

"Just one more question."

"Wait a minute. You said two."

"Yes, but I have another. When are you going to come down?"

"I promised The Portal I would work for them for a year. That ends in mid-February."

"That's too long for me to wait to see you. What about if I come up for Christmas?"

Eileen was talking to me on the phone. "How are you feeling?"

"I'm a little lonely and really looking forward to seeing you."

"Yes, but what color are your eyes?"

"Brown."

"That's good, because mine are yellow."

"Hepatitis? Since when?"

"Probably before I went to Mexico. The doctors say it takes four to six weeks to incubate."

"Are you contagious?"

"Not now, but during the incubation period I was."

"And that was when?"

"Right when you were visiting."

"So we'll skip this Christmas. There will be another Christmas next year," I said trying to be cheerful and hiding my disappointment.

"If we can't be together for Christmas, then let's both read Dicken's <u>A Christmas Carol</u>. We'll share the story and it will help us get through the holiday," she suggested.

A week later, Eileen called.

"I found someone who wants to visit his sister in Portland

for Christmas. He used to drive a taxi and doesn't mind driving long distances. Is it okay with you if he spends one night at your house?"

"Of course. But you're still sick yourself and yesterday they had to close the pass for hours because of snow."

"If we leave here by six in the morning we'll be at the pass by one o'clock. That'll be the best time to try making it over. I made a bed in the back seat of the car. Harold will do all the work."

"I'd love to see you."

"And I want to meet Natasha and Gabriel."

"Are you sure?"

"I'm sure I want to be with you."

Somehow, Eileen managed to get to Eugene, her trek across the snow bound mountain passes reminding me of heroines in Russian novels. When she arrived, we made a bed for her on the living room couch from which she occasionally rose to engage in folly.

One morning when she was resting, I took the kids out for breakfast.

"I like her, Daddy. She's fun," Natasha said.

"Did you mind us having a Christmas tree, Natasha?"

"No. I know you're Jewish. The tree doesn't take that away from you."

"I always liked Christmas trees. But until now I couldn't think of any reason to have one. Being with Eileen gives me a good excuse."

"I liked it when the tree fell down and took the bookcase with it," Gabriel added.

"What did you think of the gifts she brought you from Mexico?" I asked.

"The poncho is soooo beautiful. I'm going to wear it to school."

"She bought me a white chamois shirt and gave me a crystal this morning." Gabriel said, pulling it out of his pocket.

"Ooohh. Wooey, wooey. Can you see the future in it?" I questioned.

"Yeah. I see you and her having a big fight if she hears you call her stuff 'wooey, wooey.'"

"I see something different, when I look in the crystal," Natasha remarked.

"What do you see, Natasha?"

"I see you leaving me."

Eileen drove up to help with the packing and to follow behind me in case my car had engine trouble.

"If you put the carton containing the lamps in that corner, on top of the dining room table, your good china will fit beneath the dresser," Eileen suggested like a Mayflower moving van employee.

"Don't forget to leave room for the cedar chest," someone cautioned.

"There must be ten thousand pennies in here," Allen noted while running his fingers through a mountain of copper coins.

"More than that," I said. "I've been collecting pennies ever since Natasha was born so when I someday give them to her, I can say, 'I'm giving you every penny I ever received.'" Looking around anxiously I asked, "Where is the surrey Gabriel made out of pipe cleaners?"

"I put it with your *kiddish* cups and your grandmother's silver tea set in the back seat of the car, Daddy," Natasha reassured me.

"I put your archery bow on the back seat also, Dad." Gabriel added helpfully.

"I brought you and Eileen a box of chocolate truffles for the trip. I'll put them on the dashboard," Debbie said.

"Can I get a family hug before I leave?" I asked.

Natasha, Gabriel, Debbie and I clung to one another like a family that would never be one again.

Eileen and I left in the morning. .

That night, February 21, 1988, the fifth anniversary of the day I brought her soybeans we stopped at a motel outside of Redding. I went to take a shower and when I came out there was a vase of red tulips on the bureau.

SAND
DOLLARS

1989

Eileen's friend, Fay, created a job for me at her mobile home sales lot. In the meantime, I applied for a California teaching license and if nothing else, I may be able to teach English as a Second Language to Latino immigrants.

On April Fools weekend we drove to Tahoe. With Eileen's hectic schedule, driving anywhere long distance gives us precious hours alone in the car. Eileen is a fast driver but I compensate by driving slowly. I'd love some day for us to drive across the country.

After dinner we took a walk around the lake. Eileen found a twenty dollar bill in a snowbank. Handing it to me, she said it would bring me luck when I spent it.

Back at the cabin, we sat on the floor in the dimly lit living room, knees touching. "I have something important I want you to hear," she said.

Digging through her pocketbook she brought out a cassette. She took both my hands in her own as Sikh chants filled the room. As we listened to the sacred calling out to the Beloved, Eileen's eyes slowly closed. I met this woman five years ago. I have lived with her for six weeks. Tonight I know I have loved her throughout a thousand lifetimes.

Easter is around the corner. The only things I know about celebrating the holiday are Easter egg hunts and Easter parades.

Eileen said Easter is celebrated similarly to Christmas with lots of gift giving so I bought her a gold wrist watch.

While Eileen was in the living room meditating, I placed the watch on her pillow in a basket carried by a pink bunny rabbit. When she saw the watch she jumped around the room, clapping her hands, throwing her arms around me and kissing my nose.

"I put your gift by the fireplace."

The only thing by the fireplace was a small bag of Easter candy in a tiny straw basket.

I brought the basket into the kitchen. "You told me people give gifts at Easter just like they do at Christmas."

"Yeah. I knew this would be my only chance to trick you because by next year you'd know better."

I have an interview to teach English as a Second Language. It's only part time but beats the heck out of working at the mobile home lot.

I arrived in Santa Cruz with twenty three hundred dollars, half of which came from a church group that passed the hat when they heard I was leaving town. I had a barely functional Pinto station wagon and was paying a mortgage on a house that was underwater. By the time I was offered the interview I was down to my last few dollars.

"Let's go shopping," were the first words out of Eileen's mouth when I told her about the upcoming interview. "Macy's is open until nine tonight."

The store was deserted and a sharply dressed salesman immediately asked if he could be of assistance.

Eileen wanted to see their best dress shirts and for the next few minutes I was draped in raw silks and cottons in colors ranging from almond to puce. For a guy who thought it was uptown to shop at St. Vincent de Paul, it was surreal.

"What do you think of this one?" she said, holding up a conservative white shirt with a button down collar.

I whispered in Eileen's ear. "Eileen, this shirt is forty-three dollars."

"So?"

The salesman quickly busied himself tidying racks several aisles away from us.

"So, I'm going broke and I don't have money to throw around. You don't get it because you can spend three hundred dollars on a dress."

"What do you know about me?" Eileen was angry. "I've had to search through my pockets for lost change to buy gas for the car. And it isn't so much better now. I do twenty-five massages every week. That's an incredible work load. At the end of each month I have enough money to pay the bills and send the alimony. On top of that I'm planning to go to school three nights a week to become a family therapist because I know my body can't do this level of work when I'm older." She looked sadly at me. "I'm going home." She turned and walked toward the exit.

"Eileen. Wait. Please stop. I'm sorry. I was wrong."

I motioned for the salesman.

"I'll take the white shirt, please."

"Can I interest you in this beautiful herringbone neck tie? It's on sale for eighteen dollars, with tax just under twenty."

Eileen nodded. I reached into the back flap of my wallet where the lucky twenty dollar bill was stashed. "I'll take it."

I started teaching two weeks later.

Classes are on spring break so I borrowed Eileen's car to see Natasha perform in Rocky Horror Picture Show. For the drive, I took along a set of self-motivation tapes because I don't plan on being a part time English teacher the rest of my life. On one tape the lecturer was coaching on how to ask for a salary, higher than the one I might hope to be offered. For better or worse, how I project myself does determine how people respond to me. I have already done the worse. I'm going for better. The first time I played the tape, I asked for eighteen thousand dollars a year. By the fifth time, as I was driving by Mt. Shasta, the number had gone up to fifty thousand dollars. Definitely better.

Natasha was terrific in Rocky Horror. She was a member of the chorus of vamps who were all semi-dressed in black. To add color to her outfit she wore purple lipstick. I caught up with her after the performance and she asked me how I liked it.

"I liked it a lot. It reminded me of Lady Chatterly's Alien."

"Did you like my dress?"

"The little there was, yes."

"Mom helped me pick it out. I'm going to wear it to the Prom."

"Very nice. I hope you'll wear some clothes over it."

"How long are you going to stay in Eugene?"

"I've got to go back in the morning. I have time for a Dunkin Donut if you do."

"Sure. Hey, Dad, how hard would it be for me to get a job in Santa Cruz this summer?"

"I know the Human Resource people at the Boardwalk. If you want to work there I'm sure I can get you a job."

"Okay. Talk to them. I'll see you in a few weeks."

Natasha woke up early. She knocked on our door. "Are you decent?"

"Come in, Natasha," Eileen said. "We're in our pajamas."

Natasha stood in the doorway. "Get up you sleepy heads. Let's go to the beach."

"Have you been outside this morning?" I asked, pulling open the curtains to reveal a heavy mist.

"Don't worry. It's only hazy. It'll blow away."

"It'll blow away around one o'clock," I clarified.

"What are we supposed to do until then?"

"Climb under the blankets and tell us about the end of the school year," Eileen said, making room in the bed and in her heart for my daughter.

I've begun packing for the Oregon Country Fair. I have two tents, air mattresses and six sleeping bags. I also took a Marx Brother's book called Flywheel and Flywheel *to read aloud while we drive to Portland. We'll pick up Eden and Dylan and meet Gabriel out at the Fair. It's going to be the first time the four kids are together.*

Dylan stood staring at the fantasy castles and elaborately designed booths that surrounded us and asked, "Jay, where's your booth?"

"You're standing on it."

"There's nothing here," he exclaimed in bewilderment.

Eileen grimaced. "How many years have you had this space?"

"Eight."

"And you never did anything to improve it?"

"I never had the need."

"Well, you have a family now, so there's a need. Here, Natasha, tie this rope to that tree. I'll tie this end to our neighbor's deck and we can throw a couple of tapestries over it to give us some privacy. Jay, after you put up our tents, see if you can buy a few bales of straw we can use for a table and chairs."

Bruce and Sandee arrived while I was setting up the tents. They were my neighbors and Fair family since the beginning. One of their trucks was filled with lumber.

"We heard you were bringing someone special," Bruce said, as he began to unload crates of pottery. "Sandee suggested we make you a house. All it will take is a front wall that we can secure to a tree and to my deck."

Eileen was as happy as a kid who just hit a home run in punch ball.

"Do you think you can cut a window in it and make a space that looks like a front door?" she asked.

To Bruce, who was a chain saw carpenter, cutting two holes did not pose a problem.

"Jay, see if you can buy something pretty to decorate the window. Eden, Dylan, Natasha, help me clear this brush."

By mid afternoon we were settled in. Eileen hung a madras print in the doorway. A candle and vase of flowers sat on a windowsill which was framed in lace. About the time we stopped, Gabriel arrived.

"Wow! This is nice. Who did it?"

"Everyone helped. The only thing we're missing are some bales of hay," Eileen said.

"I know where I can get them," Gabriel said. "I passed the guy coming in. Come with me, Dad."

As Gabriel and I left on our mission, I turned back and saw Eileen inscribing the words "Home Sweet Home" over the doorway.

The weekend was a collage of wonder and elegance. On Thursday night we pressed together on the grass in front of the Gypsy Stage as belly dancers took turns swaying in rhythm to brass finger cymbals and the haunting sound of the *ney*. Friday afternoon Eileen brought out a *doumbek* which had been handmade by a famous drum maker. Gabriel was enthralled with it. She taught him some simple rhythms and then together they wandered off to the drum tower where they spent hours keeping tempo with the heartbeat of the earth. In an open field, on Friday night, fire dancers performed a flaming ballet. On Saturday Eileen insisted that I take a break from selling my books and poetry and accompany her on a shopping spree.

"I have a responsibility to support artists and craftspeople," she said as she merrily wandered from one booth to another.

The Portal ran a barbecued chicken booth on the loop. Profits from the chicken booth were earmarked for the homeless health care program I helped launch and several of the volunteers barbecuing were themselves once street people. They were a ragged group, indifferent to their disheveled appearance, cleaving frozen chicken breasts before a mostly astonished and horrified mass of hippy vegetarians, vegans and breatharians. Arnie was attending the grill when we arrived. When he saw Eileen he offered her a broad grin.

"Come meet everyone," he said, putting his arm around her shoulder.

There were wide eyed stares as men who were often shunned and taught to stay in the shadows basked in Eileen's warmth. How one of their own, me, could have a girlfriend as beautiful and accepting as Eileen both mystified and made them proud. They would have kept her among themselves for the rest of the day if a sudden fat fire hadn't brought them out of their revelry and back to work.

On the way back to our booth, Eileen purchased a rose colored floppy corduroy hat with a red rose made from fabric sewn to the brim, a carved walking stick for me, a plush velvet skirt for Natasha, jewelry for Eden, a sweater for Dylan and a drum for Gabriel.

Heralding the Midnight Show at Main Stage was an impromptu marching band playing a sprightly version of Teddy Bear's Picnic. It was led by a score of women and girls adorned with fairy wings that wound its way through the Fair, gathering musicians as it went. We followed in its wake and when we tired of the show, Eileen and I made our way to the Ritz Sauna and Showers.

The Ritz Spa is hippy opulence. There may not be a spa more grandiose than The Ritz with its one hundred seat hand-crafted sauna. Seventy shower heads are lined up in the open air where men and women lather side by side, with water made hot by cord after cord of blazing wood. After we scrubbed the dust from three days at the Fair, Eileen and I sat by a fire pit and listened to the crackle of pine and fir accompanying the sweet songs of traveling troubadours who performed for the price of a shower.

On Sunday afternoon, two of America's street poets stopped at my booth to put down their hats to passersby. I introduced them to Eileen. One was from the eastside of New York City. He recited from Sonnets from the Portuguese by Elizabeth Browning. My other buddy earned his rent standing in front of the Fillmore, reciting Alan Ginsburg. He recited from Richard Brautigan's Trout Fishing in America, one of Eileen's favorite books. Eileen was royalty. The poets were court minstrels.

On Monday morning, Eileen purchased a forty-eight piece set of stoneware, service for twelve, from Bruce. As I tried to fit everything into the mini van we had rented, I thought to myself that Eileen takes seriously her responsibilities to artists and craftspeople.

Eileen reduced the number of hours she works at the Spa and on the evenings I'm not teaching, we make bonfires and roast marshmallows on the beach. Natasha got a job selling pretzels at the Boardwalk and the others are taking surfing lessons.

Tuesday evening is family night at the boardwalk. All the rides are twenty-five cents. On the last week of summer all six of us joined the locals for a night of thrills and cotton candy.

"I want to ride the Giant Dipper three times!" Dylan exclaimed.

"I want to ride the Giant Dipper three times and reach my arms overhead," Eden said.

"I want to ride the bumper cars," Gabriel contributed to the conversation.

"What do you want to do, Daddy?" Gabe asked.

"I want to eat cotton candy."

"I like the ferris wheel," Eileen added.

"I know what I don't want," Natasha said. "I don't want another pretzel."

During the evening, Eileen and I sat in a swaying gondola at the top of the ferris wheel gazing over the amusement park lights.

"When the kids leave next week there won't be much reason to come down to the boardwalk," I said.

"I don't know, it could be fun. Let's say the ride got stuck and you and I were up here swinging at the top of the wheel. What would you do?"

"I'd kiss you."

"Good answer. Do it."

Eileen has been crying ever since we dropped the kids off in Oregon. She sobs so fiercely that her rib cage is in torment.

I grew up in the Bronx where knowing someone was watching your back was as important as having money in your pocket, especially when you were in trouble. Eileen had neither on the day she went to court for custody of Eden and Dylan. She didn't have money to hire a decent lawyer and several of her family members spoke in favor of her former husband, who, like most of Eileen's family, was a practicing Catholic. No one spoke on her behalf. It was a betrayal she has not been able to forgive. She was alone and she lost, though I think Eden and Dylan lost the most.

Hers is a sorrow that any words of consolation I could offer are lost in an abyss of pain so I drove seven hundred miles south in a silence occasionally broken by muted tones of wrenching despair.

I'm hoping the near prospect of us backpacking with Natasha in Vermont will brighten her spirit. This is the last opportunity we'll have to do the trek because once Natasha is in college there will be no time to take a week off in mid semester.

Eileen had backpacked only once. She needed boots and reassurance. Natasha never hiked with anyone but me. She, too, needed reassurance. I hadn't hiked the Appalachian Trail in twenty years. I needed a cane.

Each of us took along one totally extraneous item. Eileen chose a harmonica. Natasha selected a map of the constellations. I brought along a pair of binoculars.

We spent six days on the trail. The entire way, the path was layered with oak and maple leaves in reds, yellows and browns. It looked like G-d ran a palette across a mountain canvas.

On the first night, Eileen created an altar to the Goddess of The Trail and made an offering of her new hiking boots. For the remainder of the trek she wore a pair of old sneakers. The Goddess must have been satisfied because no one got blisters.

On Friday, we came off the trail. At 5:03 an earthquake struck Santa Cruz County, destroying homes and transforming the downtown business district into Craters of the Moon.

I was devastated. While Eileen tried to contact her brother, Owen, Natasha tried offering me comfort. "Don't worry, Daddy. Your house might not have been damaged."

"I don't care about the house. I care that I spent years preparing for the San Andreas Earthquake. I attended more seminars on "The Big One" than I can count and what happens? We finally get a 7.2 on the Richter Scale and I miss it because I'm back east. What a lousy deal."

"Maybe you can get back in time for aftershocks," she offered in consolation.

Our house wasn't damaged and the only breakage was my English bone china salt and pepper shakers. The real excitement was going to be at Red Cross Headquarters so I headed in that direction.

Eileen and Owen drove to Oregon to be with her kids for the holidays. The four of them are planning to spend Christmas with Eileen's mom and dad and no one has yet been able to talk about or process what happened in court. I'm glad she's returning to California for New Years Eve. I plan to cook a feast.

I laid down a white linen tablecloth and put two white tapers between a bouquet of red roses. I baked cranberry muffins and made a Southwest spicy pumpkin soup along with a casserole recipe from the Moosewood cookbook.

She expected to be home by five o'clock. At five thirty I turned off the soup. At six I put the casserole in the refrigerator and at seven began pacing the street. At seven thirty she called.

"Where are you?"

"Hi, Jay. I'm sorry. My car broke down. We're stuck."

"Where are you?"

"We're in Winters, about a hundred miles from you."

"Okay, I see it on a map. If I leave now, I can be there by ten o'clock. Is there anywhere you and Owen can wait and stay warm?"

"I'm calling from the Buckhorn restaurant. We'll wait here for you. I'm really sorry, Jay."

I spotted Eileen and Owen at the edge of a horde of reveling UC Davis students. I joined them, pulling cranberry muffins from a brown paper bag. We ate veggie burgers, French fried potatoes and shared a beer. It wasn't a feast but just being with Eileen made it a great way to celebrate the new year.

1990

I have an interview at Goodwill Industries for director of Public Relations and Development and Eileen is beginning graduate school to become a marriage and family therapist.

I met with Harris, the C.E.O. of Goodwill Industries.

"What experience do you have making presentations to civic clubs like the Elks, Lions and Rotary?"

"None, but I've acted in or directed more than a dozen plays. The Junior Chamber of Commerce shouldn't be too tough an audience."

"How about writing newsletters and press releases?"

"Nope, but I wrote two published books of children's stories and had a weekly column in a small town newspaper for years."

So it went. I left feeling positive about the interview but hoped G-d would put in a good word for me.

"Hey, G-d, are you listening? I need a favor. I applied for a job at Goodwill Industries. I need this job. If you'll help me get the job, I promise I won't ever again eat pork."

"You think it would make me happy if you gave up eating bacon?" I heard a voice say from somewhere within myself.

"Well, kind of, yeah, I guess. Don't you?"

"If you think so."

"So what do you think?"

"I think you have to quit eating pork because you think that will please me."

"Yeah, right. But how about this deal?"

"I don't make deals."

Harris invited me to lunch and offered me the job. He wants me to begin in two weeks.

"By the way, in case you're still hungry after the salad, this restaurant serves magnificent stuffed mushrooms rolled in bacon strips."

"Sounds good, but I don't eat pork."

I earned more money in two weeks at Goodwill than I did at The Portal in two months. But I didn't get to keep any of it.

On payday, Eileen and I went to Men's Warehouse. I bought shirts, shoes, socks, ties, slacks, and a suit. I told the sales clerk to put on hold two additional jackets and maroon suspenders until my next pay check arrived.

I wore the new clothing out the door, stopping at a trash can to discard the brown cords and blue shirt with frayed collar which I wore to work all week. When we passed a store front window I caught a glimpse of how I looked. I liked the image.

During the probationary period, Harris kept pretty close tabs on me. During one of the business forums we were attending, he leaned over and asked to borrow a pen. I handed him a gold plated, imitation Cross I bought at a flea market. When he returned the pen, I noticed the gold plate was rubbed off where he had held it with his fingers.

The red Mustang convertible glistened in the sun. I parked in front of a coffee house where several homeless looking men were whiling away the hours. Stepping out of it in a sharply pressed suit and herringbone tie I felt like an ad in GQ magazine. I shined the chrome with my hanky.

"Spare change?" one of the men asked half heartedly.

Eileen had taught me a rule: I should always have money to feed the birds, poets and those who ask. She told me as long as I was able to help others, I would never think of myself as poor.

I reached into my pocket and extended a pocket full of coins.

"Thanks mister. I didn't think someone like you would care."

"Someone like me?" I thought as I walked away. "He doesn't know who I am. He wasn't able to smell my past. If I can fool one of my own, straight people will never guess where I've been." I walked more sprightly.

At the end of the day I eased into the car. On the passenger seat was a small gift-wrapped box from Harris. It contained a gold plated Cross pen and pencil set.

Gabe is becoming a rebellious teenager.

"Hi, Debbie. What's up?"

"It's Gabriel. Last Friday, he, Misty and Michelle hitchhiked to the coast. When he didn't come home for supper, I called their mother. She wasn't concerned. Then it began to rain. I kept picturing the three of them without dry clothes getting hypothermia. I thought about calling the State Highway Patrol, but I was afraid the kids might be carrying drugs. I made Don drive to the coast to look for them. He found them sheltering under a picnic table in a campground."

"Sounds like Gabe," I ventured.

"Sounds like trouble," Debbie replied.

I need the support of the three hundred workers if I'm going to be able to do my job. I organized a coed company soft ball team, equipping them with baseball mitts and bats from donated goods, but I need a project that inspires pride in the organization. Creating a float for the Begonia Festival would build team spirit and might earn us media coverage, which is part of my job responsibilities. The floats actually have to float down a creek and since everything is made from begonias instead of paper mache, the flowers need to be picked on Friday with the float completed by Sunday morning. Natasha and I helped construct floats several times when I was teaching at the high school and she is here, visiting. She thinks we should go for it.

"We saw the parade last year and the floats are impressive. They're built by church and social groups. We won't have as many volunteers so we need to be more interesting," I explained.

"Do you still want to tie it into the war?" Natasha asked.

"The government wants a war with Iraq. Most Americans don't want this war and a lot of people are frightened for their sons and daughters. My idea is to build a giant white dove and place an olive branch in its mouth."

"Good idea but it will look pretty plain compared to the other floats and isn't going to win any prizes," Eileen said.

"I know. My idea is to rig it so the dove can flap its wings."

"What if Natasha is hidden inside the dove handling the wings and just when the float goes past the viewing stand, she releases a covey of live doves?"

And that's what happened. On the second Sunday in September our dove floated down Soquel Creek with Natasha waiting inside for the announcer to read the vital statistics usually consisting of a flower count and a brief pitch for the church or social club.

The announcer began: "Friends and neighbors, the workers of Goodwill Industries built this peace dove. The olive branch in its mouth is from an olive tree growing on Goodwill property. In a few day our sons and daughters may have to face great dangers and Goodwill asks that we take a moment in silence and pray for their safe…" she was beginning to cry and needed to compose herself… "safe return home." A great stillness blanketed both sides of the river and then a dozen white pigeons were released.

The crowd went wild. As the float continued past the viewing stand, people tossed flowers in the water surrounding the dove with begonias. We made the front page of the newspaper and took home the Mayor's trophy.

Eileen, Natasha and I hadn't slept in two days. "Let's take a nap," I suggested as we stumbled into the house.

"Let's pray first," said Eileen as she spread out prayer rugs. She took out her *malas* made of *bodhi* beads and offered me a small green silk purse that looks like it might have been purchased in Chinatown but was a gift from a Tibetan Lama. The purse contains the jade *malas* she gave me as a Christmas present last year.

As we began, I looked at her dressed in a plain beige nightgown. There is a coffee stain near the hem of the sheath. She looks like a Trappist monk in her simplicity and all I see is the radiant light of love for G-d in her eyes. Sleep can wait.

*Fay sold the Mobile Home Sales Lot and is moving to Mexico.
She is holding a garage sale this weekend and leaving for Acapulco on
Sunday night.*

When Eileen and I arrived, Fay's son was loading the living
room furniture into a U-Haul truck. Eileen boxed whatever
was going into storage and I spent the day as a barker, hawking
whatever I could sell or give away. By nightfall we were exhausted.

Eileen had crammed the Mercedes with a beach umbrella,
barbecue grill, the perishables from the refrigerator, a case of thirty
weight motor oil, a Persian carpet and a white ball of furry feline.

"What's with the cat, Eileen?"

"Fay wasn't able to find a home for her so I said we would
take her. Her name is Snowball. Isn't she beautiful? She's the first
sentient being we've adopted together."

"Wasn't your horse named Snowball?"

"Her name was Sunshine. What do you think about us leasing
a couple of horses?"

1991

*Eileen believes we have reincarnated thousands of times and
everyone we know in this present life we have known in many
lifetimes, but in different relationships. Somebody's brother in this
lifetime, she believes, might have been that person's daughter in a past
life. It's a new concept for me, but what do I know? I used to think
I was an alien and that my birth on planet earth was some form of
mistaken intergalactic postal delivery.*

*We attended a past life workshop given by Shari, the woman
who called me Eileen's soul mate. During the workshop, I envisioned
being a North African tribal chieftain who fought and died battling a
lion to protect my lover whom I knew was Eileen, though I never saw
her face. The fact that people almost always recall past lives in which*

they were kings, queens, poets or saviors didn't diminish the sense of truth that the vision held for me and it was terribly romantic.

It was enough that I wanted to know more and Shari is coming to our house for a private reading.

She sat in a wing back chair, closed her eyes and entered a trance.

"The two of you have been together many times. The furthest back I can see is in China during the time of the Middle Kingdom. You, Jay, were a scholar and born into high society. Eileen was a farmer's daughter. You saw her for the first time when she was seven years old and she had such a thirst for learning that you broke with convention and taught her to read. As she grew into womanhood, Eileen taught other girls how to read and had many students. Surrounding her always were the bewildered souls of uncountable children who had been stolen from their homes. Wielding a sword of compassion she would sever the tethers of thousands at one stroke, freeing them from the *bardo.*"

The seer emerged from wherever her mind had taken her. She looked at us and laughed. Pointing to Eileen she said, "Both of you have been troublemakers for a long time."

"Is there more?"

She resettled and resumed a trance.

"In Egyptian times you were brother and sister. You were very close and could communicate telepathically. The priests learned of your gifts and took both you from your parents and taught you their mysteries. When you came of age, you were separated and placed far apart in temples to the Mother Goddess Isis to enable the Pharaoh to instantly send and receive messages.

"There's one more lifetime you shared that I can see.

"A hundred and fifty years ago, Jay, you were an American Indian elder who took Eileen as your second wife. In the moment of her birth, a blue jay flew into the tent and when the babe was held up for her mother to see, the bird alighted on her shoulder. From that day on Eileen was known as Blue Feather. When she reached marriage age, you asked her to be your wife but she refused unless she had your first wife's blessing, which was granted. For the rest of your lives she was your most trusted counselor and sat behind you, hidden from sight, during council gatherings, whispering advice."

Shari returned to the present.

"Jay, do you have an animal totem?" Eileen asked.

"The blue jay. What about you, Eileen?"

"I have two totems, the dolphin and the crow. Jay, remember this. No matter how far apart we may some day be, I promise I will come to you on the wind."

Gabriel is having a tough time settling down.

Gabriel was on the line.

"You sound happy, Gabriel."

"I'm feeling good. I decided I'm leaving school at the end of next month and coming down to stay with you from May until June. Then I'm going to hop freight trains with Stu during the summer and go back to Eugene in the Fall."

"Why are you quitting school?"

"I'm not quitting. I'll go to school in Santa Cruz. I can have South Eugene transfer my grades down there."

"You can't transfer this late in the year. You'll lose all your credits."

"It doesn't matter. I'm flunking most of them anyway."

I cupped the phone and turned to Eileen. "We talked about this before. Are you still okay with Gabriel coming to live with us?"

Eileen nodded her head. I uncapped the phone.

"So, am I coming down at the end of the month?"

"No. But I do want you to be with me. Eileen and I hope

you'll spend your sophomore year in Santa Cruz."

"What if we can't get along and I hate it?"

"If it's beyond awful for any of the three of us, you can return to Eugene or make other plans. But at least we'll all be going into this thing with a willingness to try to make it a success."

I haven't been back to the farm in years. If Debbie and I sell it, my half would be enough for a down payment on a house in Santa Cruz.

"Eileen, I'm bored."

"Do you want to play backgammon?"

"No."

"Rent a movie?"

I shook my head. "Let's get married."

"You may be bored, but I am not crazy. I've been there twice and the bridal path doesn't get any prettier just because it's rutted."

"All right, if you don't want to get married, let's buy a house."

Now I had Eileen's full attention. "You love me that much?"

"I asked you to marry me, didn't I?"

"It's harder to get out of a mortgage than it is a marriage."

"Let's talk about the house we want to buy."

"Something small and cozy."

"By the beach,"

"With a brick patio."

"And French doors."

"It has to have a porch."

"I like bay windows."

"With window seats."

"What about a widow's walk?"

"And a fireplace."

"Two of them. One in the living room and one in our bedroom."

We stopped to catch our breaths.

"Can we afford it?" Eileen asked bringing us back to reality.

"If Debbie and I sell the farm, I think my share would be enough for a down payment."

"Do you feel bad about selling the farm?"

"I didn't want to sell it while Grandpa was alive but it doesn't matter anymore. I wish you could have met him."

"I do too. Here's another idea. I'm getting an eight thousand dollar student loan. I can add that money to the down payment."

"If you do that, how will you continue to pay for graduate school?"

"I have a plan. I need to do three thousand hours of internship to get a license. My friend Bailey created a non-profit, low cost counseling organization. I'm going to work out of her office and she is going to let me keep whatever money I earn. That should cover school costs."

"You're going to attend graduate school full time, do twenty-five massages a week and also see counseling clients?"

"I can do it."

"Okay. It's settled. Let's go look for a house. How long will it take you to get ready?"

"I've been ready for a man to pop the right question, most of my life."

I am going to miss this cottage. The sun room is my favorite spot. One wall is made up of mismatched window panes. The floor has partially rotted away where it meets the outside wall, allowing morning glories to vine their way into the room. There's a baby grand piano in the corner and Eileen plays it in the evening hours. We'll sell the piano if there is no room for it in the house we buy.

"When did you learn to play the piano?" I asked, as Eileen played Dvorak's <u>New World Symphony</u>.

"I was eleven when I decided I wanted to learn how to play the piano. We didn't have money to pay for music lessons but one of the nuns agreed to teach me, if on Saturday mornings, I would do light house keeping at the convent and visit with the sisters who were bedridden."

"How long did you do that?"

"Until high school."

"Was it scary being with old, sick people?"

"No. I liked going there. It was quiet in the convent and when I wasn't sweeping or dusting, I sat and talked with the retired nuns. It was at the retirement home that I was introduced to Padre Pio."

"Who's he?"

"A Capuchin friar. He saw G-d everywhere, taught meditation and could be in two places at the same time. He was my glimpse into Christian mysticism."

"Was it ever boring?"

"I was a mad seamstress. I always had a Simplicity pattern that needed hand stitching and I took it in a basket when I went there. There was one sister who could barely see but could thread a needle. I asked how she did it and she told me to see with my hands as well as with my eyes. I remembered her when I went to massage school and learned to see with my hands how to help heal a person."

"Did you always want to be a healer?"

"What I always wanted was to make this my last turn of the wheel and not reincarnate."

"What about you?"

"I always wanted to be with you."

Buying a house in Santa Cruz is so dang expensive.

"It's a very small house," I said, pointing to the cottage within walking distance of the harbor.

"It has three bedrooms."

"It's not in a forest but it has a liquid amber tree in the front yard," I pointed out.

"I like the porch. There's room on it for two rocking chairs. It'll be cozy."

"The dog run is dreadful."

"We could replace it with a brick patio."

"Do you really like it?"

"I love it," she said.

"Here are the keys. Happy 40th Birthday."

In two weeks, Eileen is taking Dylan, Eden and Natasha to France and Spain. Her sister, Iris, and her parents are going as well. Her dad hopes to reconnect with his family in a small Basque village where he was raised. Eileen is excited about spending the summer with her kids and Natasha is looking for an adventure. No one talks about what took place in court. I'm looking forward to moving into the new house and unpacking all the boxes.

I sought Eileen's past in the garage that awaited the moving van. I ran my hands over the potter's wheel and sought to feel where Eileen's fingers had shaped clay into art. It was an old style kickwheel with a concrete flywheel at the base that she rotated with her foot. Just lifting it would take two strong men.

Alongside of it was the floor loom I had seen for the first time when I visited her in Oregon. The half finished Navajo rug remained strung on the frame across from the spinning wheel. In the center of the garage was a utility trailer that Eileen and her father built from scratch, scavenging an axle and wheels from a dead pick- up truck.

"Do you know how to pull this behind your car?" I asked.

"Sure. I learned how to pull a trailer when I had the tofu

farm. One time I overloaded the trailer and when I put the tractor into drive, the weight at the back lifted the front wheels off the ground. I was doing wheelies and holding onto the steering wheel so I wouldn't fall off. Even after I turned off the ignition it kept going until the tractor bumped into a tree and tried climbing it."

Returning to the kitchen, Eileen asked, "How are we doing for boxes?"

"We're good. Oh, I almost forgot. We got a package from Debbie."

Saving the bow, Eileen opened the package and lifted out a set of wooden salt and pepper shakers along with a tiled house address plaque. In bright colors it read "Welcome" and beneath it, "Eileen and Jay."

Gabriel arrived yesterday.

I furnished Gabriel's bedroom with a massive six- drawer, solid oak desk. Alongside of it was a bookcase with the Tolkein trilogy, two novels by Piers Anthony and a collection of Robert Frost's poetry. On the other side of the room were a single bed and a dresser. I refrained from tacking up a Star Wars poster.

"This is great, Dad," Gabriel said as he emptied his luggage onto the floor.

"I hope you intend putting your clothes in the dresser."

"If I put them in a dresser, I'd never be able to find what I need. Ah, here it is."

Gabriel pulled an American flag out of the suitcase. It was so big the Navy could bury a battleship in it.

"Huge, huh?"

"I don't suppose you bought it at a souvenir stand?"

Eileen came into the room to announce dinner was ready. "What is that?" she asked in astonishment, pointing at the flag.

"It's the flag from a football stadium. I was thinking of

hanging it over my bed or using it as a bed cover," Gabriel said.

"I can tell the difference between a wall hanging and hanging out dirty laundry and this flag is definitely dirty laundry. I think you should send it back to wherever you stole it." Eileen turned and left the room.

Gabriel arched his eyebrows at me.

"I'll go find you a box to mail it in," I said.

I have my fingers crossed that spending Christmas with Eileen's family is going to be lacking in drama. She assures me her family does not blame Jews for the death of Christ, but I am worried that Gabriel and I don't look like the people in a Currier and Ives greeting card.

"Is this an okay time to teach me how to shave, Dad?"

"Excellent. Let's go into the bathroom. I begin by soaking a washcloth in very hot tap water and then applying it to my face. It's soothing and reminds me of Chinese restaurants. I use a safety razor and like to lather my own soap with a shaving brush.

"The trick to a successful shave is to stretch the skin on your face. Depending on the faces you make, you can stretch the skin which makes shaving easier and it's a good way to make you smile at yourself at 7:00 in the morning. Other than that, you learn by feel. If you feel like you're ripping flesh, you know you're holding the razor at a wrong angle. If you don't feel any pull on your face it means you got drunk last night and are holding a tube of toothpaste in your hand, not a razor."

"Stand still, both you guys, I want to get a photograph," Eileen said

"Thanks, Dad. This was fun."

"I enjoyed it also. Tell me one thing, however, Gabriel."

"Yeeess?"

"Why are you putting shaving cream on your head?"

"Merry Christmas, Edith," I said, lightly embracing Eileen's mom. "This is my son, Gabriel."

Edith tried to not stare at his bald head. Then she looked to Eileen for assistance.

Eileen's dad, Quinn, came to the rescue.

"Welcome to our home, Gabriel. Just let us know if there is anything we can do for you. Do you need to rest? Are you hungry?"

"Gabriel doesn't have cancer," I interjected. "He thinks Fester Adams is a distant relative."

"Grab our bags and I'll show you where we're sleeping," Eileen said, ending the discussion.

From the other side of the room, two of Eileen's teen-age nieces were eyeing Gabriel like he was a piece of exotic candy. They were stay-at-home fundamentalist Christians and were getting their first sight of the Garden of Eden Macintosh apple. Gabriel was having fun.

I, on the other hand, was forgotten in the clamor of sibling reunions which gave me a chance to observe the bigger picture.

The family was divided. The Catholic, not- Catholic, schism ran deep and family dynamics were made more challenging by the fact that there were two strong women in one kitchen.

Half of her sisters and brothers lived with Eileen at one time or another in their lives. In her mother's view Eileen was a pagan, in the eyes of some siblings she was a loving sister who went astray and to most of them, she was the one they could count on when things got rough.

1992

Eileen's excited. She received permission from Judith Durek, the author of Circle of Stones, to use that name for a women's circle she is creating with her friend, Faith. Their first gathering is on the Spring Equinox. Murshida Rabia Ana Perez-Chisti, the national representative of Sufi Movement, has embraced and agreed to be a spiritual guide to both of them.

We have created a simple, gentle nightly ritual. We select a book and most evenings I read aloud until Eileen falls asleep, usually after ten pages. When she falls asleep I mark the page and the next night we go back and find the page where she began dozing. I resume reading from that spot. Tonight we finished reading Trinity by Leon Uris.

"Conor Larkin used his last breath to say Atty's name. I'd like to die saying your name, Eileen."

"Mahatma Gandhi died whispering *Ram, Ram, Ram Ram*, not the name of his wife. I'd like to die saying G-d's name," Eileen said as she draped my arm over her and lay with her back pressed against my chest.

I turned off the reading lamp and Eileen rolled over to face me.

"Did you ever hear about Copper Colored Mountain?" she asked.

I shook my head.

"It's where *Padmasambhava* ascended when he left this plane. It's outside of karmic return. I want this to be my last reincarnation and G-d's name is one of the keys to the Gate."

"Not me. I want to love you for at least one more life time."

"Then come with me to the mountain and we'll be able to love forever. We'll have fun. I promise!"

It's all very well and good for Eileen to talk about Copper Colored Mountain, but how the heck does she think I'm going to accompany her to Valhalla.

For one thing, I never wanted to ride shotgun on that spiritual road trip. I don't have a map how to get there and my compass keeps pointing to my lower chakras. Even supposing I change my mind, I haven't done the homework much less passed the spiritual LSAT's to gain admission.

Throughout public school I got lousy report card grades. My classmates got "Outstandings" (O) or "Satisfactories" (S). Me, I got "Needs Improvement" (N) and the worse, the ones that insured trouble at home were the "Unacceptables" (U). Both "N" and "U" were written in red ink. My spiritual report card also has a lot of color.

Follows the Ten Commandments – N
Reads the Holy Books – N
Meditates Daily – U
Speaks kindly to everyone – S
Went on a tour to Israel with Hadassah – U

With grades like these, I'm pretty sure to be denied admittance. Instead, I'm going to focus on a Valentine's Day party we're hosting.

The theme of the potluck party is Hearts and Chocolate. Eileen and I made chocolate rum balls and they sit stacked alongside more chocolate than Hershey, Pennsylvania. Scattered among the cakes, puddings and candy are trays of artichoke heart dip and bowls of heart of palm salad.

The guests have been asked to share a poem, story or love song. Eileen and I are going to do a duet. She's going to read from Sonnets from the Portuguese by Elizabeth Barrett and I'll read the love letters Robert Browning wrote to her while she was composing the collection of poems.

(Robert)
Do you know I was once not very far from seeing you…(It was) as if I had been close, so close to some world's wonder in chapel or crypt, only a screen to push and I might have entered, but there was some slight…bar to admission and the half opened door

shut, and I went home my thousands of miles.

(Elizabeth)

Oh my friend! Men could not part us with their worldly
jars, Nor the seas change us, nor the tempests bend;
Our hands would touch for all the mountain bars
And, heaven being rolled between us at the end,
We should but vow the faster for the stars.

(Robert)

I love you because I love you. I see you once a week
because I cannot see you all day long. I think of you
all day long, because I most certainly could not think
of you once an hour less."

Everyone went home sick with sugar withdrawal and
chocolate smudges on their lips. With the dishes cleaned we
scrambled in bed to begin our next book, The Love Poems of
Pablo Nureda.

"I hardly knew you, when you proposed to me at Latourell
Falls," Eileen said, as she turned on the reading lamp. "I heard the
words but thought they had so little weight they would be carried
away by the spray."

"And now?" I asked.

"Now... I love thee with the breath,
Smiles, tears, of all my life! And, if God choose,
I shall but love thee better after death.

*Our adopted cat died during the night. It wasn't expected and I
feel abandoned. I wish I could talk to Eileen but she is in Washington
D.C. at a massive pro-choice rally organized by NOW. Eileen and
Eden, who is a congressional page, are going to march together. The
radio says half a million women are at the Washington Monument,
which means there are probably at least a million protestors.*

The phone rang.

"Hi, Jay. Can you hear me?"

"Hey, babe. Yeah, I can hear you. What's all the noise in the background?"

"That's the sound of a million women celebrating. It's so beautiful. Eden and I marched next to a grandmother pushing her granddaughter's stroller."

"How's Eden?"

"She's great. She gave me a private tour of the House of Representatives and introduced me to a congressman. I forgot his name. She's so beautiful. She's right here. Say hello to Jay, Eden"

"Hi, Jay."

"Hi, Eden. I'm glad you prevented your mother from getting arrested."

"Mom is so awesome. Last night she led a drum circle in the lobby of the hotel where a lot of demonstrators are staying for the weekend."

"Good for her."

"Mom's trying to take the phone away from me. Bye, Jay. Here's Mom."

"I am so proud of Eden. So, how are you doing, Jay? I hope you don't miss me."

"I miss you a lot. Snowball died last night. I dug a hole by the orange tree and put her in a shoe box. I'm pretty depressed."

"I'm sorry. I wish I were with you. I'll miss her too, but there'll be others."

"Other times like this or other cats?"

"Probably both."

I was reluctant to tell Eileen that I snore and that my parents are garrulous. She discovered the part about my snoring almost immediately and has reduced it by changing my diet, suggesting I gargle with sage and placing dozens of tiny magnets on top of the mattress. I go along with everything but I swear I can feel the nubs of those magnets digging into my back.

As for Mom and Dad, she thinks kindness and love will be the keys to spending three days in Kings Point, Florida.

Passover is a lot of work. Replacing the everyday set of dishes with Passover dinnerware is a huge undertaking and the festive meal can require hours standing over a stove. It is beyond the ability of my octogenarian parents to perform these tasks but since there are so many elderly Jewish people in south Florida, the take-out delicatessens have thrived and several were offering Passover dinners complete with matza ball soup and coconut macaroons. Eileen and Dad went together to pick up our order.

Mom and I looked up from the crossword puzzle when we heard the front door swing open. Eileen was carrying a carton the size of a large Coleman cooler.

"*Gevalt, gevalt, gevalt.* Irene you should have seen how crazy it was at Murray's delicatessen. It took forever. The place was packed and everyone was shouting because they couldn't hear when their names were called. And the pushing? Irene, it was like being on the D train."

I looked to Eileen and she nodded in agreement.

"Here, give this to me," my dad said, taking the box from Eileen and putting it on the kitchen counter.

"But, Irene, *kaynahora,* Eileen is terrific. She helped the salespeople *shlep* the cartons to people waiting on line and got ours nearly right away. Mrs. Weingarten was there and she said I have a lovely daughter." My dad was smiling at Eileen.

Before we sat down to dinner, all four of us walked one block to the canal where Dad, in his daily ritual, bent down with bread crumbs as fish came to eat out of his hand.

On the way back to the condo Eileen whispered in my ear, "Garrulous?"

The plan is to fly to Portland, rent a car and drive to Eileen's parents' home.

Snow was falling when we pulled out of the Hertz parking lot and twilight was chasing the sun. I don't like driving in snowy conditions but Eileen takes to it like an Iditarod sled racer and we had the road mostly to ourselves. Even so, we made little progress. We asked a gas station attendant where he would take his sweetheart for a romantic evening and he drew a map to a resort two miles from Cascade Locks.

The resort was aglow with Christmas lights, surrounded by a vast virgin field of snow blanketing a golf course. The only vacancy was the bridal suite and though we couldn't agree on how to register, we took the room. We dined with champagne and shared a meal of portabella mushrooms stuffed with brie. By the time we returned to the suite, a porter had lit a blaze in the fireplace and placed a small potted holly bush on the nightstand, compliments of the resort.

Sitting in plush terry cloth robes, I turned to Eileen. "Since we're already here in the bridal suite, let's find a parson to marry us."

Eileen was holding the holly. "I'm not ready yet, Jay. Ask me again when this holly has berries."

1993

Gabriel had a difficult time in school this year, but he's doing better now that it's summer and he has a job building trails in a state park.

Every morning Gabriel ran the shower until the hot water tank was empty. Then he put on his steel toed boots and stomped through the house while he prepared a Dagwood type lunch. Afterward, he'd go sit on the porch, slamming the screen door behind him, to wait for his ride to Boulder Creek. If he thought we might have fallen back into sleep he'd re-enter the house and slam the door once more for good measure.

In the evening he sprawled on the couch and reluctantly removed his Wolverines only after being asked twice to do so. From his reclining position, he furnished us with the details of how many wheel barrows filled with gravel he pushed up a mountain side and how many trees he cut down.

When September rolled around and the only available job was collecting parking fees at state campgrounds, Gabriel removed his hard hat and turned in his work gloves.

On a warm afternoon he gave me a tour of his work site. I walked on the gravel path he helped lay down and he had me peer under a handsome new footbridge. His initials were carved into the wood.

Eileen has found her teacher in Rabia. Rabia has found a student in Eileen. Last week Rabia initiated Eileen into the Sufi Movement. Her Sufi name is Tofah. In Hindi it means Divine Spring and in Hebrew it means "She will shine forth."

Next month Rabia is starting a two year interfaith religious studies program for initiates. The class meets once a month for an entire day. No one is allowed to miss a single class. After completing the class, students get the privilege of calling themselves Cherags which entitles them to do more volunteer work. I looked at the curriculum and it's a bear.

"How long are the Five Books of Moses?" Eileen wondered.

"About a thousand pages if you don't count the *Haftorahs*."

"Let me look at the syllabus. Yes. Counting the *Haftorahs*."

"Maybe twelve hundred. Do you have to read all of it?"

"Yes, but we have two months. What are the *Haftorahs*?"

"Every chapter in the Torah has a *Haftorah* that is read the same week as the Torah portion. They're a page or two in length and a lot of them are taken from the prophets. When people get *Bar* or *Bat Mitzvah* they are assigned to chant the *Haftorah* for that week and that is their *Haftorah* for the rest of their lives regardless of when it occurs on the Roman calendar.

"How do you determine the date of a *Bat Mitzvah*?"

"It should be the closest Shabbat after you turn twelve. It's different for boys.

"What's my *Haftorah*?"

"It depends. If it was this year it would be one *Haftorah*. If it was next year, it would be one or two before or after this *Haftorah*. The Jewish calendar is on a lunar cycle so it doesn't match up with our calendar.

"I don't know that I'll be *Bat Mitzvah* this year, but whatever the *Haftorah* is, I take it as mine."

"Hand me the Jewish calendar over by the computer and I'll look it up."

"So, what does it say?"

"By coincidence, because we were both born in early June it turns out we share the same *Haftorah*."

"It doesn't sound like coincidence to me," she said.

One of Gabriel's pals from Eugene has shown up on our doorstep. He's a vagabond with an attitude.

At eleven o'clock on Sunday night John and Gabriel gathered sleeping bags and filled a large wooden chest tucked in a corner of the garage with firewood.

"Where do you think you're going at this hour?" I asked belligerently.

"Me and John are going to sleep at Hidden Beach."

"It's not even legal to be on the beach at this hour and there's school tomorrow."

"Chill out, man."

"You're the one who needs to chill out. You're failing most of your classes and you can't afford to miss any more time. I get that you don't like following rules, but as long as you live here, you have to obey them."

"I'm out of here." The screen door slamming was an exclamation point on Gabriel's departing words.

Gabriel returned alone in the morning. We sat in silence drinking coffee. I broke the ice.

"Now what, Gabriel?"

"I have a friend spending his junior college year in Massachusetts. He asked me to room with him in Amherst. I could do my senior year of high school on the east coast. The problem is he won't be ready to go until June. If it's okay with you, I'll leave right after school closes in two months."

Eileen joined us at the kitchen table. "Did you put the wooden chest back in the garage?" she asked.

"Nah. It was too heavy to bring back so we threw it on the bonfire."

"But my father made it for me," Eileen wailed.

Gabriel looked crestfallen. "I didn't know it meant anything to you. I thought it was just some old box. I'm sorry."

Eileen got up silently and went into the bedroom, locking the door behind her.

"I swear I didn't know, Dad."

"I believe you."

Gabriel's idea is to buy a motorcycle and take the summer riding cross country.

After scouring the bike lots we found one that was scruffy and durable. The owner wouldn't vouch for how many miles it had, a mirror was missing and the amber brake light on the back was held together by duct tape. It was also big but, Gabriel was correct, anything less than five-fifty cc wouldn't survive the journey. My mechanic inspected it for potential weaknesses and pronounced it road ready. Gabriel paid the man seven hundred and fifty dollars from the money he earned working for the park department.

The first day, Gabriel went up and down our two hundred feet of brick patio causing the gold fish to dive for deep water and the cats to scatter into the tops of trees.

On the second day, Gabriel drove up and down our street for hours. He hadn't yet taken it out of second gear, but he was mixing it up with street traffic. I sat on the porch and every time he went past, he'd wave. It reminded me of times he'd wave from a carousel horse.

On the third day, Gabriel pulled up to the stop sign at the corner, looked both ways for oncoming traffic, stalled once as he made the turn, and took off out of sight.

Three weeks later Gabriel was up early, going over his bike and making sure everything was tied on tight.

"If you leave soon you'll beat the San Francisco rush hour."

"Let's go."

I nodded. "I'll follow you a little ways out of town. We can stop up the coast and have breakfast."

At Davenport, I took a photograph of Gabriel next to his motorcycle. He looked like James Dean.

As we came out of the restaurant, a teen, in the basement of the restaurant building, pressed his face against the wire mesh covering a casement window.

"Is that you, Gabe?" he called out.

Gabriel moved to the window. "Yeah, Leroy. How's it happening?"

"I got a job here for the summer washing dishes. It's all right. What about you?"

"I'm leaving for Massachusetts," he pointed to his bike.

"That's cool, man. Take care, bro." Leroy reached his fingers through the mesh and the two boys clasped hands.

Gabriel got on his bike and was gone.

I shot a back-to-school television commercial for Goodwill Industries. It opens with a view of a cattle drive and a voice- over saying, "Do you want to go along with the herd and shop at the mall where for fifty dollars you'll come away with half a pair of shoes, if you're lucky? (The camera pans to Eileen limping across a field wearing one shoe.) Or do you want to be an individual and get a complete wardrobe for fifty dollars at Goodwill Industries?" (The viewer sees a group of somewhat rough teens getting off a bus wearing clothing from the Goodwill Store.)

I got off cheap with the kids. In exchange for being on camera I gave each of them as much clothing as they could wear out the store. The actress who wobbled across the screen had something a little more expensive in mind. Eileen wants us to take a trip to Paris, which I'm certain I cannot bill to the cost of the commercial.

The gardens at Giverny were crowded with tourists. With so many people shuffling along, it was impossible to pause and ponder the elegance of Monet's estate. That changed when a thunder cloud burst over our heads. Those slow moving bi-peds suddenly became fleet footed, dashing for the coffee house and gift shop.

We got out of their way and sought a relatively dry bench beneath a weeping willow tree next to the lily pond. The park was empty and we nestled in its beauty. It was ten minutes before another couple ventured out into the rain and they were astonished to have the park nearly to themselves.

The man stopped by the bridge and turning to us said, *"S'il vous plaît. Avec toute cette beauté nous entourant, je n'avais pas pensé à interrompre deux personnes donc jolies amoureux."*

We all smiled at each other and they thoughtfully sought a tree across the pond under which to shelter.

"Were you able to translate what he said?" I asked Eileen.

"I think he said, 'Excuse me. With all this loveliness surrounding us, I had not thought to interrupt two people so lovely in love.'"

"Really?"

"Maybe."

The bullet train to Provence took us from the mist-laden paved banks of the Seine and the crepes we shared while watching a puppet show to the sculptured fountains of Aix-en-Provence and the Chateau de Roussan in St. Remy. I chose the chateau from a one-inch by one-inch photograph in a travel guide and when we drove up its tree lined entry was astonished at its grandeur. It was the former estate of Nostradamus and the tower in which he wrote his prophecies was still intact.

In the morning we tested the door into the tower. There was no lock and plenty of light to guide our footsteps. The room was bare. No memorials, no artifacts, no ouija boards. Regardless of his legacy, the present owners of the hotel have no wish to further his memory. We sought a copy of his book but the only one in the St. Remy bookstore was in French. We purchased it and over a lunch of baguettes, cheese and sparkling wine Eileen read a little bit and then made up any old translation that popped into her head.

In the dappled sunlight of late afternoon Eileen sat with her back against a tree at the edge of a formal lawn bounded in front by a brook where swans meandered the slow moving stream.

Does Nostradamus predict we'll get married?" I asked.

Eileen thumbed through the book. "Let's see. Aha. Here it is. He says we'll be married but you have to be patient."

"Show me that in the book," I said.

"Can you read French?" she asked.

"No."

"Well here it is, clear as day," she said pointing to a paragraph on page 195.

1994

The Ahwahnee Hotel is a towering elegance graced with views of Yosemite Falls filtering through its floor- to- ceiling windows framed in stained glass. We're sleeping in a tent in a nearby campground on the valley floor, but I have reservations for Sunday Brunch at the hotel. By lantern light, in our sleeping bags, we're reading <u>The Alphabet Versus the Goddess</u>.

Snow lay in drifts under the sheltering shadows of massive granite outcroppings and the trail to Mirror Lake was riddled with puddles of melting snow.

"Right around this bend is a friend I want you to meet," Eileen said as she scampered under a fallen tree. "Here he is," she said rushing to a stone slab rising ten feet from the ground. "Press against it and listen for its heartbeat. These stones are the bones of the mother."

We leased two horses for the year. There are wild Saturday morning canters that are straight out of the Arabian Nights with gallops across sand flats. There are Sunday afternoon slow trots through the forest glens that are as sweet as Robin Hood and Maid Marian. Many times, we tie our horses to a tree and sit in a meadow, high in the mountains. At night we're reading <u>The Three Musketeers</u>.

"I can think of at least two good reasons not to go along with your idea."

"Name one," she challenged.

"For starters, if I try holding this three foot tree while sitting in the saddle, my horse is going to freak out, buck me off and I am going to have many bruises."

"Name another," she said.

"Second, you have only a ten second delay from the time you press the shutter, to return to your horse and remount before the camera takes our photograph. That is not enough time."

"Let's try. Hold the tree and try not to move or shake too much," she said, handing me a fir that fell over in a wind storm.

Eileen positioned the camera on a boulder "Okay, keep hold of Cleopatra's reins. With ten seconds, I have enough time to slowly walk back to her and remount. She won't spook. Don't worry."

I watched the red flashing dot on the camera, forced a smile and posed for the Christmas card of us wearing winter plaids, atop our mounts, holding a tree. The caption read: "Bringing home the family tree."

Inside the card we wrote: "Merry Christmas and Happy Chanukah. We're getting married on June, 24th. Save the date."

At the bottom of the card I penned:

Winter winds
shall find no haven here,
for I am draped
in woolens of love
and clothed in fine silks
of your sweet embrace.

People choose a date for a wedding based on weather, the preacher's availability or how pregnant the bride will be when she walks the aisle. Tofah made her decision based on divination. It helps that the holly bush we planted has three red berries.

In numerology, June 24, 1995 is comprised of three sixes. June is the sixth month, the twenty fourth is made up of a two and four which equals a six. And the year 1995 is also a six, even if it doesn't quite look like one.

The number six represents love and marriage. It's influenced by Venus and goes well with pearls, sapphires and diamonds.

With the date set, it was time to explore our future through the fog of mysticism. On a bookshelf dominated by the I Ching, Enneagram For Advanced Practioners, and Handbook of Palmistry, was a stack of tarot cards. We chose the classic Rider deck.

We smudged the room with sage to clear away confusion. We lit frankincense to support spiritual transcendence. To bring us luck, we placed jasmine incense at the base of our altar. On a lace tablecloth we placed a photograph of Hazrat Inayat Khan, an image of Mother Mary, sea shells, a pomegranate and a string of prayer beads given to Eileen by Rabia.

Tofah posed the question, "Will this marriage serve G-d?"

After shuffling the deck, the first card I pulled was the symbol for the righteous and the sacred. The second card indicated a life of merriment. The final card, the one describing how it all turns out was the symbol for reaping and sharing bounty. This reading sure beat the one Guru Dev gave when he examined me.

1995

Planning the wedding has become a full time job.

Dollops of whipped cream melted in cups of hot chocolate. We were tired. We'd been to Macy's, Nordstrom's and several millenaries, but Eileen hadn't found the hat she had gone seeking.

Eileen searched through her pocket book which was considerably more exciting than a magician's hat filled with tricks. It wasn't any bigger than a sherpa's backpack but it held mysteries to make a shaman envious. The bag was divided into compartments but there was minimal logic to where she put her possessions. The bag contained a Swiss Army knife, a mini flashlight, small rocks, sandwich bags filled with flower seeds she harvested from bushes in people's front yards, five and ten dollar bills wadded with a week's worth of checks to be deposited, a pill box filled with assorted gels with exotic names from the Amazon rain forest, keys to both cars, house, counseling office, massage office and one to the apartment of a client who asked Eileen to hold it in case of an emergency, her and my prayer beads, a candle stub, watermelon lip gloss, red lipstick, dental floss, hair brush, an overflowing address book with tiny notations worthy of Egyptian hieroglyphics, tea bags, camera, recording stick, several unmatched earrings, cassettes of Byron Katie lectures, first aid kit, street map of Portland, harmonica, a canister containing corn given to her by Pueblo Indian elder, Gray Antelope, a book of the ninety-nine names of G–d, and photographs of the two of us, the kids and Rabia. She also had an assortment of pens, one of which she drew forth from the bag.

"Here's my idea," she said, making rapid pen strokes on the back of a paper place mat. "They call this a fascinator or cocktail hat. I'm going to sew a simple silk beaded lace headdress that follows the contours of my head. Something Theda Bara might have worn. It'll match the dress I'm sewing."

"Do you have time to do all of this?"

"I'll find the time. What do you think about the idea of me making our wedding rings? They're offering a class in lost wax jewelry at the community college and we could design our own bands."

"I still have my gold wedding band and a gold ring my parents gave me at my *Bar Mitzvah*. Can we melt them and reuse the gold?"

"I think if they're fourteen carets they can be melted. I'll ask the teacher. I have gold earrings and a gold bracelet that I can add to the mix."

"Does that mean we're done shopping for the day?"

"You betcha."

Jogging with Eileen is like running a decathlon. Her preferred route begins in a eucalyptus grove where the cone shaped woody seed pods are invitations to sprained ankles. Once out of the thicket there is a tree trunk spanning a dry creek- bed. It's only five feet to the rocks below but feels like the Grand Canyon when I am inching my way across its length. I especially do not like it when Eileen jumps up

and down on the tree while I'm putting one foot in front of the other.
Anyone else would simply jog down the road to the beach entrance
but this steeplechase reminds Eileen of her childhood and I would not
deny her heritage. She is a diamond in a gingham dress.

After two hours at a bridal expo we needed to breathe salt air. As we ran along the shore we reviewed where we were in preparation for June.

"We still don't have party favors to give the guests," Eileen said as she pointed out two dolphins swimming parallel to us.

"Everything is so expensive. Personalized chopsticks, seven dollars. Candy coated almonds in a heart shaped box, four ninety-five. It's crazy," I said panting.

"We could make our own."

"When? In between the time we build a wedding *chuppah* and the time we design the program?"

"I'm just saying we could go to Costco, buy twenty pounds of almonds, put them in boxes and save some money."

I spotted an unbroken sand dollar and handed it to Eileen. On the rare occasion we find one, we cradle it in our hands until we can bring it home to add to our collection.

"It would be cool if we had enough sand dollars to give as party favors," Eileen said as she enfolded the fragile sea creature in her palm.

"We'd need more than a hundred."

"G-d provides," Eileen said as she took off running to keep pace with the dolphins.

An hour later as we turned toward home I stopped at the beach entrance.

"We are not going back through the forest," I said firmly.

"Why's that?"

"Because I am not going to risk breaking the seven sand dollars I'm holding."

I'm visiting Gabriel in Northhampton, Massachusetts. He's graduating in two months. On his first day of school the principal called him into her office and said she had no legal obligation to admit him and if he even looked like he was contemplating mischief he'd be out the door. Furthermore, she told him, with what Gabriel described as a sadistic grin, Northampton High School is considered one of the strictest in the nation with a majority of its seniors being accepted into prestige universities. She expected no less from Gabe.

Snow lay in drifts, soot and slush sharing space where the sun warmed the pavement. We walked past the city park and I tried imaging the scene captured in a newspaper photograph I held in front of me.

In the photograph a heavy snow had buried the park in a thick cover of white. In the morning, a complex crop circle appeared causing wonder and awe in the people of Northhampton. The caption under the photograph was "Wow!"

"Pretty cool. How'd you do it?" I asked Gabriel.

"I was up in a tree with a laser light so I had the perspective we needed for Rob to tramp the snow wherever I traced the line."

We continued down the street and went into a chocolate store. Gabriel introduced me to the owner. She said Gabriel was a good worker except that everyone had to work around Gabriel's lacrosse schedule.

"How often do you work here?"

"Every weekday except during lacrosse and then I work when I can."

"You didn't tell me you were playing lacrosse."

"Yeah. I'm on the team. I didn't have money to buy my stick and equipment so the rest of the team chipped in to help pay for it. I think the coach did too. I usually play midfield, but I prefer to play attack. Where are we going to go for dinner?"

"How about the Outback Steak House?"

"Good idea, matey. You know, Dad, I'm thinking of going to

Australia."

"I hope not before the wedding."

"I'll be there. The chocolate shack has a heart shaped mold that I'm going to pour and give Eileen as a wedding gift."

"And what graduation gift do you want from me?"

"What do you think about a one way ticket to Spain?"

"Round trip costs almost the same amount of money."

"No. One way suits me better."

The celebration began last Wednesday. We reserved group space in a campground that rapidly filled with travel trailers, camper vans and tents. For several nights it was the belly of the party with bonfires, marshmallows and water balloon fights. Eileen and I were too busy to spend time out there but, now and then, heard bits and pieces of the goings on. Uncle Bob got drunk. Gabriel was earning a reputation as a Lothario and no one liked the tofu hotdogs Eileen brought over for their dinner.

On Sunday morning I dressed in cummerbund and tailcoat while Eileen, in another room, was having her hair braided with petite white lilies. When she stepped out to greet me I draped a necklace of pearls around her throat.

In a county park overlooking the Bay, Rabia conducted a Sufi Universal Worship honoring the eight primary spiritual pathways along with the all the Masters, Saints and Prophets, known and unknown. The chuppah was snapping in the wind as we placed rings forged by Eileen from the gold of our past into the pageantry of the present.

As our one hundred and fifty guests said good-night, each had with them a gift box with an unbroken sand dollar we'd found on the beach last month.

We plan to honeymoon at the Country Fair though I'm surprised Tofah doesn't want a bridal suite in some exotic country.

"One of the best things about driving to the Fair is it gives us time to talk," Eileen said as she effortlessly managed the twists and turns of Highway 17. "Let's talk about a Sufi retreat center. The experts think fifteen to twenty families is a workable number to create a co-housing community. If we buy a small summer camp, we could live in the cabins while we build houses."

"It can be done," I agreed. "I'm sure there are twenty Sufis who have the money to invest and want to live in a spiritual park with fountains, hot tubs, horse drawn carriages instead of cars..."

Eileen interrupted. "We could pray together every day. In the evenings we could do *zhikr*, Sufi Dancing and Universal Worships. We could invite teachers and help pay for the center from people who register for classes. It would be like Esalen, only G-d instead of psychotherapy. One of my clients told me Delarosa Hot Springs is for sale. We should spend a weekend out there. What do you think, sweetie pie?"

"Let's go for it. I'll make a list of people we could invite to our house to discuss the idea." As I dug through Eileen's pocketbook looking for a pen, I saw a brochure.

"What's this, Babe?" I asked, looking at the color photos of an elegant Balinese inn.

"One of my clients gave it to me. She said it was magical and couldn't stop talking about the bridal suite. It's within walking distance of the center of Ubud. Ubud is one of the major spiritual centers of the world. It also has a park where monkeys wander about. Want to go?"

We spent the weekend at a family reunion on the Rogue River. It's a church camp with four bunk beds in each cabin. Owen upheld his reputation as chief mischief maker and it was a guarantee somebody was going to toilet paper his cabin. Even his own family insisted he sleep in a cabin by himself.

Last night we sat around a bonfire listening to tales of the old Basque country, of lives that depended upon daring border crossings, smuggling anything that the French wanted from the Spanish. Eileen wondered if it was part of Basque history to kidnap children and sell them on the other side of the border? Even in the flickering light I could see pain in her eyes.

"Before we begin to eat, let's go around the table and say one thing for which we are grateful and then we'll say Grace," Eileen's mom suggested to all of us. Pointing to a seven year old granddaughter sitting next to her, Edith said, "You begin, Naomi."

Naomi hemmed and then said, "I'm grateful for Jesus in my life."

Edith smiled. "Your turn, Luke."

Luke turned to his mother, hoping for guidance but he was on his own. "I'm grateful for Jesus in my life," he repeated.

Edith smiled again. It was Lilly's turn next. Lilly is one of the nieces who lives closest to us.

"I'm grateful to Aunt Eileen who helps me find sea shells on the beach."

Dad had a heart attack and has been in a rehab center. He's being released and Eileen and I are flying to Florida to help him resettle in the condo. On the plane we are reading Beau Geste.

Dad's suitcase was packed at the foot of a bed and he was pacing back and forth when we arrived. When he saw us his face lit with a smile.

"C'mon. You need to sign some papers," he said propelling us down a corridor to a nurses' station as he took small steps alongside of us.

"Do you want some help, Dad?" I asked, extending my hand.

He waved it away as he pushed past a swinging door.

"Mary," he said to a woman wearing a blue lab coat, "meet my son and daughter-in-law."

"You have a very special father," Mary said, as she sorted papers, pointing to where she needed my signature. "The staff love him. If we asked him to exercise on the treadmill for ten minutes, he insisted on fifteen. When he arrived six weeks ago I was of the opinion he might need long term care, but two days ago he passed the eye exam and his driver's license was restored. He's going to do just fine living independently." She turned to dad, kissed him on the cheek and said "Good luck, Sam. You have beautiful children."

I carried the suitcase as Dad led us toward the exit. A dozen people drinking coffee in the common room stood up and clapped when they saw him. A frail woman pushing a walker she had fitted with tennis balls for rollers was holding a helium balloon that she extended to Pop. "It's for you, Sam," she said.

"Thank you, Mrs. Lefkowitz. I hope your husband can come see you tomorrow."

"He wants to come, but it's difficult. It costs thirty-five dollars, one way, for a taxi from West Palm. Is this your daughter? Such a beautiful *meydela*."

"This is Eileen. She's come to take me home," Dad said as he reached for Eileen's arm. "C'mon, Eileen. Let's go. I want to stop at the deli and buy some pastrami for lunch," and he took small steps out the door, leaning on Eileen's arm.

A dozen women spent the morning in the kitchen baking gingerbread women cookies for the monthly Circle of Stones gathering. Each cookie was uniquely shaped. One was baked holding another cookie's hand. A second had two long braids. A third wore a cowgirl hat. I got to eat the broken ones.

The overheads were dimmed and tea lights spread a glow around an altar to The Goddess. Tofah and Faith took turns speaking to the twenty-five women gathered in the community center.

"We'd like to begin this evening with a guided visualization so please get comfortable, there are chairs and *zafus* if you like. When you're ready, close your eyes.

"Imagine you are following a forest trail at dawn. You are alone and the pathway is unfamiliar. You are a tiny bit nervous but your curiosity and sense of adventure carry you forward.

"The sun rises over the horizon dappling the forest floor. You hear birds chirping and the sound of a brook lapping against rocks. Your attention is drawn to the rustling of leaves in an open glen.

"A little girl is in the field, making a house out of twigs and moss. When she sees you, she runs to take your hand. Her knees are smudged from playing in the dirt and her hair has brambles. She looks up at you, her eyes filled with mischief, her smile filled with love and trust. She skips alongside of you.

"As the sun climbs over the tops of trees, the earth basks in its warmth. Not far off, you hear singing coming from a meadow. Young maidens have gone to the forest. They wear garlands in their hair. They lie on the grass, watching clouds take form. They twirl, faces lifted to the sun, radiant in their youth. When they see the two of you, they stretch out their arms in greeting. You join them in their exuberance and they join you on the path.

"In the late afternoon your company takes a rest at a clear, blue pool. Women, round of belly, infants suckling at their breasts, are there cooing to their infants and chasing their toddlers. They stand and wrap their arms around your waists or shoulders and all of you continue on.

"In the twilight, as shadows deepen, you see dim figures moving consciously through the underbrush. They are the old, wise ones, who gather plants and flowers to bring comfort to those who are ill. When they see you, they cease from their labors and beckon to all of you to come forward.

"The journey is completed. You have arrived. There is a fire burning within a circle of stones and all who are here are welcome to share their wisdom.

"Welcome everyone to our Circle of Stones," Tofah Eileen said merrily.

1996

I made reservations for the Honeymoon Suite at Kebun Indah Bungalows in Ubud. The Balinese guest house overlooks rice paddies and each morning a man escorts a brace of ducks along a path beneath the room. There is no air-conditioning but when it becomes too hot to sleep, we doze on the veranda where there are luxurious sofas and lamps.

"Sweetie, would you bring me the banana smoothie in the refrigerator?" Eileen asked, as she settled onto a settee on the veranda.

"You'll never go back to sleep if you drink it. How about a bottle of water?"

"I don't want to go back to sleep. I want to stay up and listen to you read the <u>Ramayana</u>."

Returning with the drink, I created a *canang sari*, an offering to the Gods, as I'd been taught by our host. On a wide green leaf I placed an orchid, a cookie and a slice of papaya. Then I lit incense and offered a blessing to the Divine Spirits. The only thing missing was the sprinkling of holy water on the leaf, because I forgot to ask how to obtain holy water.

We were at an exciting point in the story. Sita was in the midst of several grotesque *rakshasa* demons who were tormenting her because she would not agree to be the mistress of Ravana. When she could bear it no longer, she determined she would commit suicide. In that final moment of desperation she received Rama's signet ring from a secret search party as a token of Rama's unending love for Sita and a promise that he would find her. She gave the messenger the last remaining jewelry she possessed to present to Rama as her oath of eternal love.

"If we are ever separated, whether by distance or death, I'll send you the feathers of a blue-jay to assure you I'm waiting for you to find me," Eileen whispered.

"And I'll send you a rose quartz crystal as pledge that I will not stop seeking." I looked at Tofah in the moonlight and she was crying. With my finger I caught a single tear and carried it to the table where I sprinkled it on the offering.

If compromise isn't possible, it's best to take turns. I like to arrive at airports two hours early, she likes dashing toward the gate. I appreciate the security of having hotel reservations, she prefers to flow with the unanticipated. This vacation is her turn. Dylan spent his junior year in Florence and invited us to attend his graduation. Afterward, the three of us are going to find a room in the Cinque Terre and hike the hills along the coast for three days. We're reading A Room With a View.

The hotel Eileen found in Florence experienced several lifetimes. It was formerly the home of a wealthy dowager, later a nunnery and today is more or less a boarding house.

Opening the shutters, we were surprised by the resemblance of the view to the illustration on the cover of our paperback book. Eileen pointed toward the cathedral. "Look, that's where George and Lucy saw the Italian man stabbed to death."

"And George catches her when she swoons. It's right next to the Statue of Neptune where we're meeting Dylan. If we hurry, you can practice swooning."

Dylan was waiting for us when we reached the square. Ceremonies at the school were beginning shortly and he wanted to introduce us to his teachers. They said he spoke Italian like a native of northern Italy and could cook like a Sicilian. Eileen beamed.

Eileen and I were given high honors when we were invited to celebrate with several of Dylan's buddies. We were the only adults in the circle of kids who roamed the streets of Florence that night, though Eileen laughed with such glee she could have passed for a teenager.

With red eyes we arrived in the Cinque Terre without a reservation two days before a national holiday when it is an Italian custom for thousands to take the train to the picturesque five little villages.

Dylan and Eileen told me not to worry and to watch the luggage while they went to find a room. They came back in fifteen minutes in the company of a short, elderly man wearing a grey vest under a black sports jacket, walking with the aid of a cane.

Dylan introduced Signore Santori. Mr. Santori's sister owns an apartment on the main street. She is gone to her daughter's house in Roma for the holiday and he could rent it to us for the weekend. He says it is very small and has us follow him down toward the sea.

"My mother's family is from Bologna," he confides as Dylan translates. "They don't like to admit it, but the accent gives them away. I love the sound of it. You have the same accent, that's why I listened when you asked a shopkeeper about renting a room."

The apartment is the top unit of a three story building. It's big enough for the three of us and has a rooftop balcony that overlooks the markets below and the Mediterranean beyond.

From our aerie we see the street come awake in the morning. With coffee and pastries we watch a fisherman pushing a cart with his catch up from the harbor. He stops in front of his house and begins to arrange the fish for sale. He does a brisk trade. In the afternoon a violinist plays Italian opera beneath our window hoping people drop lira into her violin case. We give her money and she returns each day to the same spot. Mr. Santori presents us with a bottle of wine and we toast his health watching the sunset from our roof.

The days are filled with hiking and the evenings are spent dining on the quay. At night we stand on the balcony, filled with awe, marveling at the great place Dylan and Eileen found without a reservation.

1997

Throughout small town America, being crowned Homecoming Queen is like being named Miss America. In 1967, Eileen was chosen her high school homecoming queen.

Where I grew up if someone was called a homecoming queen it meant he was a gay guy returning to the neighborhood. But even without the official title, there were a couple of dozen girls attending my high school who vied for the honor. We all knew who they were. They were the pretty girls. They dated the athletes. They didn't talk to me.

Being wed to a Homecoming Queen was not how I saw myself. I wasn't tall or blond. I didn't play golf and I wasn't planning to become a dentist. I was a river rat born under the shadow of Yankee Stadium and here I was escorting Eileen to the thirtieth reunion of her high school graduating class.

We went there like royalty. Many of her classmates had barely moved from their hometown and were enchanted by Eileen's tales of Sheherazade. They filled her dance card throughout the evening.

"So this is the place you came to neck?"

"Whenever we could sneak out of the house."

"It's beautiful. From here you can see the Columbia River and the hills in Washington."

"No one was looking."

"How many cars would be out here?"

"After a Friday night football game, the whole parking lot was full."

"And did you get out of your cars and talk to each other?"

"No. We were necking. Didn't you neck in a car in high school?"

"We didn't have cars. We had subway trains and buses. Will you teach me?"

"Here?"

"This is where you said you did it."

"Okay, but it was easier before they invented bucket seats. Lean over and kiss me."

I leaned over and kissed her and then sat back up.

"Don't break apart. Your lips are glued to mine. We only come up for air and then dive back down."

"Okay." I was really getting into it. With one hand around Eileen's neck my other hand sought beneath her blouse. She pushed my hand away. I tried again. Eileen broke from the kiss and with her palms outstretched, shoved against my chest throwing me against the driver's side door.

"Ow. Why'd you do that?"

"You told me you wanted to learn, so I'm teaching you. Girls did not allow hands to wander. You want to kiss again?"

"I want a chiropractor."

Last year we learned how to play marimbas and spent a weekend in Puget Sound dancing to the best bands on the west coast. This year we learned to zydeco dance and we are heading for New Orleans for some hot Cajun footwork.

The Annual Louisiana Zydeco Festival draws thousands of people. It is staged in the middle of a cotton field. It's more than a hundred degrees in the sun and sun is all there is. People bring blue tarps and stretch them on poles overhead to provide shade. If it's a small family they only need one tarp. Some of the bigger families tie together half a dozen tarps. The only things Eileen and I brought were hats.

"Honey child, what are you thinking?" the clan mother said to Eileen. "You can't be sitting out there in the sun. Lord, the two of you like as not will get sunstroke. Next thing they'll be saying us black folk killed the only two white people who come to the dance. You just come sit under our tarp. It's plenty big enough for two more. You want a beer to cool you down?"

Playing board games with Eileen is an occult experience. I'm not smart enough to beat her at Go and any game that includes dice is out of the question. When we're neck and neck in Backgammon she shakes the dice, blows on them, tells them what numbers she needs and they oblige. It doesn't work every time but often enough to consider a trip to Vegas though she says the dice won't cooperate if greed is involved. Still, I love to bet with her because it's a way to learn what she would like to win and I always get it for her regardless of the outcome of the game.

"Isn't there anywhere else in town we can shoot pool besides this tavern?" Eileen asked, as I racked the balls.

"This is the only place besides the one table they have at the pizza parlor. Okay, here's the rules. We're playing eight ball. We keep secret whatever it is we're betting until after the game is over. Agreed?"

"Agreed," she said as she chalked her cue stick. "But nothing gross."

We lagged for who breaks and she won. After that, the game was all mine. When the eight ball went into the corner pocket she gave me a high five and asked what I won.

"I need a button sewn on my gray sports jacket."

"Do you still have the button?"

"I put it in my sock drawer."

"Fine, winner breaks."

The second game was closer. We were both shooting for the eight ball and it was her turn. She walked slowly around the table, chose her shot and said, "Center pocket." She put a good back spin on the cue ball to prevent a scratch, but the black ball hovered leaving me with a sitting duck. She shrugged her shoulders. "What did you bet this time?"

"A fire on the beach."

She nodded. "Last game, I'm getting a headache from the cigarette smoke."

I broke and watched the balls scatter across the cloth.

"Scratch!" Eileen shouted as the black ball slowly made its way down into the corner pocket."

"You lose," Eileen said jumping up and down. She replaced her stick on the rack and ushered us out the door. In the clear night air she kissed me.

"What do you want for winning?" I asked.

"A bike tour down the Danube River for Eden and me," Eileen spurted. "We talked about it and she has time between the end of school and her internship."

"I thought you said your luck wouldn't hold if you were greedy?"

"It's not being greedy wanting to spend time with my kids."

"I suppose you have a brochure for the tour you want to take?"

"I'll show it to you. The tour comes with bike rental and van support. We sleep in a castle one night and on a river boat another. Let's go home and I'll sew your button."

1998

I wanted to do something at work to honor Mothers Day. If I can get permission for the workers to have an extra thirty minute break I'll decorate the lounge with linen tablecloths and serve tea to all the moms. If I can get Eileen to help pour, it might take her mind off how sad she feels that her kids aren't here celebrating the holiday.

"How do I look?" I asked, as Eileen straightened my red cummerbund.

"Dashing. Where did you get the tuxedo?"

"It was donated to Goodwill. I had the sorters keep their eyes open for one my size."

"The room looks charming, Jay. The pink streamers with flowers on all the tables and pretty paper plates are adorable. And I love the petit fours. Who made them?"

"Costco." I looked at my servers: the Executive Secretary, my graphic artist and Tofah. "Get ready. The first shift is coming upstairs any minute. We'll each take a table."

Altogether there were three shifts and by the end of two hours I wanted to get off my feet. I saw Eileen sitting with a woman who sorted donated clothing.

"I left Mexico when Cecilia was five and Luisa was three. The doctor said the reason Cecilia didn't speak right was she needed an operation. I borrowed money from my family and came to America to get a job so I could pay them back."

"What did you do?"

"Oaxacans are good cooks. I took a job in a Mexican restaurant in L.A. The owner gave me a room in his house but I had to clean and take care of his children whenever I wasn't working."

"How many hours a week were you in the restaurant?" Eileen asked.

"Every day it was open. I didn't miss one day in nine years. When I finished paying off the loan, I went back to Oaxaca. Cecilia and Luisa didn't recognize me. When I tried to hug them they ran to my sister crying, 'Mama. Mama.'"

"And now?"

"And now we all live together, here in Santa Cruz. My sister, too. I was very sad all the time. Sometimes I would cry in my bedroom and the restaurant owner would shout at me to stop crying. But what does a man know about a mother's pain."

The worker looked into Eileen's eyes. "But you know what I mean, don't you?"

Tofah is convinced we should buy the hot springs. The resort is located on two hundred and eighty acres a few miles above the City of Soledad, which in Spanish means loneliness. Despite its geothermal swimming pools, grassy lawns and rustic cabins, Delorosa Hot Springs is a lonely destination.

Eileen believes we can create a business by offering watsu, water massage, to help people with chronic pain and she's anxious to muscle test the water at each spring to use with herbal remedies. I'm skeptical, but the landscape intrigues me.

"Fill an extra water bottle," Eileen advised. "We'll go down first to Indian Rock to make an offering. We can ask the ancestors to guide us to the throne. From there we can swing around Paradise Peak and head straight up the mountain."

"Do you have the map?"

"If you call scratches on a napkin a map, I have it, but mostly it indicates we keep climbing and when we can't go higher, we'll see a massive golden chair."

It was noon before we reached what looked like an airfield for alien spaceships. It was flat, wide and long. From above, it might have looked like an intergalactic Chicago O'Hare. We ate lunch on the runway wondering if the throne was another of the legends told about Delarosa. This one was about a stone which ten men couldn't lift that had been finely chiseled into a chair sized for a giant. The story included strange lights that visitors to the resort swore to see coming from the summit of this hill.

"If we don't find it soon, we need to head back down before it gets dark," I said to Eileen, who had resumed walking.

Around a bend she stopped. I did too. It might as well have been the Statue of Zeus at Olympia for all it held our gaze. It was golden colored with bright veins of pyrite coursing through marble and large enough for Eileen and me to sit together. The arm rests and seat were rubbed smooth, either by wind and rain or by eons of use.

"At least this explains the strange lights people saw coming from up here," I said. "Under the right conditions, this chair would have reflected so much sunlight the whole mountain would have been lit like a halo."

"That's true," Tofah agreed. "Except that all the comments I read in June's scrapbook say they saw the lights on moonless nights."

In Salt Lake City the Mormons have amassed eight billion records of human genealogy. A person can trace their family tree from the Mayflower to Noah's Ark, but we have yet to uncover the spider web of threads that binds apparent strangers in ways that speak of connection to past lives, of soul pods, twin souls and soul mates. These connections needn't be on the physical plane. It can even be a book from a long dead author that resonates so clearly with our consciousness that we sense we knew the writer.

Tofah has a connection with Max Theon who was a kabbalist and occultist of the last century. The son of a Polish rabbi, Theon's most famous student was Mira Alfassa, who later became known as The Mother and cofounder of Sri Aurobindo Ashram in India. He also significantly influenced Madame Blavatsky who founded the Theosophical Society. The basic tenets of the society were the Universal Brotherhood of Humanity, the study of comparative religions and the exploration of the unexplained laws of nature. All of which are compatible with the Sufi teachings of Hazrat Inayat Khan which Eileen has taken as her own.

Eileen was bouncing on her feet and clapping her hands in exuberance.

"Sri Karunamayee is coming to our gathering and offered to do a concert on Saturday night. She's world famous for her performances of classical Indian music and is the music director at Sri Aurobindi Ashram"

"Did you arrange that?"

"No. I had a session with Shari to channel what the Masters and Saints had to say about buying Delarosa and if they thought the summer solstice was the right time to have a gathering. The Spirit Guides told me to go ahead and plan it and they would send help. Karunamayee was teaching in the Bay area this weekend, heard we were trying to buy Delarosa and said she wanted to support us.

"What else do you have planned for this weekend?"

"After dinner tonight, Karunamayee is going to lead us in *bhajans*. Tomorrow we're going to make spirit arrows to help us divine the best and highest good for this land."

"I'm good at making marshmallow sticks, but how do you make a spirit arrow?"

"You select a piece of oak or willow, the length of your arm, that you gather under a full moon, and hallow with a drop of your blood. You dress the arrow with colored string, beads, crystals, bird feathers or whatever calls to you. Each of the six directions has a color and each intention has a color. I brought baskets of material for people to use."

"I never did well in arts and crafts. I'll stay down in the pool or help in the kitchen."

"You should do this, Jay. You need some form of defense. If you won't make arrows, make a spirit shield. In the meantime I made you a pendant to protect your heart.

I bent down so she could slip a necklace of rose quartz and carnelian over my head.

On the drive back to Santa Cruz Eileen showed me arrows she made. One was wrapped with black string. Attached to it were beads and the vertebrae of a mammal. A yellow one was adorned with the tooth of a walrus and from a red one hung beads and a blue jay's feather.

"So what did you talk about with Karunamayee?" I asked

"She invited us to the ashram in India and asked me how I knew she was in the Bay area this weekend."

"I told her I didn't know she was in the United States. When I said that, Karunamayee looked puzzled and said, 'But the invitation was hand signed by you to me.'"

Natasha is getting married and as one of her gifts, I am giving her the pennies I've been collecting for three decades.

When my daughter told me she meant to wed her heartthrob of two years, I had the same reaction as fathers throughout the centuries: I was bewildered.

Natasha is charming, attends the opera, owns a collection of miniature porcelain dragons and reads Barbara Cartland romance novels. Her sweetie likes baseball, drives a pick-up truck and manages parking lots.

Natasha was raised Jewish and her roots are in the immigrant culture of New York City. Her future eternal was reared a Mormon and the family tree is planted deep in the Canadian farmlands.

Gabriel and his wife flew in from Australia, Dylan from Colorado and Eden along with her beau came up from San Francisco. More relatives converged from the East Coast.

At the Daughters of the American Revolution Hall we were introduced to the minister and a corsage was pinned to my suit jacket. A pianist played at the back of the room and a *chuppah*, the Jewish wedding canopy, stood at the front of the hall. The *chuppah* was sewn by a family friend and was being held aloft by two of Natasha's cousins and two of the heart throb's sisters.

The flower girl came down the aisle scattering rose petals as cameras shuttered. Following the child, my daughter's dream-come-true walked down, handsome in black tuxedo, strong and straight, someone who could be depended upon when times were difficult.

At a cue from the pianist, Natasha entered, dressed in a long white gown, delicate, angelic, someone who could be depended upon when times needed cheering. They looked the perfect couple.

They lit candles. I offered a Hebrew blessing. The minister spoke a few words. The couple offered vows. They placed rings on each other's fingers. They concluded the ceremony by breaking a wine cup. Some in the audience dabbed their eyes with handkerchiefs.

Natasha and her wedded one began the first waltz. In the middle of it, Natasha asked me to dance and her partner extended a hand to Debbie.

It was a picture book wedding, lacking only a horse drawn carriage and the sanction of the state of Washington. Natasha thought a carriage ride too extravagant and the state of Washington rejects same sex marriages because bigotry still holds sway in the legislatures and hearts of many.

Our reputation for creating Halloween extravaganzas is well known and each year increasing carloads of kids scamper up our driveway. We are part of these children's life histories. The older boys and girls remind us of what we did five years ago. The younger children tell us what happened last Halloween, as if we were not there ourselves.

"You read my palm two years ago," recalls a ten year old girl dressed as a 1920's flapper. "You said the lines showed I'm very smart and I got an "A" in math this report card." Her twelve year old brother, who was chaperoning, said, "You told me I was brave and afterward I chased away a dog who was barking at our cat."

I remember other Halloweens. There was the year when Gabriel designed an elaborate Rube Goldberg set of ropes and pulleys that swooped a straw ghost from the roof to the garage. And another time when Eileen and I, prompted by our reading Next of Kin, dressed in full ape costumes, climbed into a tree facing the street and threw candy to the trick or treaters.

But this year should be one of the best.

The front porch was taken up with a home-made plywood box sufficiently large for me to comfortably sit inside. The lid was layered with fall foliage and Indian corn. In the center of the lid was a black silk top hat hiding a hole big enough to allow my head to fit through.

Eileen was wearing a wizard costume complete with a Rapunzel cone shaped cap.

I could hear footsteps on the street.

"Ladies and Gentlemen," I heard Eileen greet the trick or treaters. "Step right up and see the eighth wonder of the world."

I heard a mommy encouraging some children to come on up.

"Would you like to see some magic?"

I heard several voices say yes.

"Would you like to make some magic?"

The yeses were more enthusiastic.

"Can you say 'Abra cadabra'?"

The kids were into it now.

"Can you say: 'Abra cadabra, Please say hello, Mr. Pumpkin Head?'"

They said it.

"Okay, get ready. When I tap the box three times with my magic wand, you say the magic words."

Tap. Tap. Tap. "Abra Cadabra. Please say hello, Mr. Pumpkin Head."

Slowly I rose up through the hole. My face was painted to look like a jack o' lantern.

"Happy Halloween, Mr. Pumpkin Head," Eileen prompted.

"Happy Halloween, Mr. Pumpkin Head," the kids echoed.

"Happy Halloween," I said, smiling at Red Riding Hood, a fairy and a squirrel.

As I slowly lowered myself down, the kids were studying the magic wand Eileen had made this morning when we walked the beach. Attached to a piece of driftwood were sea shells, sea glass and a couple of bird feathers wound with ribbon.

"Can we do it again?" I heard one of them ask.

"Of course. Abra…"

On a month to month basis, we are sharing a yurt at Delarosa with our friend Bonnie who owns a new age knick knack shop. Being full time tenants gives us an opportunity to more slowly learn the land. We're up to the second book in the Harry Potter series. Eileen wanted to give them as Christmas presents to several of her nieces and nephews, but some of her family think the books are satanic.

"Did you know Tom clears rattlesnakes from the swimming pool changing rooms every morning?" Tofah confided to me as we silently walked through the meadow thick with mist.

"Does that mean the snakes are all out sunbathing and we have nothing to fear trampling through this underbrush?"

"With all the noise we're making, everything that's alive has scooted beyond our reach. Here, it'll be easier if we follow this deer trail. Indian Rock is in that clump of scrub oak."

"The owners haven't gone out of their way to make visiting a national monument an easy jaunt."

"They're afraid if people know about it, a Native American rights group will reclaim it on behalf of the Ohlone or Eselen Indians. The rock and all the land surrounding the springs was considered sacred once upon a time. Since each of the tribes wanted to enjoy and heal in the hot water, the rule was weapons had to be removed before they came up the mountain. All the while they were vacationing here, the women were grinding acorns into meal on that rock which is why the rock has round holes."

I thought about the weapons people carry today: gold and silver bangles, credit cards, titles, indifference, arrogance and prejudice.

The air was swirling around us, whipping branches into a frenzy. We stopped and watched the mist take form. Surrounding the rock were wisps of fog that blended into the shape and dress of native people. The vapor bodies were turning to face us and we both heard a warning on the wind. "This place is not for you. You are not welcome here."

I thought this was a pretty concise statement and was ready to high tail it out of there, but Tofah stayed put.

"Who are you?" she asked

"We are those who have not found a way to cross. We remain here hoping our grandchildren will find us and take us home, but our grandchildren are all dead."

"Is there anything I can do to help?" she asked

"Find a way to release us."

"I promise." Eileen turned to me and motioned for us to start walking back the way we had come.

"I thought you told me that because of all the noise I was making everything living out here was going to move out of our way."

"They're not alive, Jay, they just don't know they're dead."

"Have you ever helped a soul cross?"

"Yes, I have. The first time was in the 80s. I rented a downstairs apartment from a guy and soon afterward we became lovers. On three occasions I awakened in the night to a woman standing at the foot of the bed demanding to know why I was sleeping with her husband.

"After the third time, I asked Herman to tell me about his wife. She had committed suicide in a shed many years back. After the body had been removed, Herman padlocked the building and never set foot in it again.

"The next three nights I lit candles on my altar and called to her. I explained what happened to her. I told her she was dead and to follow the light beings who volunteered to help release her soul.

"On the third night I could feel the last of her presence slip away and I gave gratitude for the love and responsiveness of spirit.

"The next day I returned from work and saw the smoldering remains of the shed. Herman, not knowing what I had done, had sensed she was gone and he was ready to move forward with his own life.

"I never told him what happened but within a month we separated. I believe spirit brought us together so I could help release a soul locked in the in-between place."

Money can eat a hole in Tofah's pockets.

I was asked to dress as Santa Claus for the Christmas gathering in Washington. The idea conjured up salacious thoughts of Eileen sitting on my knee and telling her she would have gotten a bigger gift if she had been a little more bad this past year. But, I think she will be pleased with the gift I bring. I've contracted with a fine woodworker to build a cedar chest from Eileen's own design to replace the one that Gabriel accidentally burned on the beach.

It was a festive mood. The economy is healthy and all of the sisters and brothers are doing well financially. The only one struggling is Ruth who is a single mom with seven kids. She works as an in-home caregiver. She has the opportunity to buy the house she's rented for the past five years if she can come up with a down payment.

After dinner the entire family attended midnight mass at seven in the evening. I sang the carols with gusto and held the hand of six year old Charlotte as she walked down the aisle to place a handful of straw in the manger.

Back at the house, White Russians were being quaffed as each of us got to open one gift; the deluge of opulent gift giving would have to wait upon me to distribute in the morning as St. Nick.

The little kids got toys that only someone who watches Saturday morning television cartoons would ever desire or play with for more than ten minutes. Owen received a box of home-made cherry cordials so drenched in rum they competed with the Bailey's Irish Crème, so we all had to taste them. Santa gave me four pair of wool socks with a card that said, "Merry Christmas, You've come a long way, baby and I love you so." Ruth got a ceramic Department 56 Christmas house and checks from Owen and Eileen, to cover a down payment on a home of her own.

1999

Someone else purchased Delarosa. In the next couple of weeks we have to move out of the yurt. Eileen has been despondent for days. She was sure G-d was directing her to build a community.

It was difficult seeing the oak grove. For two months I've been cutting the strangling vines that are tangled in the branches of the trees. It takes an entire morning to free one tree and there must be at least a hundred trees that are dying from a lack of care. At the most, I saved half a dozen of them.

As I was returning to the yurt, I heard a young oak call out to me: "Jay! You promised you would do me next. Please don't go!"

I turned to the tree and said, "I'm sorry. I'm out of time."

By late afternoon we had filled two pick-up trucks and the Pontiac Skychief. The only thing left to do was scrub the bathroom and say goodbye to a dream. Eileen was crouched over the medicine wheel she built a year ago.

"I could never get anything to grow out here," she said as her fingertips caressed the circle of rocks and spokes that reached in four directions.

"Do you remember when the lama came and did a *puja*? He only had a handful of twigs and they burned for hours but even he couldn't awaken the land," she said

"Let's go down to the spring and search for wild turkey feathers, Eileen. Bonnie will have dinner ready by the time we return and we'll have one more night of watching desert silhouettes."

We found three feathers and a postcard of Shiva that someone had placed in a hollow of a tree.

We awoke early for the drive back to Santa Cruz. Coming out of the yurt, rubbing sleep from my eyes I gazed on the open field.

"Eileen and Bonnie," I called, "come outside." The field was blanketed with tiny blue flowers.

We stood in silent awe. "They came to thank you," I said, taking Eileen's hand.

"Do you think we'll ever be able to build a community, Jay?" Eileen asked, as we climbed into the vehicles.

"If we sell the house in Eugene, you and I could buy something by ourselves. It won't be as big as Delarosa but at least we wouldn't be waiting for someone else to write a check."

Driving away I looked through the rear view mirror. The flowers had disappeared.

THE ROSE ZHIKR

2000

Eileen is disconsolate. There are other hot springs for sale but her faith in The Goddess is shaken. She wonders if she misunderstood her purpose or if this was a test to love G-d, despite disappointment. It's easy to give thanks when the sun is shining overhead. It's not so very easy when the forecast calls for forty days of rain.

I have an umbrella, if she wants it. I wasn't able to raise four million dollars, but if I sell my house in Eugene, we'll have the down payment for a small center in Santa Cruz. It won't be two hundred and eighty acres, but it will be our own, with no one telling Eileen what she can or cannot do. She's never worked for someone else and I don't think she would have done great with a board of directors whether or not it was based on the Iroquis Great Law of Peace. I think she has more Taurus than Gemini in her chart.

This place?" I was standing on hard caked dirt in front of The Winchester Mystery House meets The Bates Motel.

"It has plenty of parking and it's legally zoned. The rest is just money," Eileen said casually.

"A lot of money," I said not so casually

"Not so much. We'll get it cheap because it's run down."

"It's falling down."

"It'll be fine, Jay. We can repair the office building and I can make it into counseling offices. That way we'll save the money I'm now spending on renting an office. We can rebuild the wall on the other side of the building and make it into a sanctuary."

"When are you planning to do this?"

"If you agree, we'll start as soon as you go in for knee surgery. That way it will be clear there's only one boss on the work site."

None of the doctors have been able to explain why I have holes in my knee but between the holes and a torn Achilles tendon, I can barely walk. The solution is to repair the tendon and fill the holes with bone marrow taken from a cadaver. It's hit or miss whether my body will accept the marrow since there are no tests for compatibility, but the doctor performing the surgery assures me the procedure is unlikely to be fatal.

So why was I convinced I was going to die? If the surgery isn't life threatening, maybe the danger lay with the anesthesia? We studied the date astrologically and bio-rhythmically and it all looked copacetic. I wasn't worried. I just knew I wasn't coming back home and I had sixty days notice to clear my desk and karma.

In the morning, Eileen drove us to Stanford Hospital where I was prepped and kept waiting half a day. At lunch time, an apologetic nurse told me the bone marrow they ordered was unexpectedly needed by the patient who had gone ahead of me. I needed to return another day when they would have more bone marrow on hand.

I leaped off the bed. My premonition of death dissolved.

"How'd they do?" I asked, groggily.

"The doctors say it went smoothly. You'll be on crutches within a month."

"And I didn't die."

"And you didn't die. The doctors were nervous that you weren't coming out of the anesthesia as quickly as they anticipated so I went into your psyche to see what was going on."

"And?"

"That's what I asked you. I said, 'What are you doing, Jay?

Come back.' And you said, 'I don't want to come back.' And I said, 'Come and dance with me.' And you said, 'I don't want to dance.' I said, 'You always wanted to espalier a fruit tree. If you'll come back, it'll be the first tree we plant.' Your face became more relaxed, like you were enjoying the idea of training a tree and then you woke up."

"That's it? I came back to plant a tree?"

"Maybe. What kind do you want to espalier?"

"How about an apricot?"

"Great choice! When I was growing up there was an apricot orchard across from the house and I was Annie Oakley. I could hit a moving target at twenty-five yards."

Eileen found gold when she found Chris, a contractor, who can do it all: framing, plumbing and electrical. His buddy, Craig, will do the grunt work. They start work right away. My "brother" George is my attendant until I am on my feet. We are reading Endurance, the saga of Shackleton's failed attempt to reach the Antarctic.

Craig spent his junior year of college in the jungles of Oaxaca introducing improved wood cook stoves to skeptical villagers. Before returning to the States he invited his new friends to visit if they ever made it across the border.

Cesario, Hilberto and Aquillino showed up at his doorstep a few weeks ago, unannounced, exhausted and terrified by the two thousand mile gauntlet getting from their pueblo to Monterey Bay and the fifty mile death run through the Sonora Desert.

"Can you put them to work?" Craig asked Eileen.

"I don't speak a word of Spanish."

"That makes you even. They don't speak a word of English."

"Then how am I going to manage them?"

"You can use hand signals to show them what you want and I can always translate."

"What do you think, Chris?"

"Give them machetes and have them hack the blackberries. When they're finished cutting the vines, give them shovels to dig out the roots. If they're still here a week from now, you'll have three good laborers and we can use the muscle."

Yesterday Craig came to Eileen, agitated.

"My landlord is threatening to evict me because of the guys staying in my place. Do you think it would be okay for them to sleep here at the work site?"

"Craig, this is a complete remodel. There are times when we shut off the electricity and water for days. How are they going to live here?"

"In the jungle, the only running water is in the creek at the entrance to the village."

"What's the word for sleep in Spanish?"

"Dormeer," Craig volunteered.

"Hand signals, huh?" Eileen muttered to herself. She walked over to Cesario, the unspoken leader of the three young men. She put her palms together and leaned her cheek against them as if she were napping. "Dormeer?" she said and pointed to the house.

Cesario imitated Eileen and said something that sounded like the word dormeer.

Eileen nodded her head. Cesario spoke rapidly to Hilberto and Aquillino who both rested their cheeks against their palms and said "dormeer?" Eileen nodded again and suddenly all three of them were vigorously shaking Eileen's hand and repeating the word "dormeer."

Call them *mojados*, wet-backs or illegals. Eileen only saw three boys the same age as Dylan. She didn't know the word for family in Spanish but she knew her family had grown.

2001

We are celebrating Halloween differently this year. The Garden is on a dead end, unlit street and Freddie Kruger would be reluctant to trick or treat our neighborhood. Instead, Tofah invited the emerging Sufi community to come to a party dressed as their favorite saints.

The aroma of home made chai bubbling in a two gallon pot reminds Eileen of the months she spent with Yogi Bhajan and Guru Dev. It was from them she learned the healing art and science of *Sat Nam Rasayan* as well as the recipe for the tea.

"Yogi Bhajan was the first to open my eyes to non-Western healing. Instead of antibiotics, he taught balancing the earth, water, fire, air and ether elements in a person to heal them of their illnesses. We spent hours meditating and the way we kept awake was by drinking cup after cup of yogi tea.

"It was during that time when I realized most allopathic medicine is a corporate sham. The doctors coming out of medical school have no training in diet, homeopathy, massage or a dozen other modalities. They prescribe pharmaceuticals because it's the only thing they know. I wanted to know more."

"That's how you approach spiritual teachers. You always want to know more."

"What I want to know right now is why you are wearing an empty toilet paper roll tied around your neck with the word rum written on it?"

"I'm coming to the shindig dressed as Saint Bernard."

2002

Dad had a second heart attack and we booked the first flight leaving for Florida. Dad lived his life like the strong man in the circus protecting his carnival queen but that fantasy is finished. Even before this, he'd been in pain, nearly blind and could hardly walk.

Coming out of E.R., he was placed in the hospice wing of the hospital. The doctor thought he would pass during the night but when Eileen and I arrived he was awake, conscious and refusing food. He continued like that for nineteen days, taking sips of juice, fasting and waiting to die. During that time two of his roommates died but Dad got stronger. Hospice recommended he be transferred to a nursing home and suggested one nearby. We signed the papers for the transfer but before Eileen and I could return home, I had one last task to complete.

"Are you sure you completed all the forms?" he asked.

"I'm sure, Dad. I made a copy of your last year's taxes and used it as a template for filling out this year's return. Only a few numbers change, mostly on Schedule B. Let me show you."

"Give them to me," he said feebly grasping the sheets of paper. "Help me sit up." I waited anxiously while he studied the return I had prepared. If he found an error he was liable to start yelling.

"It looks correct." He turned to Eileen who was sitting on the edge of his bed. "Eileen go over the addition, make sure he got it right. There's a pen in the top drawer. Everything needs to be perfect. Irene never did the taxes and I don't want her to worry about them this year."

Not everything is right in Florida. The nursing home is a nightmare. Nearly all the patients are on welfare with no one to act as their advocates, all except Dad who is paying two hundred dollars a day out of his own pocket. It's too far away for Mom to visit and my sister, Harriet, hates to go there because it is so depressing. When she does visit, Dad begs her to help him die.

After reading mostly useless books on compassionate dying I've made a decision to assist his suicide. I spent hours researching and couldn't come up with a good way to help him die until a kindly retired physician handed me several pills. He didn't ask for money and he warned me to be very careful. Assisted suicide at home is rarely prosecuted. Assisted suicide at a nursing home is much more likely to be prosecuted because the people who own these places see it as theft, since each of their patients is a revenue stream and regardless of whether the residents are in pain or in a coma, each day they occupy a bed is money in the pockets of these corporations.

I argued until I was blue in the face but Eileen wouldn't budge. If she's with me when my father dies she could be considered an accomplice to murder. She said that unless she keeps watch at the door, there is a greater chance of my being discovered and she couldn't accept me going to prison. If I was going, so was she.

Dad looked like a gristly, pale rider. When we entered his room he struck a bony finger at us and said over and over, "Jay. Eileen. Jay. Eileen."

We sat by his bed. "Oh my G-d. Why did you come? Why did you come? I didn't want you to see me like this. Oh Jay. Eileen." He kept kissing Eileen.

The other bed in the room was empty. Eileen kissed Dad and left the room, closing the door behind her to stand sentinel.

"Listen, Dad. We don't have a lot of time. I have these pills that will cause you to have a heart attack almost immediately and you'll be out of pain. There's only one thing. I'm not willing to put them in your mouth. You have to do it for yourself. You have enough strength to take them from my hand and swallow them on your own." I opened my palm and showed him the three small capsules.

He closed his hand on mine. "Jay, if I take these pills, I won't know if you got in trouble for giving them to me. You might go to jail and I'd rather be in pain for another few days than die not knowing you're safe."

"Then at least we're going to get you out of here."

"Jay. Jay. Don't bother."

"I am going to bother. We'll be back this evening."

I opened the door. Eileen looked at me expectantly. I shook my head. "I'll tell you once we get outside."

The best residential care was one of a chain of Marriott nursing homes. The room looked exactly like an upscale hotel room with a hospital bed instead of a king. I put a deposit down on the room and we returned to the dungeon of despair for a meeting with the director.

"I am very sorry, Jay" the director said, leaning back in his desk chair with his hands crossed behind his head. "It's not possible for your father to be released from our care until all the paperwork is completed. At a minimum I need a letter from the patient's doctor and authorization from Medicare."

"What are you talking about? My dad didn't come here under a doctor's supervision and he's paying out of pocket, so Medicare has nothing to do with it."

"Even so we have our own paper trail and regulations to follow. That can take days. Today is the beginning of a three day weekend, so I suggest you come back on Tuesday and we can discuss his transfer. Until then I'm afraid I am unable to assist you. I myself am leaving for a fishing trip to the Bahamas and will be out of reach. Would you like to schedule a meeting for first thing Tuesday morning?"

If the director was going to be out of reach maybe we could bluff the staff. On Saturday morning we appeared at the nurse's station and said we had been told to come promptly at nine to transport my father to the Marriott.

The acting administrator was startled. "Mr. Bineglass didn't say anything about this. I have no instructions and it will take an hour to prepare the paperwork. I'm so sorry. He must have forgotten in the excitement of his fishing expedition."

We acted a tiny bit indignant at being inconvenienced but said we understood.

"Can I help in any way?" Eileen asked.

"Well thank you, honey. I'm always short staffed on the weekends. Would you mind photo copying your father's medical history? They'll need all of it at the Marriott."

Eileen took the binder and went to make copies.

"I'll go pack my dad's clothing and call an ambulance," I said to the exasperated nurse.

"Thank you. Again, normally we would have everything ready to go. I'm so sorry."

"Don't be," I assured her, and hoped the ambulance would hurry up and get here.

An hour later Dad was wheeled into the Marriott on a gurney.

The director of nursing care showed us to his room.

"Hello, Sam. My name is Cynthia."

Dad said hello in a shallow voice.

"You sure do look something, Sam. I'm going to call the beauty salon to come straight up here to give you a shave and haircut. How does that sound? After all we can't have you joining everyone in the dining room looking like you've been riding a freight train."

Dad chuckled. "I can't go to the dining room. I can't get out of bed."

Cynthia took his hand. "Oh that's not a problem. We have special beds that help you sit up to eat which can be wheeled anywhere in the building. We have a lovely aviary that some of our patients enjoy. Do you like birds, Sam?"

Dad nodded.

"And for heavens sake, let's get you into some clean clothes. I'll bet your t-shirt was white before it became yellow."

A handsome young Haitian man was placing a warm towel on dad's face in preparation for a shave when Eileen and I kissed him goodbye.

On the way to the airport, Eileen stopped at a pizza parlor where she ordered two large pizzas be delivered to the staff at dad's former nursing home. "It's small thanks for all the grief Bineglass is going to give his workers when he finds out what we did."

Dad died this morning. He was alone.

There is something really, really wrong festering in the soul of America. We are the first generation to die alone. Seventy percent of us are dying in hospitals and old age homes. We die with a nurse looking in every ten or fifteen minutes and if we are lucky, with someone at our bedside to hold our hands.

We have a culture that adores youth, beauty, happy endings and minimal emotional truth. Most of the time, when people die they aren't young, beautiful or happy. The easiest way to avoid this reality is to hide from it by removing sick people from our sight.

It takes a community to help a person cross and despite the legion of words spoken about communities, they barely exist. It requires a great many people to cook, run errands, mow lawns and walk dogs. It can take weeks, months, even years for a person to die and during the journey they may need twenty-four hour care. How can it possibly be done, given the world in which we live? The answer is, it can't. We need to change the world in which we live.

The Women's Circle of Stones is moving to the Garden Sanctuary in time to celebrate Beltane, the Celtic May Day festival. It's the first large event Tofah Eileen is hosting at the Garden and she expects twenty-five women to attend. It'll be a challenge to park twenty cars on our property but there's more space next door in the county park. I don't need to read the tarot to know my future job description is going to include parking lot attendant.

Tofah Eileen purchased a mountain of various colored ribbons to dress a May Pole and intends to build a fire in the caldron in honor of the wedding feast of the God and Goddess.

A fire engine was pulling out of our driveway when I got home from a late night rerun of Shrek. Tofah was standing under a lamplight waving good night to Faith.

"What did you burn down?" I asked, peering nervously at the house.

"Jay, it was so great. Come see the May Pole," she said, leading me onto the labyrinth where the cauldron still held burning embers.

"Fifty women came."

"How did you park fifty cars?"

"I don't know. Janice was in charge of that but you would do a much better job. I was busy smudging people."

"So go on."

"Somebody down the street saw the smoke from the cauldron and called the fire department. When they arrived I poured them cups of yogi tea.

"Did they give you a ticket?"

"No. They were very nice. They said the next time we're having a fire we should call and let them know."

"So they'll have it on record?"

"So they'll know to bring marshmallows."

The ideal location for a koi pond is in the upper left corner of the garden, but there's a eucalyptus tree at the edge of where I would be digging. Even if I could dig around it, which I doubt, it will be constantly dropping leaves and depositing an oil slick the envy of the Exxon Valdez into the water. I asked the tree if it would allow me to chop it down and it gave me a dirty look.

I am rapidly losing interest in the Harry Potter books, but Tofah loves them.

Aquillino, who is training to be the chef at an Irish pub owned by a Persian, took the afternoon off to help Cesario, Chepe and I move the statue of *Quan Yin,* Goddess of Compassion, that I purchased at Goodwill.

As soon as I saw her in the warehouse, I wanted to buy the statue for Tofah. The Goddess is seven feet tall, carved from a single piece of wood and took all four of us to lift into the truck. She is brightly painted, leading to speculation she was crafted in

Bali. She is standing on a turtle instead of the usual lotus flower or dragon, which is perfect, if she were standing alongside the koi pond.

Eileen went to have a conversation with the eucalyptus. She returned to the house an hour later.

"I asked the tree if it would be willing to be a pavilion for a Goddess. At first it didn't answer me, so I drew a diagram of what I have in mind. I promised we would take her down in ten foot pieces and use her trunk as the corner posts. The pavilion will be open on all four sides with a curved Japanese style roof topped with wood shingles."

"What did the tree say?"

"It said okay."

Yesterday was my birthday. Eileen baked a chocolate cake and the guys taught us a custom of their village which consisted of them chasing me around the kitchen table attempting to throw a bucket of water on my head. Eileen gave me a gift of a brand new shovel.

I lived in downtown Brooklyn for six years. It was nasty, dirty and desperate. To reach the Botanical Gardens I passed a knot of the most wretched prostitutes in New York City, those who did it against a wall for thirty dollars. But within the Botanical Gardens is the first Japanese Garden ever created in an American public park. It is three acres of hills, waterfalls, arched bridges and an island. If I ever stopped being poor, I was going to have a Japanese Garden of my own.

The pond, with a cascading waterfall, is going to be three feet deep to prevent raccoons from eating the fish, but before I can buy the fish, I have to dig a hole. Unfortunately no matter where I stick a shovel, I uncover shards of glass.

This presents a problem. I am wheelbarrowing the excavated dirt to an undeveloped extension of the county park across the way, creating a small knoll among the eucalyptus and blackberries. But I feel responsible to remove the glass from the fill.

To take the task from a purely ecological responsibility into a spiritual practice, I decided to say, "Thank you, G-d," each time I removed a piece of glass from the sifted dirt.

I was out there early this morning, digging, when I uncovered the mother lode of glass. In that one shovel full of dirt there had to be at least fifty opportunities to say "Thank you, G-d." It would take me half an hour before I could make any more progress on the hole. I was so frustrated I threw the shovel down. The shovel immediately jumped back up and smacked me in the center of my third eye with the wooden handle.

As I stumbled into the house in search of an ice pack, I heard a still small voice say, "Did I get that you're tired of saying 'thank you?'"

Mom accused Dad of bringing home stray cats. I accuse Tofah Eileen of bringing home stray people. The house has four outside doors facing the four directions and folks enter without knocking. On the rare occasion when someone does ring the doorbell, we get fidgety thinking it's the border patrol.

Eileen was talking to someone in a parked car. I figured the station wagon belonged to someone visiting a neighbor because it had been there throughout the night. Then I saw a twenty something boy get out from the driver's side at the same time as a girl his same age emerged rubbing sleep from her eyes.

Eileen introduced our guests. "This is Jasper and Lilly. I told them I'm making pancakes if they're hungry. Jasper and Lilly have been on the road for months, sleeping in their car," Eileen clarified.

Jasper apologized. "I'm sorry if we frightened you. It was late at night and we didn't know where to park. This looked like a church so we took a chance."

"That's okay. Do you want to take showers before you eat?"

Eileen asked.

Lilly beamed. "Yes! I haven't showered in days."

"The bathroom is around the corner. There are towels in the closet. Take your time. I'm just starting on the pancakes."

Lilly contributed oranges from their ice chest and we sat down to eat.

"So what do you guys do?" I asked.

"I'm a muralist," Jasper said with confidence. "I was working on the wall of a bank in Sacramento but had a squabble with the manager. I have a friend in L.A. who's opening a gallery and wants me to lend him a hand but I don't know if I want to live down there."

"What about you?" Eileen turned to the girl.

"Nothing much. I play the violin sometimes. I was first string in the Junior Symphony before I met Jasper. Is this place a church?"

"It's a Sufi *konka*. We have classes in the big room that I showed you and on Sunday evenings we hold dances in there. Would you play your violin for the dance tomorrow night?"

"Well, sure. If I saw the music I could."

"I'll show it to you."

"So what's next for you, Jasper?" I asked.

"We're not sure. We're practically broke. I'm hoping to find someone in Santa Cruz who wants a mural."

"I want a mural," I said.

"Me too," echoed Eileen. "I love murals that make flat walls look three dimensional."

"That's exactly what I paint," Jasper said, pushing away from the table to retrieve his portfolio.

We browsed his work. "Could you do a mural of Mt. Hood on the wall behind the hot tub?" Eileen wondered. "Jay and I both miss seeing the mountain."

"I could if I had a photograph to work from."

"Would you trade a mural for a couple of months of free rent and three hundred dollars?"

Jasper looked to Lilly for guidance. She nodded.

"Will you supply the paint?" he asked.

I nodded.

"Then it's a deal."

"I'll show you to your room," Eileen said, taking Lilly by the hand, holding another woman under her wing.

2003

On Friday nights we have dinner together with all of the guys living upstairs and whoever else is around. I had to add a leaf to the table because more fellows from the pueblo arrive every month. Lawrence, a newly acquired friend, calls this place The Sufi Bar and Grill.

I was stirring the soup with a spoon big enough to paddle a canoe. Lawrence was staring. Lawrence spent a year in Guatemala as a volunteer with Peace Brigades. These are possibly the bravest volunteers on earth – even braver than Doctors without Borders. Each volunteer is assigned to stay close to a person who has been targeted for political assassination in the hope that thugs will be weary of endangering an American in a shoot out. Lawrence is able to translate when Spanglish fails.

"This reminds me of when I was cooking for the Catholic Worker in Salinas. We used to use a broken row boat oar to stir," he said.

I looked up from my cooking. "The first volunteer work I ever did was at the Catholic Worker on the Bowery."

"I knew it!" Lawrence chortled. "I can always spot another Catholic Worker."

"Dinner's ready," I announced, and there was a clamor of

footsteps on the stairway.

We said a prayer over the wine and bread and filled our bowls with miso soup.

"*Porque ustedes vas a Estados Unidos?*" I asked without regard to gender or tense. It was enough for me to string words together.

Cesario came to earn money to send to his wife and children. Hilberto was ordered by his father to come as sort of a boot camp. Aquillino came because his best friend is Cesario and he didn't want to miss out on the adventure. Jesus, the sixteen year old child of the village came because he wants to marry his grade school sweetheart and needs money to build a house. Chepe came because his family is the poorest in the village and often go to sleep hungry. Fernando came because his cousin Aquillino was here to help him.

"Lawrence, explain to the guys that Eileen and I want to give something back to the pueblo for all the help the guys gave us. We'd like to create a small business venture that could earn money for the village and maybe help keep one person from having to cross the border. Do they have any ideas?"

"Un ro-day-o," declared Chepe.

"A rodeo?'

"*Si. Un ro-day-o. Es muy popular en Meh-he-co. No existe un rodeo en la selva.*" The guys became animated and Lawrence gave us the gist of their conversation.

"All the big towns have a rodeo arena but there are no rodeos in the jungle. If the pueblo had a rodeo grounds, they could throw a fiesta once a year for the surrounding pueblos and earn money."

"*Quantas dinero?*" I asked.

"*No sey,*" Cesario answered thoughtfully. *Po-see-blay seis o siete cientos dolares.*"

"Six hundred dollars?" Eileen asked.

"*Mas o menos. Sole-a-men-tay necessita dinero for gas-o-ly-nah y hammers. Mis amigos trabajarán gratis.*"

"Can you write home and ask if the villagers want to do

this?"

"*Si. Este noche.*"

Lawrence turned to me. "What do you think about a couple of old Catholic Workers making tortilla soup for two hundred on opening day?"

"No problem. I'll borrow an oar from someone at the marina."

To the Tohono O'odham tribe of Native Americans living in Arizona and Mexico, the Man in the Maze is a mystical labyrinth representing a journey into balance. Unlike a maze found in amusement parks, where the intent is to confuse, walking the seven concentric rings of a labyrinth will bring a person to the center where the Divine Source blesses the seeker's dreams and goals.

Creating a labyrinth was the first landscape design project Eileen completed. Cesario and Hilberto spent a week excavating a perfectly level circle, four inches deep and thirty feet across. Eileen arranged crystals and copper wire in the eight directions on top of which we laid rebar to strengthen the poured cement.

Koge assured Eileen he could duplicate the Hopi design onto the concrete. When the work was finished, he was the first to walk into the center, holding his greatest desire in mind and heart.

Recently, Suzanne asked if we wanted a gazebo. It was a kit that could be disassembled and reassembled but she was moving and couldn't take it with her. She did ask to periodically visit the Garden and sit in the wood paneled garden room.

We accepted the donation and in one hectic week took it apart piece by piece, trucked it forty miles and put it back, piece by piece, alongside the labyrinth.

Last month Suzanne visited the gazebo. Koge was walking the labyrinth. They met. They walked the labyrinth together and sat in the gazebo. Last night they announced they were flying to Japan for their wedding ceremony.

Mom doesn't want to live alone. Tofah Eileen agrees it would be best if she lives with us.

Florida was a bit nippy for Mom's taste. Weighing ninety pounds she was always cold. I think she was the only person in the Sunshine State who paid more to heat her home than to air-condition it. I couldn't imagine how we could make her comfortable considering the thermostat didn't go as high as her metabolism required.

Eileen proposed we knock out a wall and install a wood stove. Even though we couldn't keep the entire house at ninety degrees Fahrenheit, we could convert that niche into a baker's oven.

The flight across the continent was difficult for Mom, Harriet and the stewardesses. When they arrived in San Jose all of them were exhausted. The stewardesses headed for a bar, Harriett was searching for an Excedrin and Mom was shivering.

"Why didn't you tell me Santa Cruz is so close to Canada?" she queried several times on the drive south. "I knew I shouldn't have given my mink coat to Natasha. I'll freeze to death without it," she moaned as Eileen draped a crocheted car blanket around Mom's shoulders.

I had banked a fire in the stove before leaving for the airport and a roaring bed of hot coals remained when we arrived home. I helped Mom into a wheelchair and rolled her into the alcove near the stove.

"Is this better, Mom?" I asked, feeling sweat beading on my forehead.

She nodded.

"I'll get you a cup of tea, if you'd like," Tofah offered.

"Thank you. I like Liptons. Jay, put another log on the fire."

I needed to make serious budget cuts but my budget was already lean. I could pink slip my assistant or retire. I chose the latter. Harris and me are going to barbecue lunch for the workers as a going away party. But before then, I wanted to do one last grand fund-raiser.

142

I rented a nine hundred seat performing arts theatre and advertised a sing- along to "The Sound of Music." We offered the audience ice- cream- stick puppets so they could participate in "The Lonely Goatherd" and confetti for them to throw at the wedding scene. I hired an over- the- top performer to be on stage encouraging the audience to far flung antics as the movie played on the wide screen. I filled the theatre and earned Goodwill Industries twenty percent of my annual salary.

Eileen and I were back stage. I was wearing lederhosen and she was in a Julie Andrews pinafore.

"When Amos gives us a signal for the finale we're going to skip along downstage, carrying these suitcases singing 'The Hills Are Alive With the Sound of Music'," I told Eileen.

"Will anyone actually be able to hear us singing?"

"Not over the sound track, but they'll be able to see the words "So Long, Goodwill" that I painted on my luggage.

"I don't look a bit like Maria. Not even with my hair tucked under this scarf."

"That's okay. I don't look anything like Captain Von Trapp."

"You're as brave as him. Are you at all afraid of retiring?"

"Not as long as I have you and Mom making lists for me to do each day. By the way, what did you paint on your suitcase?"

Eileen turned her suitcase so I could read the words. I looked at the writing and said, "Hello, Nepal?"

"Your Mom isn't going to be here much longer, Jay. After she crosses I want to trek in Nepal and celebrate the Urs of Hazrat Inayat Khan in India."

"That's what you want?"

"There's only three things I want, sweetie pie. I want you, I want my kids and when it's time for me to cross, I want to dissolve in the arms of the Beloved. Listen. Get ready. We're up."

2004

Sufi dancing began with Murshid Samuel Lewis of the Chisti Order during the height of the Haight Ashberry counter cultural revolution. Sufi Sam, along with Ruth St-Denis, chose short prayers from the world's religions, put them to music and choreographed very easy dance steps that reflect the prayers being sung. The dances are now done around the world. Tofah Eileen leads the dances every Sunday night and whenever else an opportunity arises: the equinox, solstice, new moon, my birthday, they'll all work as far as she's concerned. Eileen's favorite instrument is a drum and as she leads thirty or forty dancers, I see a sparkle of Miriam leading the Israelites.

Tonight Tofah stands in the center of the circle, a *doumbek* in the crook of her arm, possessed of a joy that makes her face glow. She is blossoming without arrogance. Her heart embraces each of the dancers and her eyes twinkle in welcoming a latecomer to the dance. When the song begins, Tofah moves like a mirror within the circle. If dancers are taking steps backward, she moves toward them, like a gazelle on Mt. Zion. If the dancers are turning to the left, she turns to the right and when dancers lift their arms in supplication, her voice and her drum carry their prayers toward heaven. She transforms Sufi dancing into a courtship ritual to The Divine.

I never know what's coming next.

A three alarm fire emptied several fire stations and the clamor they created battered nerves and shattered crystal. A dog, locked in a car outside Eileen's counseling office, was in a frenzy.

Within an hour the German shepherd gnawed the dashboard, chewed the wiring, tore up the driver's seat and ripped apart the driver's door panel. Eileen's client was in shock at the damage. The car couldn't be driven. I expected a dog foaming at the mouth to leap from the car, but instead the dog stepped out, whimpering and contrite.

"Jay, drive Linda to Santa Cruz Elementary, pick up her son and take him to baseball practice. In the meantime we'll have the car towed." She turned to the woman. "Do you have Triple A?" The woman shook her head. "That's all right. We can use my card. Where do you want the car taken?"

Such a direct question brought the woman out of panic. "My brother-in-law will know what to do. He lives over by the park."

"Good. Give me his address and we'll have the driver take it over to him."

Eileen looked at the interior. "Jay, take the sheepskin seat cover from your Saturn and put it on her driver's seat, it'll keep the springs from poking out."

"Anything else?"

"Yes, bring Linda back here, then return to the baseball practice and cheer for her son."

I haven't known many people who've died. My dad died as he lived, in confusion. A couple of others died suddenly, probably in surprise. Fran is the first person I know who is dying consciously. She has brain tumors and has chosen not to do chemotherapy. Tofah is volunteering to accompany her through this journey.

Lawrence was seated behind his harp, Fran sat next to him on a cushion. Fran was concerned if they delayed too much longer, she wouldn't have the strength to lead prayers. As many as the sanctuary could hold, we sat in a circle made sacred by the occasion.

"Tonight, we are here to sing and praise G-d," Fran said, in a voice still rich and velvety. I turned from her because I was crying. She continued, "for all the blessings I have known, for all the gifts that I have received. Tonight, there will be no sadness in our circle. Let our joy be so triumphant, that we rest in G-d and say amen."

We all said, "Amen."

"The words of the first chant are familiar to most of you. *Om Namah Shivaya Shivaya Namah Om.* I humbly bow to you, Lord Shiva."

Shiva, Lord of transformation. Fran is in the arms of Lord Shiva. Death has become Fran's companion and serenity her maid servant. She's shed most of her attachments and what remains is beauty. I thought of the Hebrew prayer that says, "The soul you put within me is pure."

Fran is offering herself as a sacrament.

I think requiring three thousand hours of internship to practice marriage counseling is punitive. It's more than a year of full time work and interns consider themselves fortunate if they find any way to get paid for their time. Most of them don't.

Eileen is one of the fortunate few. Bailey created Pine Knoll Counseling Center to provide low cost/no cost counseling in Santa Cruz County and allowed Eileen to keep whatever fee she received from her clients, usually ten or twenty dollars an hour.

Eileen approached her internship as an opportunity to explore ways to heal the body, mind and spirit. She read Jung, delighted in art and sand tray therapies and increasingly was drawn to EFT and EMDR as emergency first aid and restorative health modalities. Still, when all the textbooks were dusted and put on shelves, she based her practice on Theravada Buddhism's four attributes: metta, karuna, mudita and upekkha-loving kindness, compassion, sympathetic joy and equanimity.

There was a week of rain and Bailey's house, alongside a creek, was in danger of flooding. In the rush to leave, her dad, Frank, fell down a flight of steps. He wound up in a nursing home until Bailey could figure out a long term plan.

Settling under the blankets to continue reading The Milagro Bean Field War, Eileen turned to me. "Jay, we need your help."

"Doing what?"

"Bailey's dad is having memory problems. He's confused and doesn't understand why he's in a nursing home. Everything is unfamiliar. He needs to see some faces he recognizes."

"I'm sorry to hear that. He's a good guy."

"He's the one who financed Pine Knoll Counseling Center. He paid all the bills out of his own pocket so poor people could get help, now he needs some."

"So what do you want me to do?"

"Visit him. I'm taking Monday and Wednesday afternoons. Can you go over for an hour every Tuesday and Thursday?"

"What am I supposed to do?"

"Just talk to him."

"You think that will help?"

"He doesn't need therapy. He needs kindness and compassion."

"Back to Buddhism, is it? Sure, I'll go over."

Eileen snuggled in and sang softly into my ear. "You are so beautiful to me. Can't you see? You're everything I hoped for. You're everything I need. You are so beautiful to me."

"Ssshh. Be quiet. I'm reading."

A few weeks later, Eileen came into the living room holding a subpoena. One of her clients is in a child custody battle and her husband claims she is an unfit mother. Tofah is testifying on behalf of her client and she's like a mother bear in defense of the woman.

"Where's your equanimity?" I asked.

"I have equanimity but I'm going to stand by her side and help fight for her rights. No one should have to do that alone."

After traveling around the world, Gabe settled in Australia and enrolled in the School of Architecture in Melbourne. In lieu of a high school transcript, he was accepted based on a Franklin wood stove he constructed from auto parts and the schematics of a parade float he designed and entered in a festival. In a couple of days we will join in celebrating his achievements and until then have been visiting sacred sites along Australia's coastline and meeting with other bishops of the Home Temple. Yesterday we climbed Mt. Wollumbin, considered a sacred site by the Aborigines. We are recuperating from the climb in Byron Bay which is considered the Australian counterpart to Santa Cruz complete with palm readers, cannabis and beach.

Coming out of the movie theatre in early evening, Eileen looked shaken.

"I don't feel right. Something is wrong. We need to light candles."

"We passed a gift shop on the way over here. They'll have some," I suggested.

In our hotel room she placed bed pillows on the floor.

"Something very bad is coming this way and we need to pray. Let's do the Sufi invocation, 'Toward the One, the Perfection of Love, Harmony and Beauty. The only being, united with all the illuminated souls who form the embodiment of the Master, the Spirit of Guidance. *Bismillah Er Rachman Er Raheem.* We begin in the name of Allah who is mercy and Compassion.'"

The last candle flickered and died at one in the morning and we stopped chanting.

On Boxing Day, while celebrating Christmas, Australian style, with a barbecue in a neighborhood park in Melbourne, we heard of a tsunami racing across the Indian Ocean savaging Indonesia, India and Thailand. Thousands lost their lives.

2005

Cesario is living in the capital city of Oaxaca. His wife disappeared along with the money he sent her each month but he met a local woman and they are planning to marry. It is too arduous and expensive for his mother to travel from the jungle to the city for the ceremony and Cesario asked if Eileen will stand in her stead. He also invited Craig to la boda. Afterward, the wedding party is going to travel to Cesario's pueblo.

It took six hours for the van to cross the mountains. Eileen got sick twice and no one looked out the window at the sheer drops alongside the highway. The driver dropped us off in Puerto Escondido, a tourist town and international surfer destination. From there we had to take roads diminishing from paved, to gravel, to dirt, to imaginary. Word traveled faster than our vehicles and when we arrived at the pueblo the entire town came out to greet Cesario, his new bride and *la abuela Americano*, Tofah, the American grandmother.

Imagine what it must be like for a mother to watch helplessly as her children leave home on a journey fraught with danger, with the possibility her sons and daughters will never return to her hearth. Everyone has heard the stories. Tales of bandits, the desert, standing in front of lumber yards hoping for a day's work, sleeping eight to a room in a country that cheats them out of justice and robs them of their dignity and no way to visit home for the holidays.

These women light votives in their thatch roof church praying to G-d to watch over Tofah. Tofah, a white woman, who knows nothing about Mexicans, but took in their children, again and again, providing them with a safe home, protecting, defending and nurturing the babes of their wombs. Without grandchildren of her own, Tofah was grandmother to a village.

Jesus pulled me aside. "Don Jay, were you *haciendo una broma quando usted dije* to buy me a calf for my wedding?"

"I wasn't kidding. Have you picked one out?"

"*Si*, I have *cinco* I like, *pero* I want you to see them first."

"When?"

"Manana. Tomorrow we will see the calves."

Magically, a *colectivo* appeared in the village after a breakfast of fresh eggs and tortillas. Magically every kid in the pueblo squeezed onto the Toyota pickup truck along with Jesus, Eileen, Craig and me.

At the edge of the next pueblo the children scrambled from the truck and with one hundred pesos in their hands, a gift from Craig, they raced off to buy treats. Just as the truck arrived mysteriously, Jesus was gone for five minutes and reappeared with a horse to lead the calf home.

A half mile up a mountain we came to a clearing where five calves were milling in a make shift coral. Their owner invited us to step over the railings to inspect the heifers.

I whispered to Jesus, "Which of these calves do you think is the best?" He pointed to a three hundred pound Holstein.

"I agree, completely. Buy her."

Jesus put a rope around the calf's neck tied the other end to the saddle horn and led the horse down the mountain.

When Jesus returned to the village he tethered the calf to a tree in front of his house and spent the afternoon accepting the well wishes of his neighbors. He was now a man of substance and his wife beamed proudly.

When children become Bar or Bat Mitzvah, they often receive a prayer shawl from their parents. The traditional tallis is white with broad black stripes though they also come in rainbow colors and artistic designs. They are made from finely spun wool and are draped across the shoulders and cascade in folds gracefully down the back. As the tallis is wrapped around the body, the person recites: "How precious is your kindness O G-d. For with you is the source of life and by your light may we see light"

I didn't receive one on my Bar Mitzvah and didn't want to buy my own so throughout my life I was volunteer custodian of the spare tallism loaned to guests at whatever shul I attended. One night I heard a still small voice whisper, "It's by your mother that you will earn your tallis."

Eileen was away for the evening. A shaman was conducting a crystal bowl healing in the sanctuary. The cat was on my bed dying. Mom was in her bed dying.

The cat and Mom were taking turns going into stress. On the quarter hour the cat would cry for comfort. On the half hour Mom did the same. I went from one bedroom to the other sitting with their pain.

Mom was heavily perspiring. It may have been insulin shock but she didn't want an ambulance. She said she preferred to die. I dampened her brow with a wet cloth while she entered semi-delirium.

"You're a fool!" she shouted, again and again. "You help everyone but no one helps you. You think they're your friends but they just want to use you." She was a mother desperately trying to protect her son from life's cruelties and she spoke it in the only voice she knew to command. "Your faggot friend, why does he hang around? Are you a faggot?" She barked. For someone on her deathbed she still had a lot of spit.

She was singing her own lament. People had been unkind to her and she never got past the hurt of human disappointment.

Mom fell into a calm sleep after about an hour. As I quietly shut the door to her bedroom I heard a still small voice say, "Now you can have a tallis."

The cat died that night. Mom lived a few weeks longer. I own a white on white silk prayer shawl that I purchased at a Jewish gift store.

The mortuary sent Mom's body back to Florida to be buried next to Dad. The ceremony was brief but sweet. Mom was the last survivor of her generation.

Harriet and her husband, Sy, hosted a reception at their Florida home. At the gathering we were introduced to an east coast niece, Devorah, who is to be Bat Mitzvah this year. By coincidence, the portion of the bible that she is studying is the same portion discussed in the book we're reading, The Jew and the Lotus. This gave the three of us something in common. We gave Devorah the book and she said she hoped we would attend her Bat Mitzvah.

"I'm glad we decided to come to Key West after the funeral because I swear I am never coming back to Florida. What did you think about the people applauding the sunset?" I asked Eileen.

"It was spectacular. I trilled. It was ten minutes when everyone on the promenade took a break, stopped chattering and witnessed wonder. The Algonquin Indians say as long as one person greets the sunrise and sunset the world will continue. Jay, look over there in that pile of cut branches."

"What?"

"A giant air fern." Eileen picked it up with both hands.

"Eileen, it's crawling with ants."

"We need to wash it and take it back to the hotel."

"And then what?"

"Then we buy a second hand suitcase and take it home."

"Because?"

"Because it's been sent to us. This fern lives solely on the breath of G-d."

I envisioned the scene at the airport. "I hope I don't get arrested," I muttered under my breath.

Eileen has been driving on the wrong side of the road throughout England. She was totally awesome driving out of Heathrow and across London. We used mantra to calm us in dicey traffic snarls and we chanted Hazrat Inayat Khan's zhikr until we were well into the country. Our plan is to spend two nights at The Chalice Well in Glastonbury and from there travel north. Eileen's Doctor of Theology thesis is on stone circles and we hope to sleep in at least one of them. We are reading <u>The Wind in the Willows.</u>

Glastonbury is a town of history and myth. The Chalice, the Holy Grail, that caught drops of Christ's blood, was possibly brought here. Many believe it was the Chalice which birthed the well that has poured rust colored water for two thousand years. But, before there was Christ there were Druids who came to the well to worship the mystical feminine.

Excaliber is also hidden somewhere in these hills. Here is Avalon, King Arthur and the Knights of the Round Table. For five years I yearned for my Guinevere. It was an ache that Sir Lancelot would have understood.

Outside our window I could hear people singing.

"Eileen, come look." A parade of one hundred Goddess clad women was entering the gates of the Chalice Well and circling around the pool.

"They must be coming from the Glastonbury Goddess Convention the waiter was talking about. Get dressed. We'll go join them," Tofah exclaimed throwing on a dress.

With pomp, poetry, and song the women took turns going around the circle offering their individual expressions honoring the Divine Feminine. When people were looking in the direction where Eileen and I were grouped, a person from across the pool cried out: "Tofah?"

An Englishwoman who took sabbatical in Santa Cruz for a year had recognized Eileen. "Tofah lead us in a Sufi dance," she called aloud.

Eileen nodded her head. She turned to a woman holding a doumbek. "Will you drum?"

"Can everyone hear me?"

"Louder."

"Is that better?"

"Good."

"Okay. The words of the dance are: "Isis, Astarte, Diana, Hecate, Demeter, Kali, Inanna. Let's say them together.""

We skipped Stonehenge but spent two days at Avebury, less famous and more accommodating to touch and taste. Far north of there, the road ended in front of a ferry terminal. In a blinding rainstorm, we spoke to a crewman who was pleased the weather was mild and assured us an easy passage.

Crossing to the Outer Hebrides, all the time bemoaning the absence of Dramamine, we talked of what awaited us on the Isle of Lewis. One of the largest stone circles in the world is Callanish. There, the stones are oriented with a line of hills where the moon skips along the horizon once every eighteen years. We would be there to celebrate the Goddess and witness her dance.

From the bed and breakfast, which was the only one inland, we borrowed blankets and knew we were still going to be cold. Come dark, the storm was in full regalia. It wasn't snowing, but it made a good case for being slush.

We were the only two people out in the weather. Eileen hoped to physically and spiritually enter the burial chamber at the center of the stone circle and asked if I would drum and hold place for her on the outer plane.

We walked down a long avenue marked by smaller stones on either side of the path and parted at the entry to the circle. "I'll see you later," I said.

Eileen squeezed my hand. She moved toward the burial chamber and I found myself standing between two of the thirteen giant stones of the circle. Time and consciousness wandered until a voice overcame the gale.

"Are you prepared to become a brother to the stones?" It was a twenty-five foot tall pillar to my left that asked the question.

"Yes," I said, though I hadn't the faintest idea what I was agreeing to join or with what spirit entity I was conversing.

The tall stone spoke to the other twelve. "Will you have him?"

Each in turn answered "yes" except one close to me on the right. That stone hemmed and hawed and finally went along with the others. I felt relieved.

I waited for an explanation or at least to learn the secret handshake, but nothing more was said. Sometime later the storm blew itself out. The clouds moved over the Atlantic and the moon was dazzling. I came out of my trance and Tofah came out from underground. We stood together as the moon traced the voluptuous shape of the hills. A kiss given only once in eighteen years. We watched for some minutes and silently made our way to the car, struggled to open the door and huddled over the vents as the heater thawed our bodies.

"What happened back there?" she asked.

"I was invited to join The Brotherhood of the Stones and I said yes."

"That's cool. What does it mean?"

"Heck if I know. What happened to you?"

"I asked permission of the Mother to enter the chamber and she allowed it. Inside I spoke to the stones. I told them what was happening on earth and how we really need their help. They said they knew the earth was calling to them and they promised they would give their help. The bones of the Mother are awakening. There's hope for the planet."

"Is there any hope we won't get pneumonia?"

"We're not going to get sick, silly. We've both been blessed tonight."

My interest in predicting the future consisted largely of Chinese fortune cookies though eventually I progressed to reading the daily horoscope about once a month. I was born in the Year of the Rooster but that's as far as it went. My birth certificate omitted the time of my birth and though Mom said I was born "late at night," such vagueness made it impossible to determine my rising sign, moon sign or natal chart. To Eileen, who studies every means of divination, this is a serious character flaw and she is tireless in trying to secure my records from a hospital that had been torn down to make room for a White Castle hamburger stand. To conceal my spiritual disfigurement I tell people I was born around midnight but now Eileen thinks she may have found a way to determine the actual time of my birth.

For two years she has been studying Jyotish or Vedic Astrology, which is based on the Indian Vedas. The Vedas calculate differently and according to their astrological calculations, Eileen is not a Gemini but a Taurus.

Eileen invited Sanjay, a renowned Vedic Astrologer, to stay at The Garden for the next six weekends while he teaches an advanced course to his American students. In exchange for free rent, Eileen was given a scholarship and she is encouraging me to schedule a reading with the master.

Sanjay and I were sitting by the wood stove, becoming acquainted, when I expressed an interest in an astrological reading. He peered at me and said, "I always wonder what energy propels me to stay at one home and not another, but when we met, I knew I was here for a reason. Let us look immediately at your chart."

Sanjay had developed a sophisticated astrology software program which his students were learning to use. Tofah had my chart ready at hand. He studied it intently then arched his eyebrows and said, "Something very important happened to you one month ago."

Four weeks ago I was shivering among a circle of stones that were talking to me, but I didn't want to share that information. I nodded.

Sanjay's fingers traced my chart. "Yes. Very odd. Your chart can explain."

"There's a problem. I don't know the exact time of my birth. My mother told me it was late at night so I tell people I was born at 11:57 p.m., but I don't really have a clue."

"That too is unusual, but I can find the time of your birth." Sanjay moved to the dining room table where his students were awaiting a bowl of soup and words of wisdom. Sanjay explained the situation to everyone.

"When I look at Jay's chart, I learn many details. If I learn something that is not true, it is because the chart is mistaken. By statements and answers we can determine when our host was born.

"It is true you have one sister and no brothers?" I nodded.

He went on. "Your sister is older than you and has two children?" I nodded again. "One of the nephews, the older one, is an artist, a painter perhaps or a writer?" My nephew was an editor of a prestigious magazine. I nodded. "And the other son inherited the family business?" I nodded again. "Your brother-in-law had a back injury. Was it his right shoulder?"

I corrected him. "He had surgery on both shoulders."

"Ha!" Sanjay exclaimed. "Tofah, make this correction and give me a new print out."

Sanjay resumed. He turned his attention to Natasha and Gabriel and whenever his conclusions were incorrect, he had a new copy of my chart created before proceeding. He spent two hours astounding us with how much he accurately read of my life from the astrological chart.

"If I had many more hours, I could determine the exact minute when you were born, but it is close enough to say 1:20 on the morning of June 12th. Your mother was correct. It was very late at night."

Everyone was tired and Sanjay was scheduled to begin teaching at eight in the morning. He and his wife retired to their room and our guests left for home. Eileen and I stood at the sink washing dishes.

"That was the most amazing thing, I've ever seen." He even knew I was born in the Bronx."

"Jay, anyone who hears you speak knows you were born in the Bronx."

I rented the largest SUV that didn't require a commercial truck license to drive and we packed for a cross country camping trip timed for us to attend Devorah's Bat Mitzvah.

We saw the pink Cadillac at Graceland, sat in rocking chairs on the front porch of Loretta Lynn's ranch and cheered the horsemen at Dolly Parton's Dixie Stampede Equestrian Show.

We sat with Hopi elders on Three Mesas in Arizona, said

Kaddish for Murshid Samuel Lewis at his burial site at Lama
Foundation in New Mexico and prayed in the Lotus Shrine at Sri
Swami Satchidananda's ashram in Virginia.

Harriet and Sy were gracious hosts in New York City. We
ate potato knishes at Katz's Jewish Delicatessen, where my
Grandmother stood in the doorway for two decades collecting
nickels and dimes to first fight fascists and later to plant trees
in Israel. We rowed around Central Park Lake and lazed in the
sheep meadow. We rode the elevator to the 86th floor of the
Empire State Building and I confided to Eileen that I occasionally
thought of myself as King Kong. On the way out of the building,
Tofah gave me a gift of a stuffed gorilla.

At the *Bat Mitzvah*, Eileen and I were given the honor of
chanting the Hebrew blessings prior to Devorah reading from the
ancient Hebrew script. We had known ahead of time we would
be called upon and Eileen sang the melodies as she had learned
them from me, in a thick Bronx accent.

We gave Devorah a gift of a *shofar*, a ram's horn, used in
Jewish ritual.

"We call this a Jewish alarm clock. When it's blown, it
awakens the soul and gathers the community. It's also sometimes
used in a crisis to summon your clan," I explained.

"What if I can't learn how to blow it, Uncle Jay?"

Eileen hugged Devorah. "Call us on your cell phone. We'll
come."

*Tofah is not Jewish. Her mother is Irish Catholic, for G-d's sake!
Still, there are people in Santa Cruz who think she's a rabbi and call
her "Reb." When the Jewish Renewal congregation began renting the
sanctuary for Friday night services, Tofah quickly found heart space
with the community, often joining in the prayers and singing. The
rabbi gave Tofah her Hebrew name, Tifereth bat Chava, Beauty born
of Eve. Now they're taking it one step further. She and the rabbi are
planning a combined Sufi/ Jewish Renewal Sukkot celebration here
at the Garden.*

In the Bronx, Orthodox Jews erect four poles on their fire escapes and toss palm leaves over the tops for roofs. If the weather is hot, which it often is in September, they eat and sleep in their sukkahs.

In the last half century, the holiday has become more widely celebrated and people take pride in the huts that they erect for the eight day celebration, even though most of them are still made small enough to fit on a Brooklyn fire-escape or a West Palm Beach balcony.

Not the sukkah Eileen intends to build.

"We need a building permit to construct a *sukkah* this size," I said.

"It needs to sit eighty people," Eileen reminded me. Turning to the construction outfit who volunteered to build the *sukkah,* she went on: "We can attach it so the gazebo becomes part of the *sukkah* which gives us twenty-five of the seats we need. But we don't want a box shape. We want to build it so the energy is directed toward Jerusalem. What if we build an octagon with the fifth wall facing east? Will that be much harder to build?" Eileen asked.

"We can build anything. We're wood butchers," boasted the boss.

Snake and Butch, who introduced themselves as radical fairies, own a decorating business and volunteered to decorate the walls. They came with suitcases crammed with tapestries from India, batiks from Bali, belly dance hip scarves from Turkey and carpets from Persia. They draped great swaths of silk and hung strands of crystals until the sukkah became the magical abode of a desert princess. From the rafters we strung Christmas lights and thatched the roof with pine boughs, leaving space so the light of the stars could shine through.

On the night of *Sukkot,* the *sukkah* was filled to capacity with Sufis and Jews. The rabbi opened the service with a familiar melody. Then it was Tofah's turn.

"There's not enough room for us to do a standing *zhikr* so we'll do the *hadra* seated. We inhale, bending our necks backward, not so far that we hurt ourselves, sweep our heads from left to right, cleansing our hearts, and exhale bending forward. Then it repeats. The words of the song are: '*Shalom Aleichem. Aleichem Shalom, Asalam Aleikum, Aleikum Asalam.* Peace be with you and with you be peace, in Hebrew and Arabic. Join me when you know it."

My heart rate soars and my anxiety level goes off the chart every time I go near a hospital, but it's a long drive and Eileen wants my company when we visit our former house contractor, Chris. The latest news isn't good. The gall stone surgery went well, but his lung got ripped by a surgical tube and the doctors can't get the bleeding to stop. He's growing weaker by the day.

We arrived a little before the end of visiting hours. Husbands and wives were saying their good-byes and the nurses were putting their patients to sleep. The hallway was empty and we were alone with Chris and Ilana in his room. He did not look well.

Eileen gave him a foot massage while they discussed the bleeding.

"I spoke with the homeopath and the acupuncturist. They both agree these Chinese herbs are worth a try. In any case, they won't cause harm and they may stop the bleeding," Tofah explained.

Chris reached for the capsules.

"Take three of them tonight and three in the morning. I'll leave the bottle with Ilana. If there's any improvement within the next twenty four hours continue taking them twice a day. But don't tell anyone. They're liable to cancel your medical insurance if they find out you're self medicating."

"Will you come back to see me?"

Eileen looked to me. I grimaced and nodded.

"We'll try to get here a little earlier tomorrow evening."

We returned in two days, by which time the doctors were patting themselves on their backs for successfully stopping the hemorrhaging. Who knows? Maybe they did. Nevertheless, his doc recommended Chris remain for several days for observation.

"Let's get you out of here, Chris. The sooner, the better," said Eileen. "Ten thousand people a year die from staph infections they get in hospitals. You'll be safer at home, where we can take care of you."

Chris rang for the nurse. As we said goodbye, Ilana was helping him get dressed and he was filling out the discharge papers.

2006

I get confused by similar sounding names. Qi Gong, Tai Chi and Tian Gong all collide in my brain, particularly because each one of the systems for healing has been taught at The Garden. Lately, Tian Gong has taken center stage. Tofah believes Grandmaster Letian, a renowned healer in China, receives celestial transmissions of higher consciousness and she is grateful to take his classes in healing the body, soul and planet. Grandmaster is teaching a week long class in Majorca in how to avert bird flu. Tofah is attending the workshop.

"I told him I can't continue to study with him," Tofah said over a cup of chai. "He gave us hours and hours of exercises to repair our physical organs and strengthen our immune systems in the event of an outbreak of bird flu but then told me I could not share the techniques with others. He feels only he has the complete knowledge to teach these exercises correctly. I told him if I saw people suffering and had knowledge, even a little bit, of how to heal their illness, I wasn't going to turn my back on them because I wasn't fully trained. So, in fairness to Grandmaster, I quit the program."

"Did you learn anything that can help others?"

"I learned amazing things. Grandmaster has been called upon by the universe to clear karmic debt. He taught us how to coalesce and radiate energy to sever the bonds that keep souls tied to the earth plane. We did a mass clearing in Majorca of five thousand souls."

"People who died in Majorca?"

"People anywhere. He chose Majorca because it's a vortex and because of its sacred and mystical connections to *Atlantis, Mu* and *Lemuria*. When we did the practice, I fulfilled my promise to the spirits of Indian Rock. Their souls were singing when they were released from Delarosa Hot Springs."

Eileen is hiking with a group in the foothills of the Himalayas and then taking a plane to Delhi to commemorate the Urs of Hazrat Inayat Khan. Sufis believe Sufi saints die into a wedding with the Divine Source of Life and the annual memorial ceremonies are an occasion for prayer and celebration.

(From Tofah's journal)

We have climbed Poon Hill this morning to see the sun rise. A thousand foot climb on a packed snow and ice pathway. We begin with flashlights and they soon become unnecessary as the first light of the morning informs the day. The moon is full above us, the stars bright and the mountains all ways round are receptive to the pink and then gold light that first marks the day. Again I am awash in emotion at this beauty.

My heart feels like it has broken open and flown out as far as these mountains extend.

We stop on the descent at a power spot marked by a Buddhist/Hindu shrine and a thousand prayer flags. After praying to the wisdom beings of many different traditions we mount our own Sufi heart and wings flag given me to take to the top.

We smudge with incense from the Peruvian Andes and I leave a stone from there as well. Donna brought me the incense and stone to take on this trek to be used as a greeting from one sacred mountain to another.

I find I can't look at these peaks without a fountain of tears rising up and overflowing. Ascending joy the Buddhists call it.

"When did you learn there was a revolution taking place?" I asked.

"Not until we came off the mountains into Pokhara."

"Then what did you do?"

"Some of the group were afraid of driving to Katmandu because of the rumors the Communists had taken control of the roads leading in and out of the capital but I meditated with my spirit guides and they said no harm would come to us. I shared with the group what I heard and we decided to chance it. We hired a Communist driver, as insurance, just in case we came to a roadblock. I sensed we were never in danger because the last thing a revolutionary group would want to do is antagonize the United States by capturing fifteen American tourists."

"Did you run into trouble?"

"The only problem was all the computer lines were down so we couldn't write to tell anyone we were okay. Once we were in Katmandu, it was a short hop to Delhi."

"What was the weather like?"

"It was cold. On the third day we hiked into a blizzard. That was pretty edgy. The stone steps were slick and Gary got altitude sickness. The guides put him on a pack horse and we hoped he would manage to hold on. When we got to the hiker's hut, I did massage and Reiki on him and the next morning he was stronger. Some people brought food supplements and mountains of energy bars, but they were the ones who suffered the most. When we reached the huts each night, the host asked us what we wanted to eat and I asked for whatever they were eating out of their garden. Underneath the table where we ate, there was a fire burning and though I never took off my down parka my feet stayed toasty."

"And Delhi?"

"The *Urs* were incredible. There were hundreds of people chanting throughout the day. Hazrat Inayat's *dargha* is located in a poor neighborhood in Delhi and The Sufi Movement opened a school for street kids across from it. It's called The Hope Project. I spent most of my time over there when I wasn't praying. The *Pir* made me a *Sheikha* in the *Ruhaniat* during the *Urs*. I was waiting for him to ordain me before accepting ordination from Rabia in the Sufi Movement. This way I can continue to be a bridge between the two Sufi orders. Rabia and I talked about it and she will make me a *Sheikha* at this year's summer camp."

"So the fact that my feet have felt ice cold this entire time wasn't even sympathetic pain because you were feeling fine?"

"I think it's cute. Here, put them in my lap and I'll warm them."

What is it among sisters that without a phone call and having seen her only once in a decade, Eileen knew within hours that Sita's son had died in a motorcycle accident. The two Sirens of Silverton raised each other's children and are now sharing heartbreak.

Eileen belonged to Sita's family and Sita belonged to the Lakotas. I was there by myself. The only person I knew was Hawk. Hawk is an Apache warrior and he looks bad ass. Standing next to him I always feel small and Jewish.

Chairs and benches were placed in a semi-circle around a blazing fire. The first several rows were reserved for family and dearest friends. Sita's mom looked to Eileen and patted the chair next to her. I went and stood in the back with Hawk.

It was hard to bear witness to the ceremony. The drum and the chanting and the outpouring of grief became a symphony of sorrow. Shamans prayed and the owl was made silent by the lamentations.

The ritual progressed through the chilling afternoon and the fire became more enticing. When the service was finished, dinner was announced and nearly everyone headed to the community hall. The perfect bench, close to the fire, was vacant. I hunkered down and stretched out my hands to warm them over the embers.

Eileen was sitting with Sita's family. They had turned the

beach chairs into a small circle with mother, daughters, grand daughters and Eileen holding hands and telling stories about Jeremy and recalling his adventures. They were smiling, crying and catching up on each other's lives. Sita's mom had raised a litter of wild women. They're shamans, coyotes and red tailed fox. Eileen ran with the pack.

A young girl sat down on the bench next to me and leaned into the fire. We sat in silence. I was poking the fire with a long stick watching the embers dance in the nightfall.

Eileen returned from the community hall juggling three plates of food. "I didn't know if either of you were hungry, but I made up some plates, just in case."

We ate in silence. Eileen took the long stick from me and *patshked* the fire. She had already said goodbye to the clan and we stood to leave.

The girl looked up and said: "Thank you for sharing the bench and food. I live up the road. Jeremy was my friend and I didn't want to be alone tonight. I needed to be with family."

Who are we? How is it we know when we're among our own?

2007

Every time we go to an airport, I think this time we're going to be on a no-fly list because of Tofah's role in Sufi leadership. If not that, I'm apprehensive about the contraband Tofah often packs in her suitcase, like when she flew home with the air fern. If I offer to help her pack she becomes suspicious and orders me from the room.

"Is this your luggage, Miss?"

These are dreaded words. Eileen nodded her head.

"Please step over here."

I went to join her but was told to wait behind a white line.

165

"What is this button glued to your cell phone? What does it connect to?"

"It's a system designed to defend against electromagnetic radiation coming through the phones into our brains."

The officer stared at the phone like he was expecting it to explode. "Hey Bill, come over and take a look at this thing."

Dang. The situation was getting worse.

"The lady says this button she glued on her phone prevents brain radiation. What do you think?"

Bill took the phone and studied it like an archeologist, "How does it work?"

"There's seventy-five feet of superfine copper wire wound up in the capsule. There's also a resonating cell inside to magnify the frequency of the copper. The radiation we're exposed to by the cell phones is harmful to our brains and the copper sets up a shield."

"No kidding?"

"And if your supervisor insists that all of you wear Bluetooths, I think you should talk to your OSHA representative."

"Well, I'll be. Thanks, lady," Bill said, as he zipped up Tofah's suitcase. "Do you need any help with your luggage?"

"No I've got it.

"Good luck, lady."

"Thanks. We need it." I said. They just erected a cell tower across from where we live."

As we walked to our departure gate Tofah turned to me and said, "You always worry. I told you there's nothing to worry about."

Bonnie closed her New Age gift shop and donated thirty cartons of miscellaneous trinkets, beads and sacred statuary to the Sufi community. Tofah thinks we can sell the stuff to provide emergency assistance to people in need. I hope she is correct because the boxes take up the majority of the floor to ceiling space in my office.

There are contests where winners are allowed a limited amount of time to run down the aisles of a store, throwing whatever they want into grocery carts. I am reminded of the glaze in their eyes when I watch Tofah sitting on the floor, surrounded by a mountain of Bonnie's donations. In one pile are a dozen eight inch, cast iron statues of the Buddha. In another pile are display cases filled with sterling silver earrings and costume jewelry. There is enough incense to meet the needs of the entire Greek Orthodox Church and more refrigerator magnets than there are Kenmores.

"How are we ever going to sell this?" I said sifting my hands through a carton of African trade beads. "I took samples to the bead store and they don't want any of it."

"We'll take five or six cartons to the Sufi dance each week and set up a display table," Tofah said confidently. "And you and I can string *malas*."

"Once upon a time I had this fantasy that together we would weave prayer shawls while praying," I confessed.

"Prayer beads take a lot less time to thread than it takes to weave a shawl. There are enough jade and *bodi* beads to make several *malas* and we can infuse them with whatever prayers we chant while stringing the beads.

"Carol is worried that Carl might have stomach cancer. Let's make a pair of *malas* for them out of these opalescent beads. The white color in the beads will help bring peace to their inner selves and might calm the cancer cells. We should begin with clearing our own egos. We'll chant 'Let me do thy will, Oh Lord, Allah, Allah', a hundred and eight times and then we'll begin stringing."

So, Tofah and I sat for an hour, creating *malas*, chanting Hazrat Inayat Khan's *zhikr*, which aches with love, envisioning Carol and Carl healthy in long life.

2008

Eileen missed her flight. Fortunately, the paddle wheel steam boat isn't scheduled to sail down the Amazon River for another three days.

I was eager to be away from the Spanish language immersion program in Cuenca and to meet Eileen at the airport in Quito for a vacation on the Amazon River. Fortunately I received the message she would be arriving eighteen hours later than expected. With an entire day to spend alone, I sought the advice of a taxi cab driver. He suggested the Metropolitan which is one of the biggest parks in all of Latin America.

In the middle of the week, on a windy afternoon, the park was empty, the playground was silent and the concession stands locked tight. I ambled down slightly beaten paths and where two or more intersected, I chose the one more defined. Scattered about were gigantic art works, high grass growing and swallowing them in mute testimony to nature overcoming human accomplishment or the municipal authorities' reluctance to hire a groundskeeper.

A circle of stones called to me. They were a one-fourth replica of the stones of Callanish. The shapes of the stones were nearly identical, as was their placement in the circle. People had scrawled graffiti on some. Remnants of a picnic lunch were lying about. Cigarette butts were as plentiful as the weeds.

Cautiously I stood in the same position to the stones as I had on the Isle of Lewis and I waited. The stone to my right, whose grandfather in the Outer Hebrides had been reluctant to admit me to the brotherhood, eventually spoke.

"Deep pangs of suffering are like the flapping of a bird's wings against a stone's face. Pay them no heed."

I stared at the stone. It was the second time a stone spoke to me and I was still not accustomed to these chit chats.

"Since we're having this discussion, would you mind telling me what is the Brotherhood of Stones?"

But he was all talked out.

I made reservations for a cabin on the Manatee which will take us deep into the Amazon jungle. The accommodations are fit for the wealthy and the meals are Ecuadorian gourmet, all at a price the moderate Ecuadorian can afford.

There are fourteen of us traveling together. The pilot is a passionate environmentalist. His goal is to acquaint middle class and professional Ecuadorians with the jungle, that they might experience its majesty and fight for its survival. Tofah and I are the only non-Ecuadorians on the paddle wheeler.

I'm not fluent in Spanish and I was sure I misunderstood our guide when he said the Amazon jungle was three hundred miles wide.

"*No senor. No es de trescientos. Es de tres mil. El Amazonas es mas grande que los Estados Unidos.* Three thousand miles wide and airplanes won't fly over it because there's nowhere to land if they have engine problems. Three thousand miles and we hardly know anything about it, except to kill it.

Twice a day we leave the comfort of our air-conditioned, mosquito free cabins to explore the jungle. We are told there are actually two jungles, the sunlit jungle and the jungle of the dark, very different from each other.

On our first night-time excursion, the boat harbored next to a family compound of *Kitchwa* Indians. A youth of the compound, along with our tour guide, led us down a path and had us turn off our flashlights. I could not see my hands. Further along, our flashlights barely detecting tree trunks and boulders, the youth motioned for us to stop and be quiet. He pointed to a tree fifteen feet away where a skinny three foot long Fer de Lance serpent was giving live birth to tiny poisonous snakes. These little darlings were crawling up and away from mom as quickly as they were able, since the Fer de Lance has a habit of eating its young. I suggested we also leave but our tour guides assured me we were in no danger and that it was so rare a sight that they would tell their grandchildren of this night. I thought, so will I.

On another night we visited a *Kitchwa* shaman. Each of us in turn sat in front of the aged, gaunt figure, as he chanted, beat us with branches and spewed alcohol on our heads. He spoke to his son who translated into Spanish whatever the shaman had seen. After examining Tofah and me, he pronounced us well, so I thought it a waste of good alcohol. He was, however, concerned about another of the passengers and offered to take *ayahuasca* to find a way for healing the man. He promised to return in the morning with what knowledge he gained. As we left his hut, Tofah gave him a gift of a page of sacred geometrics that she has been duplicating and placing everywhere in our house.

In the morning he came aboard the boat and had a private meeting with the man. Before departing he asked the captain to introduce him to Tofah. Using his son as translator he thanked her for the gift. In the swoon of the *ayahuasca* he saw that these geometric shapes had strength to protect and empower. In return for her kindness he said a great prophecy awaited her.

During the week we fished for piranhas, drifted in an outboard boat looking up at the Southern Cross, and clapped with glee when pink river dolphins swam by our canoes.

One morning we trudged through a swamp, the faster walkers going ahead and the slower walkers lagging half a mile behind, accompanied by a second guide. Tofah and I were at the back of the first group.

"Jay, the hair on my neck is standing straight out. Let's pick up the pace and rejoin the rest."

We found them around a bend in the path. A few minutes later the guide for the second group arrived and excitedly informed us that a jaguar crossed the path between the last person in our group and himself. We scampered back to the spot where he saw the prints. Bending down he measured the footprints and whistled. "*¿Quien fue la ultima persona en su grupo?*"

We all turned to Tofah. "I felt something back there, but didn't see anything," she said.

"*No vera el jaguar. Ataca por detras.* You do not see the jaguar. It attacks from behind."

The mood in our group suddenly shifted. A mother whose child often wandered, grabbed his hand and yelled at him to stay close to her. A wife quarreled with her husband, demanding to know why he insisted on coming to the Amazon. Eileen and I held each other's hands and wondered at what just happened.

The jaguar is worshipped by the Mayans, Aztecs and Incas as G-d, Ruler of the Underworld. Why had he sought out Eileen?

2009

On Wednesday afternoons, people bring harmoniums, drums and guitars to our house and sit in the living room playing sacred music. Recently they have been rehearsing a zhikr composed by Tofah.

This zhikr is not like any others I've heard. zhikr is usually very masculine and aggressive, almost like men have to fight their way into G-d's presence. But Tofah's zhikr is feminine and melts into the arms of the Beloved.

When Tofah leads Sufi dancing on Sunday nights she lights the sanctuary with her light, but when she leads *zhikr* on Friday nights, she lights each of us.

"Tonight, we're going to do things a bit differently," Tofah told the twenty people who regularly attend *zhikr*. "We'll start with Hazrat Inayat Khan's *zhikr*. When it's finished, maintain silence and sit in a circle. Once you're settled we'll begin the Rose *Zhikr*. It's in five parts, each part chanted separately. Listen to each part until you are sure you have it.

"It begins with *Ya Khabir*, one of the ninety-nine names of G-d. The Aware. The Seed of Potential. Allowing the rain of the Name to fall on the parched earth of the heart. Think of yourself as a seed soon to germinate. You lie in the soft earth of the mother, awaiting the form that G-d has chosen for you in this lifetime. You are patient for you know G-d intends for you to emerge in the right time and place to be a glory unto the Maker of heaven and earth.

"*Ya Musawwir*, The Fashioner. Remember patience. Allowing yourself to be trained and designed. You feel yourself in creation, not yet known by name or form but growing into being.

"*Ya Tawwab*, Acceptor of Repentance. Returning to Rhythm. Come, come whoever you are, Even though you've broken your vows ten thousand times, come, come again. You are emerged from the earth and you rest in the pleasure of the now. You are in harmony and sympathy with all that surrounds you. A red rose in the garden of Allah.

"*Ya Malik ul Mulk*, The Power of the Cosmos. You are radiant in your flower essence. You are a Divine manifestation brought to bloom in splashes of color. You are grateful to the One G-d who has fashioned you with such beauty and are opening and accepting of the Sun.

"*Ya Muta Ali*, The Exalted. You are a blossom in the garland of the Shekinah. It is no longer enough for you to bask in your design, but to share your G-dliness with all those whom you meet. Your petals, though seemingly frail, are strong enough to host a honey bee and your aroma sweetens and softens the hearts of all living beings. You are a rose, fully open, ripe to receive and to give.

"Nancy, will you pass out these papers? They have the words and music."

Eventually the voices merged in harmony, chanting together, becoming a bouquet to set upon an altar.

Either I am exceptionally discerning or else everyone prefers to go along with the pretence. We've been in Portland for four days, waiting for the birth of Eileen's granddaughter and I am covering for Tofah's failing strength as best I am able. When she and I cook dinner for the family, she keeps me company and I do the prep work. Five minutes before dinner is ready, I ask her to help stir this and season that so it will seem as if she has cooked the meal.

On the drive up she told me she thinks she has a brain tumor, but believes her practice of German New Medicine can send the tumor into remission. She has scheduled a brain scan to analyze the tumors within a German New Medicine context and thinks if she resolves her feelings of familial betrayal and rejection, the tumors will dissolve. I don't know what to think.

Lucinda Rose was born on April 15th. She is a healthy, beautiful child. There is a photograph of Tofah cradling the baby in her arms; the infant, with a wide mouth grin, instinctively gripping Tofah's finger. They look like each other.

In the morning, under a blooming plum tree, Eileen did a naming ceremony, welcoming the baby into the family.

"Who is she named after?" Eileen asked.

"Chance's grandmother was named Lilly and Rose comes from your Rose *Zhikr*."

"She's being called to remember the elders," Eileen said softly as pink flower petals rained down on us. Tofah bowed before the *Shekinah* and asked that the baby be sheltered under the wings of angels and guided by the light of The Divine. Tofah placed her hands, palms downward, a few inches above Lucinda's crown or seventh *chakra* and intoned:

> May the blessings of G-d rest upon you
> May G-d's peace abide in you
> May G-d's presence illuminate your soul
> Now and forever more.

That night, Eileen had me write a letter to Lucinda.

"Precious light,

"When Eden was having difficulty getting pregnant with miscarriages I asked my guides to bring a spirit being to her and Chance. I saw you come in like a falling star and Eden became pregnant in the next month. Lucinda, remember that you are a very special being that has a very important purpose and is dearly beloved. I am going to watch you from the other side and delight in you.

"One of the first things I learned was to tune into my truth. Lead from your heart. I would have liked us to have known each other. I loved life, and delighted in taking on a project and going full tilt; the adventure of new things.

"I threw pottery as a young women. I liked working with my hands, creating art and beauty with my hands. I was excited to create environments of beauty. I loved growing plants, gardens, making environments where people could experience G-d. I have a spiritual center that is of great joy to me that has a 35 foot Hopi labyrinth and a sanctuary where spiritual classes are held.

"I first experienced nature as the Divine Mother at the Creek where I played as a child. I knew the Divine Mother as healer, comforter and bringer of solace. I wanted other people to experience it too. I taught lots of classes, women's groups and sang.

"I experienced G-d at the Creek, as a child, and continue to experience the Beloved through meditation, music, Sufi dancing and prayer. I loved doing *zhikr*, playing the harmonium, harmonica, guitar and drums.

"I am honored to be one of your spirit guides. Think about me, take a picture and hold it to your forehead. Call anytime you want help, need a protector, have concerns, questions or need guidance. Keep your eye on the amount of joy you are having as a measure of how well you are doing in your life. I want you to have this amber necklace for protection, a gift from your nana (spirit Guide),

Love, and love beyond love,

Nana Tofah

I put down the pen. "Brain tumors?"

Tofah nodded her head. "Make sure she gets this letter if things don't work out."

The ride home has been a nightmare.

Once outside of Portland, away from the kids, I rearranged the front seat into a makeshift bed and Eileen went in and out of restless sleep. Stopping for lunch, Eileen had trouble holding her fork, twice dropping it on the floor. Her left hand is hardly functional and her left leg is becoming numb. When she was awake we listened to an audio book of <u>Phantom of the Opera</u> and I fear the unseen phantom who is riding in the back seat of the Honda.

By mid-afternoon we were nearing Silverton. We passed a make-shift, unattended fruit stand and Eileen had me stop. She selected a bouquet of home grown flowers and left a ten dollar bill in an empty mason jar. "Do you know where Grandpa Sorensen is buried?"

I nodded.

"Let's go the cemetery. I'd like to say hello and introduce myself. This way it will be easier to recognize him on the other side."

We arrived at the home of Eileen's sister and brother-in-law in mid afternoon and I helped Eileen out of the car. In the presence of her sister, Eileen perked up and the four of us went for a walk in the woods. Iris walked beside me.

"Jay, what's wrong with Eileen?"

I looked at her. "She thinks she has a brain tumor. She's been studying German New Medicine and believes she can cure it by herself. I think she's getting ready to die."

ELEVEN WEEKS

June 1

Dear Friends,

On May 28th, Tofah and I took a morning walk on Rio Del Mar beach. After returning home, while sitting in the garden, Tofah had a massive seizure. It lasted twenty-five minutes. Despite intermittent screams of pain, Tofah directed me to put my thumb on her third eye and the other thumb on her belly button to connect the energy fields between the two to lessen the seizure. She and another woman chanted Buddhist mantras and at one point, Tofah indicated she was merging her prayers with Bhakhu Tulku Rinpoche, an illuminated Buddhist lama with whom she has taken refuge. Twenty minutes into the seizure, Tofah instructed me to call 911. They arrived one minute after she lost consciousness. The paramedics were astounded. They never encountered anyone remaining conscious for more than one to two minutes.

In the emergency room, the doctors stabilized the seizure. An MRI was performed and it showed several tumors and hemorrhaging. Without a brain biopsy, the doctors can't do any further diagnosis.

Tofah diagnosed the seizure according to the German New Medicine system as the epicrisis of a complete healing. She sees it as the highest point in the advancement of the cancer; from here on, she believes that the healing phase has begun.

As word of Tofah's cancer spread, the outpouring of love, prayer, song, and healing energy has been a magnificent affirmation of our community. During the two days she was in the hospital many women sat at her bedside chanting and sending healing voices throughout the corridors of Dominican Hospital. The nurses wanted to know who was in that bed. "Is she a guru?" they asked.

Since returning home, Tofah's strength and clarity of thought improves each day. On her first day home, she walked ten steps with assistance. On the second day, she walked with assistance throughout the house. The third day, she walked in and out of our labyrinth, essentially by herself. This morning, day four, she walked up half a dozen blocks to an overlook of Santa Cruz, and only needed slight assistance on the way home.

No one knows the length of their days but what we do know is we have the capacity to choose our own responses in each and every moment. For Tofah, the work is to offer gratitude and praise to the Divine and to give thanks for all the gifts she receives. This is no different today than it was before her diagnosis.

Tofah has chosen, at least for now, to forego any further Western medicine. She places her faith for her healing in prayer, in alternative healing modalities, and in the tenets of German New Medicine.

As her beloved, I stand in support of whatever choices she makes for her healing and delight in every moment that HaShem gives to us. We ask that you support Tofah in her decisions and respect her beliefs.

Please do not call. Fielding phone calls is difficult at this time. I hope by keeping all of you informed through email it will reduce the need to speak.

Baruch HaShem

Jay Lev Shalom

On Friday night we hosted a Jewish Renewal /Sufi dance service on the labyrinth. It's an annual tradition and Tofah was unwilling to cancel the popular spiritual event.

In the past, she and the rabbi created simple dance movements to accompany the prayers. Too frail to lead the dances this year, Tofah sat in a chair in the center of the circle maintaining the rhythm on her doumbek. Iris, stood behind Tofah, massaging and supporting her sister's neck.

June 4

Dear Friends,

Yesterday, for the first time, Eileen did not take Ativan. Ativan is used when she has tremors, most frequently in her stomach, but occasionally in her arm or leg. Up until yesterday she had these tremors every morning and I gave her one milligram of the medicine. The problem with Ativan is that it makes her woozy, creates depression and is highly addictive. Yesterday, when the tremors began, we substituted skunk cabbage extract (an herbal alternative with no side effects). We coupled the extract with focused meditations and within minutes the tremors ceased.

The mantra Eileen and I use when the tremors begin is, "Om ah hum, vadja guru padma siddi hum." Padmasambhava brought this mantra and Buddhism to Tibet. The mantra connects the practitioner with the mind, voice and actions of the Guru. They are seed syllables and energize the body.

Nyla recited this mantra hovering over Tofah's body from the very beginning of her seizure, long into the emergency room procedures and well into the first night at the hospital. When Tofah was able to achieve small levels of mental clarity, she joined Nyla and me in reciting it.

The second mantra Tofah is using to calm the tremors is from the Hebrew tradition. It consists of just two words, Modeh Ahnee. It means thank you and are the first words spoken each morning. The complete prayer is "Thank you for returning my soul to me with compassion and faithfulness."

The third mantra which Tofah started using this morning is "Peacefully releasing," to let go of any resentments she may be holding against others. She feels like these resentments are lodged in her stomach and that is why the tremors appear in her abdomen.

Because it is late and I am very tired with work still to be done, I'll say good night.

Much love,

Jay Lev

For two hours, the Dakini Band played music in the living room, singing psalms and prayers derived from all the pathways to Divine Light. One of the prayers they sang was Ashray, Yoshvai, Baytechah. It means Praise to those who sit in the house of the Lord, they shall be praised for all eternity. I joined them and was certain I could hear a shofar being blown in heaven calling upon the angels to smile upon these women.

June 7

Dear Friends,

This morning, in her meditations, Tofah saw the tumors transformed into lotus blossoms on which sat the Buddha. It's a good vision and Tofah asks that we refer to the tumor in this way. As the lotus blossoms encourage and create the space for new beginnings, Tofah committed herself to expanding her psychic and physical place of joy. Joy in body. Joy in mind. Joy in the union with the Divine. She welcomes you to celebrate with her. As we begin to open our home to visitors, (a schedule of available times is being developed by the care team) we hope you will bring games, jokes, funny movies and anything else that makes you cheerful.

Twenty years ago, Tofah, Natasha and I spent a week hiking the Appalachian Trail to experience the grandeur of the autumn leaves in Vermont. When we were within two days of reaching the trail head and the end of our trek, we crossed paths with several men who were coming from the opposite direction.

They were overweight and struggling with back packs that tipped the scales at fifty pounds or more. As they came nearer, we saw one of the fellows reach into his back pack and angrily toss a family size can of Dinty Moore stew onto the forest floor.

After they went past, barely gasping out a greeting, I bent down and hefted the can of food they had abandoned. It weighed sixty-four ounces. It must have been very uncomfortable for the man to feel it bouncing around inside his Kelty. The unforgiving metal edges of the can would have dug into his back and the heavy, non-nourishing food would have made his shoulders ache.

Had no one advised these first time hikers to carry freeze dried food? Had they not heeded advice that less is more when walking a trail? As we continued to wend our way going where they had recently been, we saw a bottle of ketchup resting against a tree, a mile further on a jar of sauerkraut. At the lean-to where they had spent their first night, a shiny new three burner Coleman Stove was tucked away to one side.

We each carry cans of Dinty Moore stew for days, weeks, months and years. We carry them for so long, we actually think they are part of who we are. And when we think they are a part of us, they become part of us. After a while, the food rots within the can and still we cling to it.

We proceed through life in denial of the weight of the cans, even when they cause deathly illnesses. But we can also embrace and love them for the lessons they have to offer. We can examine them as the doorways through which we discover clarity, forgiveness of self and others and enter into wholeness and healing. And we can leave them at a wayside anytime we're willing to become more light-hearted.

June 10

Dear Friends,

Sunday was Tofah's birthday. This year June 7th was also Wesak, the birth date of Buddha, and the monthly gathering of the Home Temple Priesthood. After completing her Doctoral thesis on stone circles, Tofah was ordained an independent Bishop in the Synod of Home Temple Bishops. The congregation meets monthly at the Garden and at the conclusion of the service, Tofah was presented with eight dozen containers of red worms.

According to Buddhist teachings, a person who saves the life of a sentient being that was destined to imminently die is rewarded with a million- fold blessing for each being rescued when that rescue takes place on Wesak. Since the worms were intended for fishermen, Tofah is releasing them into our compost pile resulting in a gazillion blessings.

In the evening, Nina brought over a prepared dinner and a rock she absconded with from the burial site of Murshid Samuel Lewis at Lama Foundation. The people who maintain Lama have a great deal of trouble holding on to anything as so many people wish to carry away a memento of their visit. I imagine they hide the silverware whenever a visitor arrives, but Nina managed to squirrel away the rock. As a devotee of Murshid Sam and a certified teacher of the Dances of Universal Peace, Tofah was delighted with the gift.

Mordecai and Fawn also came by with a bottle of soap bubbles and a CD of a movie about a man who owns a magical toy store. With our eyes barely open, Tofah and I managed to watch the first few minutes of the movie, me wrapped in a blankee and Tofah resting her head on the rock.

June 14

Dear Friends,

As long as I've known Tofah, she awoke in the pre-dawn darkness, settled herself upon prayer rugs and meditated for two hours. Since the seizure, Tofah has established a new routine. From force of habit, she continues to rise between three and four in the morning. But now she remains in bed holding my hand. We talk and process what is going on in her body, heart and soul. We talk about death and dying, about the meaning and purpose of life, about clearing karma and which is better, dark or milk chocolate. These hours are so sweet, a person could gain ten pounds inhaling them.

Walter, Ariel and Tony came to the Garden and led three dozen of us in *Kirtan*. Walter set the tone for the evening. He reminded us that they were not here to perform. This was prayer. An evening of calling on the Holy Ones to heal their sister, Tofah. We began with a call and response to the chant, *Ganesha Sharanam, Sharanam Ganesha.*

Among all the deities in the Hindu pantheon, the most endearing and charming is *Ganesha*. Here is no painfully suffering soul, but a chubby pink elephant who is widely revered as the Remover of Obstacles and more generally as Lord of New Beginnings.

With Walter playing the harmonium and Tony holding rhythm on tablas, we clapped in time and our singing built in gleeful fervor. *Ganesha*, please remove the obstacles. *Ganesha*, we take refuge in thee.

This morning as the hour of awakening came upon us, Tofah took my hand and said she was going to go to her prayer room and meditate. I followed behind, to arrange her texts, light candles and burn incense, because Tofah has trouble making her hands do those tasks. When all was as it should be, I closed the door and returned to bed. Lying down, I looked at my hand, remembering the joy of entwining Tofah's fingers and prayed to the pink elephant who is sitting in the middle of the room.

June 16

Dear Friends

Eileen's sister, Iris, has to return to her nurse's job in Oregon and suggested I take the time while she is still here for a break from the house. I agreed to go for a walk, but am reluctant to be out of sight of Tofah.

The beach was nearly perfect. It was too cold for a bathing suit and too hot for a sweatshirt. The ocean waves were gentle. The sky was dappled with faint clouds and families were playing Frisbee and digging holes in the sand.

Staring out to sea, I saw the tail of a whale flash out of the water and splash back down into the ocean causing a great spray of water. In twenty years of beach walking I can count on one hand the number of times I have seen a whale. And here was this whale waving to me, sending Tofah and me a message that G-d's miracles are ever before us, if sometimes hidden.

June 20

Dear Friends,

Over the years I've had many nightmares of being lost and unable to arrive at my destination, which is usually home, a train or a boat.

In my dream, a vessel leaves port as I am frantically trying to get on board. Years into therapy, there was finally the night when I again missed the boat, dived into the water and swam to the slow moving channel crosser. Alongside the ship I found a rope and like a pirate of old, went up, hand over hand, until I reached a porthole and scrambled into a cabin filled with bunk beds. Moments later, a sailor entered the room and addressing me as Captain told me I was needed up on the bridge. I scampered up a flight of stairs, entered the pilot house, took hold of the wheel and never again had this nightmare.

When a person is in a major health crisis there are many people, who in good faith and best of intentions, want to either take command of the vessel or at a minimum strongly suggest a course of navigation.

Doctors are the worst. They instill fear coupled with a demand for urgent decisions that make it very difficult for people to judiciously steer their sacred human vessels in a way consistent with how they have lived their lives. Following close on the heels of docs are those who are close in love and friendship. They too can be unrestrained in their suggestions for treatment and are eager to share their opinions, stories and knowledge. Sometimes it's just too much and I am grateful that Jackie has volunteered to be an intermediary between us, the medical profession and good hearted souls who mean the best for Tofah.

Much love,

Jay Lev

I asked Tofah to describe the vehicle she is steering. In the past, her transportation of choice was a magical and mystical carpet but since the seizure she has switched vehicles. She said that at the height of the seizure she saw a bright silvery white light above her crown *chakra* that, as she reflected more on it, was the shape of a chariot.

She asked me to describe the vehicle I've been driving all these years. I told her in my early days I rode a buffalo, but as I've aged, I now hold the reins of a team of horses, pulling a sleigh. We promised one another that if it is *HaShem's* will, this coming winter we will find a high mountain resort and take a moonlit sleigh ride with all the bells a' ringing. Just in case it turns out otherwise, we lay together describing in detail the snow covered hillside, the red blanket tucked around us and the thermos of hot cocoa to keep us warm as the team of horses pranced through the white frosted forest.

(Dictated by Tofah)

June, 21

Dear Friends,

For the past fifteen years I've co-led ritual gatherings to honor the solstice. I am not doing that this year and want to use this day to offer my gratitude and blessings to all of you for the love, prayers, wisdom and encouragement you have sent my way. I first had a chance to read your messages yesterday and was moved to tears, over and over, as I read your delicious words.

Of all eight cross points in the yearly Goddess cycle, the summer solstice is the most powerful. It is the day when the sun, representative of the masculine G-d nature is at its fullest. It is the day when the Goddess, the Divine Mother, Gaia opens herself to receive the deepest bounty that the sun may offer. Her meadows, forests, vineyards and orchards absorb the gifts of sun light, become pregnant with its seed and bear their fruit at the equinox.

This joining together of God and Goddess is mirrored on Shavuot. It's on Shavuot that Ezekiel saw the chariot with a wheel within a wheel. The gospel tune says, "the little wheel turned by faith and the big wheel turned by the grace of G-d." Some believe Ezekiel's vision came as a result of a seizure. I had my seizure on Shavuot.

How then do we live our days? With no guarantees and limited means to determine what comes our way, we can hold our breath, squeeze shut our eyes and await the worst; be in denial of our powerlessness and assume the best; or we can find within ourselves a faith in the Divine and trust in the grace of G-d to bring us to the fullness of life.

My beloved friends, my blessing on this solstice is for each of us to have faith. With eyes filled with awe and wonder may we greet the solstice and embrace its majesty. May we have faith that the sun will nurture us, heal us, make us fecund and fertile. And may we have faith that by the grace of G-d we will sit together at the equinox, under an apple tree and share the juicy fruits.

Beloved Lord, Almighty G-d,
Through the rays of the Sun
Through the waves of the Air
Through the all-pervading Life in space
Purify and revivify me and I pray
Heal my body, heart and soul.
Amen (Nayaz)

Much, much love

Tofah

June 22

Dear Friends,

A week ago we held a prayer circle on the labyrinth. After everyone left, Suzanne, Koge's wife, spoke to Tofah about Dr. Andrew Wu. Dr. Wu is an acupuncturist in Cupertino who is extraordinarily skillful, intuitive, spiritually sensitive and has had success in treating lotus blossoms. Suzanne has been working with Dr. Wu for two decades and urged Tofah to meet and schedule an appointment with him. The three of us are going up there tomorrow.

Much Love,

Jay Lev

The waiting room was decorated with extraordinary six foot high wooden sculptures of the Buddha, a gift from a grateful patient. It felt reassuring to be seated next to these statues. The receptionists greeted Tofah like a celebrated guest, which maybe she was, considering Dr. Wu scheduled her before his first patient of the day and wouldn't accept any payment. Within minutes Tofah and the doctor established a trust and a shared confidence in an ability to heal and be healed. Despite an overwhelming work load, Dr. Wu gave Tofah two treatments last week, including one on Sunday morning when no other clients were scheduled.

At the first of this week, after treating dozens and dozens of patients, including Tofah, Dr. Wu telephoned Eileen inquiring about her health and wanting to know if she could detect any changes in her body or mind. He suggested they both find quiet spaces, facing the setting sun and meditate together for twenty minutes on dissolving the lotus blossoms in Tofah's brain. Throughout the week he has called and together they have melded their minds for a complete healing of the tumors.

As they meditated, fifty miles apart and yet as close as a flower petal and its stem, I went out to the labyrinth and slowly circled seven times. I thought that no creative instinct in a writer's mind could have constructed the labyrinthian turns that led Tofah to create the Garden, to orchestrate bringing together two souls in marriage who would lead Tofah to Dr. Wu, who would take Eileen down into the Kiva, into the shadow world, where the power of the shaman is great and where healing takes place beyond our limited wisdom. And as I stood in the eighth circle, the circle within the seven circles, the place where the brain reaches beyond the boundaries of self and into the realm of universal love, I knew that Tofah was there as well, connecting to a power that heals in ways that circumambulate our linear awareness.

(Dictated by Tofah)

July 1

Dearly Beloveds,

I will be meditating from 7 a.m. to 9 a.m. this Saturday, July 4th, Independence Day. I dearly hope some of you will meditate along with me, from your own homes, perhaps for fifteen or twenty minutes during those two hours. My intention is to meditate on a complete healing and for the lotus blossoms to dissolve. I would be so grateful if you will visualize me walking, running, embracing and dancing. Picture me snapping photographs at my new baby grand-daughter's high school graduation. Hold me in light that my light may grow bright and reflect back all the love I have for each of you.

Thank you for your many blessings.

Tofah

p.s. On Sunday I hope to tell you how my spirit was invited into two sweat lodges in New Mexico last week.

July 7

Tofah thanks all of you who joined us during the morning meditation on July 4th. We are in deep gratitude for your love and caring and know that of all the healing modalities we are engaging, there are none so powerful as the healing power of love.

At 7:00 a.m. Tofah was warmly settled on a glider in our back yard. Her shoulders and head were covered in a prayer shawl passed down from Murshida Vera Corda who, for many years, wore it when she was leading new moon ceremonies. Tofah's feet were resting on a heated bean bag.

On a table stood a smoothie filled with fresh fruits, kefer and a concoction of powders and spices that would have been the envy of an apothecary. In one corner an incense burner was filling the air with the smoke of tiny cedar boughs we collected in Yosemite. In another corner stood a statue of Padmasambhava.

Tofah purchased the statue a month ago and noticed that the paint on one of the eyes of the statue had scraped off. A lama at Pema Osel Ling repaired the statue and filled it with mantras. Placing prayers in a statue of Padmasambhava is extremely intricate with specific prayers delicately ensconced at the different chakra points.

I sat across from Eileen draped in a tallis and holding my own talisman, a steaming cup of coffee.

We began by chanting "Modeh Ani." We then called upon Tofah's angels, guides, masters and saints asking them to lend their spirit to this meditation and finally expressed our thanks for the many friends who were joining us in this prayer service.

In the breath practice we called on the angelic natures of earth, water, fire, water and ether, seeking to align with their energies. For the next ninety minutes Tofah led the two of us in the Rose Zhikr.

As the time of our meditation came to a close, I looked over at the statue of Padmasambhava and was sure I saw him winking at me with his newly painted eye.

Tofah wanted to lead the Rose *Zhikr* on Friday night but didn't wish the community to see how weak she had become. The plan was for Tofah to be settled in her place before anyone was allowed into the sanctuary, and participants would be asked to silently leave when the *zhikr* was completed.

The room filled up. Twenty people who had been coming for the *zhikr* throughout the year were present and twenty more friends came to be in the company of Tofah. I stood in the back by the door and remembered Fran leading us in prayer weeks before she died. What is it about *bodhisatvas* that as they near the bridge their surface fades and what remains is radiant beauty?

Tofah began. "When the *zhikr* first came to me I was instructed to lead it for a year. This week marks a year."

July 12

Dear Friends,

When Nina and Faith asked if I wanted help organizing dinner deliveries, I was confounded. I couldn't understand why I would ask for help preparing meals when that is what I have mostly been doing a good part of my life? What a mistake! I didn't realize what this journey entails or the strength that it requires.

There have been times driving home from Dr. Wu's office when it was already past dinner hour. I would be behind the steering wheel asking myself where I was going to find the stamina to prepare a supper. Tofah and I would discuss Chinese take-out or possibly making a quesadilla which always led to the conclusion that these were not good food items for Tofah. By that time we had reached home, entered the house and there on the table would be a beautiful meal. Then I bawled.

I was never much for crying. A tear drop here for a dead bird, a sniffle at a sad movie ending, a sob when they canceled the Buffy the Vampire series, that kind of thing, but bawling was not in my repertoire. Not so anymore.

I bawled in gratitude for what had been given to us. It didn't matter whether it came in Pyrex or Ziplock. It didn't matter whether the quinoa had been soaked overnight or whether there was chicken stock in the soup. It had been prepared with love, it was eaten in gratitude and together in distant communion, the threads of kindness wove another strand in a blanket of humanity.

I want to especially thank Flo and Dwayne. Every Friday morning, I wonder how I am going to summon the time and energy to get a challah for Friday night. Every week I say to myself, "I have more important things on my list to do today, G-d will forgive me for this omission" and every week Flo has quietly brought to the front door a challah, flowers, candles, once even a piece of chocolate cake. She doesn't ask to spend time visiting, she knows we're tired. She simply gives me a silent hug and leaves. What she leaves behind is the precious jewel of loving kindness that we can offer up to Shekinah, the Sabbath Bride.

Much love to all,

Jay Lev

July 18,

Dearly Beloved Friends,

Tofah was in the middle of a massage when she had a major seizure. None of our efforts were successful in calming it. After forty five minutes we called 911. Even at the hospital it took a huge amount of Ativan to control the seizures which continued for three hours.

Clearly we do not know what the future holds, but this morning, lying in her bed, she and I sang, " Modeh Ani."

My heart is heavy,

Jay

We celebrated Shabbat in the hospital. A friend baked a vegan challah and others brought a full feast from our favorite Chinese restaurant. While we were eating, Fernando entered the room. Fernando is the last guy still living in Santa Cruz from the pueblo in Mexico. He insisted on giving me a twenty dollar bill because where he comes from, people die in hospitals if they don't have money to buy services. He told Eileen the mothers were lighting candles in the village, praying for the American Grandmother to get well quickly.

July 23

The oncologist showed us the x-rays. Tofah has two large tumors, one near the back of her head, the other to one side. Without a biopsy, there is no way to be sure of the type of tumors but neither of the two possibilities are curable. If she allows the doctor to remove a small part of her brain, they can determine a treatment plan that includes radiation and chemotherapy which may or may not prolong her life for two to five years. Despite the imploring from friends, lovers and teachers, Tofah won't do it.

The following are the words she spoke into a tape recorder:

"I'm ready. I'm ready to go back to the Beloved and I don't want any ugliness in between. I have lived my life with the integrity that this body (crying)—sorry about that—that this body is a temple and I've never poisoned it. I've never eaten food that was really yucky for it. I tried to live with integrity honoring it, like I would want to honor anything of the Mother. And I just can't see a biopsy and chemo and radiation having any integrity whatsovever. So I say no. I'm not going to do it.

I want to die easily. I don't want ugly scenes and pain and puking and I'm hoping you (looking at her close friend, Spring, who is a Hospice Chaplain) know how to do that. I'm really hoping you know how to do that, Spring.

I'm ready to go to the Beloved. I'm joyful to go to the Beloved. The only reason I wouldn't run for that doorway is because I feel there are people here who are going to be sad and that feels like a stupid reason. I can't do it for everybody else. I've got to do this for myself. (crying). So, I love this idea of giving everybody a bead. Whatever. (laughing). We have some really rare beads. Some are hundreds of years old.

I want to go down with integrity. I want to go down the way I lived my life. And I absolutely love the Divine Mother and -(sniffling)- and I know she will walk beside me in this journey. She is walking beside me. And I really appreciate all the beautiful sisters I have surrounding me right now. - (laughing). One of them just brought me chocolate cake. You know, I'm really going to eat the chocolate cake right now (laughing) cause I never really let myself do that.

July 23

Eileen is returned from the hospital. Her condition is very much changed. She no longer has any but the smallest use of her arms or legs. On the other hand, she continues to awe and inspire with her spiritual consciousness and it is an honor and privilege to be in her presence. Throughout the days and nights one or more of us thought that Eileen would pass. Last night about midnight, our housemate, Don, heard chanting and singing coming from our bedroom. He came downstairs and all of us were asleep. What he was hearing were chorus upon chorus of angels singing to Eileen.

Yesterday she sang devotional chants with her women's band for three hours. Later she "walked" the labyrinth (in her wheelchair) along with four of us, holding the intention that whatever pathway unfolds for Eileen in the crossing over, it contain less doing and more joy. She then went on to give a spiritual transmission to one of her students. That's the type of days she is having.

This is now a full time job for at least two people and finding time to write is nearly impossible.

Jay Lev Shalom

July 28

This weekend Tofah had two marathon seizures, lasting three hours apiece, leaving her exhausted but still able to rejoice in the arrival of Damon, Eden and Lucinda Rose. She was still able to sing with a women's circle that gathered just prior to the Sunday night dance at The Garden. She was still inspired and cried at the beauty of music created and performed by Ariel who dedicated a composition at a concert to Tofah. She was still able to delight in a paper mache lamp created for her at Mendocino Sufi Camp.

A couple of days ago, Tofah began working with a new protocol developed by Donny Yance at the Center for Natural Healing in Ashland, Oregon. It includes thirty-five different botanicals and medicines. Donny is optimistic that the lotus blossoms can be shrunk. We place our prayers and blessings for him to have wisdom and insight.

Much love,

Jay lev

Tofah was raised amidst the soft brown foothills of high desert eastern Oregon, along the Columbia River.

To the Columbia River Indians, the river was known as Wy-Am meaning "echo of falling water." It was here the native peoples erected scaffolds over the raging waters and fished for giant chinook salmon. The river was so plentiful that within a fortnight, a man could gather enough salmon to feed a family throughout the winter.

To Tofah, the sandy shores of the Columbia were a scavenger hunt. Here she found arrowheads and here she heard the ancestors' call that led her to the echo of falling water. The creek behind their house flowed into the mighty river and became the gateway for Tofah to enter the home of The Mother, a pathway leading to reverence for the earth and a connection to the native peoples. The creek became a second home, a refuge and a sanctuary. The large boulder that stood sentry over her favorite swimming hole was a warm place to sit in the summer and a place that sheltered the small creepy crawlers that found respite behind its protective flanks when the waters ran fast.

Tofah continued to honor that place within herself that stayed connected to the earth and to the native people. The honor was reciprocated in Monticello, New Mexico.

Spring and Hawk, a Dakota Sioux Medicine Woman and her Chiricahua Apache warrior husband went to where White Buffalo Calf Woman was last seen and invited others to join them in a sweat on native land. The women's sweat lodge was held on the solstice with a focus on enlightenment. The men's sweat lodge was held on the new moon and had as its focus new beginnings. Tofah's presence was invited into both lodges.

For a week, Tofah wore a heart shaped abalone shell around her neck to absorb all the illness within her body. She then gave it to her friends to take to New Mexico. Once in the women's lodge, the shell was placed above the water bucket, the place of healing. For two days, Tofah's spirit sweat. For two days the echo of falling waters bathed her soul, healing her wounds, binding her heart with the Elders and the Mother of us all. Spring returned the necklace, overflowing with *baraka* and Tofah lay with it in bed, her son and daughter both at her side.

August 2

Time has taken on new meaning. It has become both less and more. I no longer am able to conceptualize the idea of a month from now. Even the idea of a future that extends beyond the space of a few hours becomes a challenge to the mind. What I do comprehend is the now.

It's 9:16 p.m. I have been lying on a cot alongside Tofah's hospital bed for about an hour. She's restless, her eyes open wide. Her right arm raises and lowers involuntarily, so does her right leg. It's 9:19 p.m. I look for signs of a pending seizure. Tofah helps. When she feels one approaching, she commences to chant Buddhist mantras. I administer a couple of drops of a homeopathic remedy under her tongue. I place my thumbs on pressure points. I chant with her. A minute passes. The seizure stops.

I do not think of morning. Morning is eight to ten hours from now. It's non-existent. It's an imaginary world. There is only now. The nights are long.

Eileen's sister, Ruth, is providing relief for Iris to return home for a week. In the morning she taught us a Sunday school song. "In the name of Jesus Christ of Nazareth, rise up and walk. I'm walking and leaping and praising G-d, walking and leaping and praising G-d. In the name of Jesus Christ, of Nazareth, rise up and walk."

After a few minutes of singing, Tofah said she wanted to stand up and walk. I was frightened because I do not have the strength to hold her up all by myself and she has almost no strength in her legs. I shook my head but her sister said, "If that's want you want to do, Jay and I will help."

Ruth, a home health care provider all of her life, was not frightened. She braced herself, reaching behind Eileen, she clasped her hands together around Tofah's waist and lifted her out of bed. I held one arm. Ruth held the other.

"Where do you want to walk?" Ruth asked.

"Into the living room."

Slowly the three of us stepped over the bedroom threshold and as we walked we sang. " In the name of Jesus Christ of Nazareth, rise up and walk. I'm walking and leaping and praising G-d, walking and leaping praising G-d. In the name of Jesus Christ of Nazareth, rise up and walk."

August 9

Dearest Friends,

Tofah has very little breath. She speaks very few words. Last Wednesday, she sat in a wheelchair in the living room while a group sang chants to the Divine. They sang: "God is Love, Lover and Beloved." They sang it looking at Tofah, each person willing themselves not to cry.

When they finished, Nina who had kept her ear close to Tofah's lips, heard her whisper.

"What did she say?" they asked.

" She said just one word 'lovely.'" Everyone gave a sigh of happiness and Tofah smiled at each of them in turn.

Last night I was lying alongside Tofah and she kept pursing her lips wanting to be kissed. I gently placed my lips on her, allowing them to linger. I said, "That was sublime."

With words that caressed my heart she said, "Do not be afraid to linger in the sublime."

Much love,

Jay Lev

The days are filled with the sounds of sacred music and Buddhist mantra pouring forth from the garden. People ask if they can come for just an hour and sing, not at Tofah's bedside, for that is asking for far too much, but to bring their voices, their devotion and their love to the place where the ethers might carry their songs through the open window of her bedroom.

Bhahku Tulku Rinpoche drove here from San Diego. In the living room, Eileen sat in a wheelchair, Iris stood behind her, holding Tofah's neck upright while the lama sat beside her on the floor playing the flute. When he put the instrument down, he faced us and said, "She is very important." He bent his lips to her feet and kissed them.

Iris said, "I feel like crying," and Tofah whispered back, "Stop crying. Can you sit in wonderment with me?"

August 11

Dear Friends,

I don't have much more to say. There is so much beauty here, along with so many bittersweet moments that it becomes a challenge where to go with this post. You will never know how much your comments have given me strength when strength was needed. They made me feel we were being accompanied by so many friends, laying down rose petals all along the pathway.

The journey has become so hard. It's funny that the hours which are the most difficult, changes with the days. In the first weeks, nights were hardest and I had a lot of fear. I was afraid Tofah would need to go to the bathroom and I might not be strong enough to prevent her from falling when she was half asleep. But now the nights are what I look forward to most.

The kids and Iris, who are here until this ends, and Don, who has lived with us for the past four years, all vie for alone time with Tofah yet everyone is respectful of the preciousness of this gift and tries not to take more than their share. Most of us think the best shift is from 10:30 p.m. to 3:00 a.m.

We each do it differently. Eden brings the baby into bed and rests alongside her mom. Don sits in a chair by her head and does silent and near silent healings. Me, I prefer to place one hand over her heart to feel for changes in her body and the other hand against her right hand, where the seizures almost always arise. In that position we doze together. For much of that time her eyes are open. She is awake. We whisper.

I whisper to her, "Thank you for offering me this honor."

She whispers back, "It's mutual."

We smile. We wait for the next seizure, my hand in hers.

Jay Lev

August 15, 2009

At 11:53 this morning, Tofah Eileen crossed to the other side. As she wished, she was surrounded by her family. In the same way that she traveled this entire journey with grace, beauty, tranquility, and reverence for the Divine, she did so with her last breaths. A quiet separation. Like pieces of cloud dissolving in sunlight. This is how she wanted to die. This is how she died. A stepping aboard a chariot and not looking back.

Buddhist mantras played softly. Above her head on the hospital pole were hung her favorite malas along with mine, her yamulka and a couple of sachets of amulets. At the top of her bed was a statue of Padmasambhava and alongside of that a poster of Tara.

Tofah's breathing began to slow and then it stopped. Her eyes were open, serenely gazing at a poster of the Amitabha Mantra which is handsomely adorned with holy paintings and a photograph of the Dali Lama. On the back side of the poster Lama Zopa wrote, "Look at these mantras (the ones on the flip side of the poster) when you are leaving from this old body... all the buddhas and bodhisattvas love you and you are in their care."

Don says he saw her neshamah flow from her crown chakra straight to Tara. I did as I promised her I would. I sang her across.

Good night, my princess, my queen. Daughter of the Goddess,

Sister to the Stones." Be welcomed by the many prophets, saints and illuminated souls. I return you to their care with the deepest gratitude. Tell Grandpa Sorensen we'll all be together soon.

Jay Lev

Thirteen Months

GRIEVING

Most people have reasons not to traverse the darkness. It's not possible to grieve and go to work. It's not a process that can be multi-tasked and it's a benign employer who will consent to a week's bereavement leave, much less a year's paid sabbatical.

It's not fun. It hurts real bad. The only way to get through it is to burn and when we think the fire can't burn any hotter, the flames burn hotter. When we burn we don't know if all that will remain is ash or if there's a speck of a diamond at the core of our souls or anything in between.

If there are kids that need to eat breakfast before leaving for school, grieving has to be put on the back burner behind the oatmeal. When there are elderly parents who need tending, it's nearly impossible to say: "Sorry, Mom, but it's more important for me to focus on myself and someone who is dead, than on you, who is living."

Regrets and recriminations, the "wish I hads" and the "wish you hadn'ts" don't make it any easier to grieve. It's hard enough to jump hurdles without having to worry about splinters. The diversions are a lure to turn us away from introspection. I'll keep them handy for when things get really rough, but otherwise, I'm in for the ride.

Grief plays havoc with our sense of time. I figure me and time are in a trial separation.

For eleven weeks I watched time progress from one minute to the next. It's hard to imagine how slow time can get watching a person you love die. When it's 2:37 a.m. in the morning and you are timing the intervals between seizures, 2:39 a.m. is so long in arriving that I could get in a nap or begin a laundry. Possibly what happened is the hands on the clock gradually slowed down so much that they stopped moving.

I don't have a job, a time card to punch or television shows I want to watch. My preferred routine is to slip under the covers at dusk and arise in the pre-dawn which further separates me from a wristwatch culture. I'm not complaining about it, but it is unsettling.

I am worried about my inability to tell time. There are wall calendars in practically every room in the house and I write meticulous notes to help me remember when something took place. When I am unable to sequence events I become consternated and a chill runs up my spine.

I told my grief therapist I'm frightened this is the first symptom of a brain tumor or that I am becoming crazy. She told me the word "crazy" isn't in the psycho-therapist's lexicon. She asked if I possessed a book called The Power of Now by Eckhart Tolle. It had a lot to say on the subject

I've spent weeks organizing Eileen's library and after she described the book, it was easy to pull it from the shelf of miscellaneous New Age texts. The therapist started turning pages. "Here it is. You have the page book-marked."

"That's not my book-mark. I never read the book."

"Well someone put this book mark here. Let me read to you."

"Whereas before you dwelt in time and paid brief visits to the Now, have your dwelling place in the Now and pay brief visits to the past and future when required to deal with practical aspects of your life situation."

"You should read this book, Jay."

The next day a friend suggested I read a book called The Power of Now. Holy Cow! That was an incredible amount of coincidence. But Eileen didn't describe me as a bull dog without reason. Yesterday someone came to visit and brought me a gift: The Power of Now. Okay, I surrender. I will read the book.

The guys from Oaxaca didn't speak or understand any English. No matter what I said to them, they nodded their heads and said yes. That's how I feel when people ask me anything about time. I have become a mojado.

A friend says, "Can I bring you dinner next Thursday?" I say, "yes." She watches me write it down. Once it is in print she feels assured I won't forget, but I do not understand what I have affirmed. The words "next Thursday" are from a language that includes the future and mine's been surrendered.

The future is part of our lives either because we hope something will continue to be as it is or something else will happen or not happen. I don't care about the future. I don't want a future.

The past is more problematic. I do what I'm able to blot from my memory those eleven weeks, especially my promise to hurry and join Eileen. Mantra, walking and gardening help to divert my attention but none of them work all of the time. When nothing works, I burn.

I've discovered time is neither constant nor linear. The days are not of equal length but none of them are short. There have been days that continued for half a week and weekends that lasted a month. Sometimes the days roll back on themselves. What happened yesterday appears to my mind to have happened last month and what took place last month I think happened last week. Over and over I am surprised when someone tells me what month we are in.

"Imagine that," I respond in awe and wonder. "Who would have ever thought it was November?"

I am tired. I remember how tired I was during the eleven weeks. I remember thinking I had never been so tired in all my life. Then I was measuring sleep in minutes. It's different now. I sleep seven, eight, even nine hours.

Then my exhaustion was compounded by the anguish I felt in watching my beloved decline. Today my exhaustion is birthed in resignation. I am keenly aware that Eileen is never going to share with me again on the earth plane. I want to resign from life.

It would be nice to reduce the amount of clutter in the house before I die so it won't be such a burden on Natasha. It would probably also be a good thing to complete the taxes for the year, but what the hell. If I go to sleep with a lit cigarette next to a gasoline soaked something, presto, no clutter, no taxes, no me, no tomorrow.

I feel like a modern day reinterpretation of Job. Instead of hardship, G-d increases the gifts to test my resolve. My days are sublime and ever more beautiful. I wander, mystified in the opulent ballroom of the Divine, caressed by the wind and made love to by the ocean. I do not deny this beauty nor am I boorish in my gratitude. Still, I seek my black clad mistress, Lady Death, for the last waltz of the night. I simply do not desire attending this gala tomorrow.

New Years Eve was never my favorite holiday. It bewilders me. I wonder if the revelers swirling and twirling amidst confetti are celebrating that last year is finally over or welcoming the prospect of new adventures in the year to come. Maybe it's neither. Maybe it's simply an excuse for getting tipsy.

What year is it? I have a calendar tacked to the wall over this computer and I can tell by the notes I've written that today is Friday, March 26th. But nowhere on the page does it print the year. I freak out. How can I be so oblivious to time as to not know if this is 2009 or 2010? I want to tear the calendar off the wall and look on the cover but I refrain. I do breathing exercises to calm my mind and gradually the truth comes to me. I am totally delighted knowing it is 2010. I am what is known as a "cheap date."

Today was the anniversary of Eileen's first seizure and I observed it, as I do every day, by walking along the seashore. As I walked a woman coming toward me waved in greeting. She was the woman whose dog had gone berserk.

She began, "I was a psychological mess when I started working with Eileen. I am doing okay now, but I don't think I'd be alive if not for her. I wish I could tell her how much she means to me."

"She's probably listening."

I collect New Year anniversaries like other people collect baseball cards. I mark December 31st by composing a list of resolutions. I mark The Jewish New Year by throwing my sins into a creek. Now there is a third New Year anniversary: August 15th.

I don't know what rituals I'll do to commemorate the holiday, but for the present, it is enough to know that it is only ten days before the New Year.

I took a walk with a mother whose teen age son recently died. As we walked we heard a siren. She shuddered at the sound. I remember how the sight of an ambulance used to make me gag.

She said, "It's been seventeen days since the ambulance came to our house…"

Grief begins with counting the hours, then the days, then the months and here I am ready to begin counting years.

KADDISH

English translation:

Exalted and holy, G-d's name is great. In the world
that G-d created, according to Divine Will, may G-d
reign in majesty, in your lifetimes and in your days
and in the lifetimes of the entire family of Israel,
swiftly and at a time that comes soon. And let us say
Amen.

May G-d's great name be blessed forever and for all
eternity. Blessed, praised, glorified, exalted, upraised,
honored, elevated and lauded be the name of the
Holy One. Blessed is G-d beyond any blessing and
song, praise and consolation that are uttered in the
world. And let us say Amen.

May there be peace that is abundant from Heaven and
life upon us and upon all Israel. And let us say Amen

May the one who makes peace in the high places
make peace upon us and upon all Israel. And let us
say Amen.

*I rage against HaShem and rail against the Voice. Is this voice
self talk, soul-talk, channeling or schizophrenia at the doorstep?
Whose Voice is it? It doesn't sound familiar and it's not saying what
I want to hear. Why does it urge me to recite the Mourner's Kaddish
every day for eleven months? Even if Tofah was Jewish, the law
simply requires reciting Kaddish for thirty days for a wife. It is only
when a parent dies, someone who is irreplaceable, that mourners are
expected to say Kaddish for eleven months. I, who do not want to live
eleven more hours, will not promise to do this. I am going to have a
conversation with myself.*

"I might be willing to recite the prayers for thirty days, if I
have an assurance I will die immediately after the final Amen."

The Voice was non-negotiating.

"Why!"

"Majesty is adorned in honor. Clothe Eileen's soul with prayer and dignity."

"If I do this, if I can figure out a way to do this, will you promise after eleven months to take me home?"

"We'll talk about it then."

"How am I supposed to do this? There has to be a *minyan* for a person to say *Kaddish*. Among the Orthodox, a *minyan* is considered ten men. Within the Conservative and Renewal movements a *minyan* is ten people. The Reform are willing to define a *minyan* as nine people with The Torah, in a pinch, counting as a tenth presence. Nowhere in Santa Cruz can I expect any of these groups to muster a *minyan* for me to say the mourner's prayer every day for eleven months."

"It'll happen," the Voice replies.

The first to come forward was a rabbi from the Reform synagogue. She offered to form a *minyan* every Tuesday morning for the eleven months. The Conservative shul took Wednesdays and Saturdays, the Renewal congregation supported me on Fridays and Chabad on Sundays. Mondays and Thursdays I can pray at home. If I stay alive, I can do this.

The future was determined during the seven days of *shiva* when a mourner remains home and others gather there at night for the *Maariv* prayer service. I was hoping we could at least form a *minyan* on each night but that would be unusual in Santa Cruz, where most mourners hold an evening service only once or twice during the week.

Each night the sanctuary filled with friends. Each night more people arrived to pray. Each night different rabbis, both men and women, led the service. By the sixth night, the sanctuary overflowed. Dozens more recited evening prayers on the lawn, by the pond or in the gazebo.

A web was being woven and there were people who wanted to be a thread in the weave. Political and theological differences ceased to separate the community. Reform Jews who never owned a *tallis*, prayed alongside those who put on *tefillan* every morning. Even the Chabad rabbis came and though they were forbidden by their beliefs from entering the sanctuary because of the religious images draping the walls, they stood on the steps and *davened* in the darkening hours.

The *Kaddish* is an affirmation when the alternative is despair. It is a challenge to sing praise when it's raining. It's the challenge to sing praise when the rains won't stop and won't ever stop as long as you're alive. The *Kaddish* is a rite of spiritual warriorship.

It's akin to the Sun Dance, a Native American ceremony found among the Plains Indians, in which people pierce their chests and hang suspended from a Tree of Life. Saying *Kaddish* takes a heart pierced by loss and offers it as a gift to the glory of the Divine.

In the face of the inexplicable, unalterable, unceasing and unendurable, stands the Mourner's *Kaddish*, a gateway to the kingdom, guarded by fire. The *Kaddish* doesn't even have anything to say in regard to death, grief or consolation. It's all about praising G-d. I struggled with each word.

The first word in the prayer is "*Yis-gah-dal.*" It means "exalted." "You're exalted? Eileen is dead and You're exalted? Pardon me, but right this minute, You don't feel so exalted."

The second word is *Va-yis-kah-dash*. It means "holiness." Tofah was a holy person. She sang Your praise on her breath. As Saint Teresa said: "If this is the way you treat your devotees, no wonder

You have so few friends."

I stood at the back of the *shul*, pulling the *tallis* over my head, so no one would see me cry as I fought to give You praise. I seeped deeper into prayer. I walked for hours before daybreak, chanting the *Kaddish*. When the best I could do was hold onto a guard rail and sob, the prayer was on my lips. As the months wore on, as my heart opened to so much beauty, to so much pain, the *Kaddish* became a map to navigate my way back to a relationship with the *Shekinah*. Turn me and I shall return.

It's Purim. People celebrate the holiday with costume parties and gaiety. I could go to one of these parties dressed as the Grim Reaper but the sound of laughter rasps against my soul and as long as I am saying Kaddish I avoid music and revelry.

This morning the rabbi asked how I would fulfill the obligations of Purim to celebrate and feed the hungry.

"Could you invite one person to your house today, say a blessing and drink a cup of wine? It would be enough."

I baked two honey cakes. As they were coming out of the oven, someone unexpectedly dropped by. We offered a blessing and ate warm cake. We said goodbye. I looked at the other honey cake.

A friend's father died a couple of weeks ago and my friend is staying close to home. I know about wanting to cocoon. I wrapped the second pastry and delivered it to her door. Back home I made an eighteen dollar donation to The Hope Project in India. That's enough Purim for one year. G-d, I miss Eileen so badly.

Two dozen men prayed in the back yard. It is Friday night and I am still saying Kaddish for another five days. As the men began to circle I moved into the dark shadows of the garden. I will not dance. I am not prepared to let go of my grief.

A Modern Orthodox rabbi arrived in Santa Cruz on a grant to provide teaching to the Conservative congregation which does not employ a rabbi. This year he brought along a friend, also a rabbi, whom he had known since childhood.

They are both kind, good men who pray with fervor. For them, Friday evening prayers are an occasion for exultation which reaches a crescendo at the moment in the prayer service when the community rises to greet the *Shekinah* or Sabbath Bride. Joining together, men take hands and dance in a circle. They sing, "Come let us go out to greet the Sabbath Queen." The circle spins faster as their hearts and souls go to the vineyards, led there by the light of the Divine.

Today was the last time I said Kaddish. From now on I will be like everyone who has had a death in the family and recite the Kaddish only on the anniversary of Eileen's crossing and on four holidays. For the final time I spoke aloud the words. At the conclusion of the service, someone asked what goes through my mind when I say the prayer. I tell him the Kaddish is the samurai way to die unto G-d. The words are in place of the sword and instead of slicing the stomach, the Kaddish slashes the heart.

At the bottom of each of Eileen's emails was the message: "To each and all it is given to dance. The one who joins not in the dance, mistakes the event."

It was Friday night. I was at the rabbi's vacation rental. The men had risen in a circle to greet the *Shekinah*. I began to move away. Suddenly the circle was broken. Avram dropped the hand of the man in front of him and stopped circling. The men danced in place and they waited as my friend waved for me to join the community. I shook my head and he waved again. It was an unwillingness to leave behind a year of mourning that froze me in place. No words were said, all the men were looking at me as they sang: "Come let us go out to greet the Sabbath Queen" Avram continued to wave. And then with tears welling in my eyes, I joined the circle and my tears were met by others who cried along with me. It was time to dance. To each and all it is given to dance. The one who joins not in the dance mistakes the event.

WALKING

It is a Jewish tradition for a mourner to take a short walk on the seventh day of Shiva. It's a pretty metaphor but I become afraid when I leave the house. People continue to bring me dinner so there's no reason to leave.

A woman brought along her dog to sit in the *sukkah*. She is gaunt and moves slowly. She is wrestling with terminal cancer and a care team has been organized to assist her on the journey. I am emotionally unfit to be with the woman, but maybe I can walk the dog. I volunteered to do it every Wednesday morning. Afterward I panicked.

It was more than a month since Eileen died and the furthest I walked was one and a half blocks to the donut shop which opens at 4:30 a.m. and sells fair trade coffees. I was the only customer in the store at that hour. During daylight hours I occasionally crossed the street to visit neighbors, now I was going to walk a dog, who knows where, during the day and around strangers. I prayed that it was not anywhere near Rio Del Mar Beach.

The woman lives in the country. There are more trees than houses and a creek runs alongside the road.

The dog's name is Mila. She is a pure bred, fawn colored pug, with a squat face. For an ugly, bulgy eyed dog, she is quite feminine. I renamed her "Pretty."

I was shown her leash, doggie treats and where to deposit her when we returned from our walk. We started down a long, steep driveway toward the creek but halfway along, Pretty stopped, sat on her haunches, and turned her face toward the house.

I got down on the blacktop. We needed to have a heart to heart talk.

"You know your master is dying and you want to stay by her side, don't you?" Pretty turned her face to me in agreement.

"You do know you can't do anything to prevent her from dying no matter how much you love her, don't you?" Pretty turned her face back to the house.

"I know something about what you're feeling. The person I loved the most in the whole world died this summer and I couldn't do anything to save her. So, here is my promise. I will never take you for a walk if I think she is close to dying; but she is not going to die today, and it would be a good thing for you and her both if you went for a walk. What about it?"

Pretty rose from her haunches and we commenced our weekly walks.

Pretty was eager to go for a walk this week and whenever the pace slowed, she tugged at her leash. A limpid creek continually shifts from one side of the road to the other and tall maples, aspens and redwoods create a moldy beauty. The frogs and salamanders are in bliss.

There was a brisk wind and a continual cascade of brilliant leaves in yellow, orange and red swirling water colors layered the ground.

The leaves are attached to thin stems which at some unknowable instant loosen from the branch and pirouette to the ground. The stem doesn't grasp, grip, or clench the branch nor does it force itself from the tree. It would be a good thing if I can become like the leaves and accept that my autumn hasn't arrived.

I felt Eileen's beauty in every tree, stone and dew laden droplet. "How can I live with the pain of your beauty surrounding me everywhere I turn?"

And that voice answered, "With surrender."

If I could walk on a country road without panic attacks, could I also walk in other places? I couldn't walk on the beach or the forest trails familiar to Eileen and me, but West Cliff Drive was a possibility.

West Cliff is an uninterrupted three mile promenade edging Monterey Bay. It is so close to the ocean that in big weather, waves cascade over the seawall and onto pavement. The walk begins at Natural Bridges, a favorite among Monarch Butterflies and ends at the Santa Cruz Boardwalk, a favorite among tourists. There are trees and benches along the route. Without an alarm clock, I awake at three, feed the cats, soak in the hot tub and wait for the donut shop to open.

A Cambodian woman owns the shop and everyone who works there is Cambodian. The baker is the only person working when the doors open. His speech is limited to Khmer, but it's not necessary that we speak. I pour my own coffee and put two dollars on the counter. He knows to call out, "Thank you." The one time I had a conversation with someone behind the counter, she told me in broken English that everyone in her family was murdered by the Khmer Rouge. After that, I was content with, "Thank you."

I wear a coat Eileen bought in Nepal to hike the Himalayas. It's warm, though the zippers are beginning to fail. It has many pockets. The pockets are useful. They hold a tape recorder with Hazrat Inayat Khan's *zhikr*, a camera, recording stick, pen, paper and most important of all a head lamp. At 5:00 a.m. West Cliff Drive is dark, except for the light of the moon.

I am among a tiny group of pre-dawn strollers. There are less than twenty people who walk West Cliff before sunrise. They have become familiar faces. We do not speak but I know them by the names I've assigned to each. There is the elderly woman jogger named "Bumble Bee" because she wears a jacket with broad yellow stripes. There is a man who walks an ancient, slow moving border collie. He's "Dog Man." There are two men and a woman who walk together and speak an unfamiliar language. They are "The Russians." There is a woman who pushes an empty stroller designed for twins. In the light of my head lamp there are tears on her cheek. I have not given her a name.

Sometimes I wonder what others call me.

Much of the time when I walk, I chant mantra or sing into a tape recorder. Two nights before Tofah died, I promised to sing her across. I didn't know what that meant or how to do it but since then I've been singing for hours at a time. Maybe calling what I do "singing" is too fancy a word. It's more like a broken record. A thought or phrase comes pouring out of my heart and I sing it over and over. Sometimes it's something I want to tell Eileen. Sometimes it feels like it is something Eileen is telling me.

I have no reason to walk in downtown Santa Cruz. There is nothing of interest in the store windows and I do not like the bustle of commerce. I am also afraid. People are brusque, loud inconsequential noises that hurt my ears bounce off brick buildings and the restaurants are closed to me. This much I know, grief dines alone.

Amidst the craze of Christmas shopping, I ventured downtown, side stepping news stands filled with lies, seeking an automatic egg poacher. The poacher we use on Wednesday mornings at the synagogue melted and I volunteered to replace it.

I was hyper vigilant and constantly turned my neck like a chicken in a barnyard. My steps were halting and erratic. I sensed I did not look normal. I wondered what provoked me to this mad quest.

Walking is an affirmation. The Jews walked into the desert. The Indians who followed Gandhi, walked to the sea. I think of Peace Pilgrim who walked the length of America. I think of me in downtown Santa Cruz.

I have learned the only thing necessary to affirm life is to continually put one foot in front of the other. I do not know where I am going or how long it will take to get there. I wish the journey would end today, but there is no evidence it's going to end any time soon. There are no short cuts on this pathway. It's a long journey, sometimes going barefoot over coals. Coming down here was an affirmation that I still have strength to support community. It doesn't matter that I didn't find what I was looking for. I was looking for what I found, courage to come downtown.

It's too cold to wear Eileen's windbreaker. I switched to wearing Eileen's heavy red down coat. But what do I do with her jacket? I won't put it in the garbage can.

I have discovered the sunrise. I spend the first hour walking west in the darkness, turn around, and spend the second hour walking into the dawn light. It takes that long to experience night becoming day. Staring at the horizon for minutes before the full radiance of the sun bursts onto our consciousness is mimosa but being in and being a part of the cycle moving from moon-and-star-lit restriction to sun jubilant expansion is epicurean.

I am grateful to have Eileen's digital camera because it doesn't cost anything to take photos. But then I look at the Canon and remember hundreds of times Eileen set the timer on the camera so we could be together in photos and I wail. On West Cliff Drive my wail merges in the boisterous serenade of breaking waves.

A woman came to the house who mentioned she enjoys bicycling before sunrise along West Cliff. There are some bicyclists out in the morning, but they ride in the gutter and it's nearly impossible to identify them in the darkness. I told her I too walk on West Cliff those same hours and reached for my fanny pack to display all the neat things I keep in it. As I pulled out the head lamp she became gleeful, 'Oh! You're head lamp guy!'

Baruch HaShem. I kept my promise to Pretty. I was visiting Natasha in Seattle so the dog wasn't walked for two weeks. Her master died with Pretty by her side.

There was something strange happening on West Cliff this morning. The nearer I approached the green lawns of the lighthouse field, the more people I encountered. I felt invaded by these pilgrims. Then I realized they were smartly dressed, walking as families and looking very well washed. I am time challenged, but I figured it out. It's Easter Sunday!

The lighthouse parking lot was filled with church buses. On the lawn a bevy of matrons was preparing a sunrise breakfast while a growing crowd of worshippers gathered by the cliff. At the edge of the crowd a man was distributing a program with the psalms and prayers to be offered. He was filled with light and pointing to the assembly said to me, "Isn't this beautiful?"

I nodded and said, "I have a secret to share."

"What?" he asked conspiratorially.

Pointing to the horizon, I said, "It's going to be just as beautiful tomorrow."

I've seen and been part of many changes on West Cliff Drive. When I began, I listened to Hazrat Inayat Khan's *zhikr* on a tape recorder. But it was too much noise to hear the voice of G-d, so I reduced. I swapped the tape recorder for *japa* beads and chanted whatever came to mind. But it was too much noise to hear the voice of G-d so I stopped wearing the beads and tried listening. I'm not too good at it, but sometimes I hear a whisper.

There are subtle changes that occur constantly. I didn't know that where on the horizon the sun rises depends upon the season. All that *wiccan* emphasis on equinox and solstice is important.

Also, I no longer view every rock jutting into the ocean as a possible launching pad for drowning in the surf. The two men and woman who spoke the unidentified language moved back to Russia and the ancient border collie died. I talked to the dog's owner. He said the dog died peacefully and that they had been friends for a long time. At his feet scampered the cutest border collie puppy. This man is going to be all right.

I am in training. I am building endurance for the hike into Yosemite in September. I know my destination but I don't remember how far it is from the trailhead. If it's five miles in, that means a ten mile hike in one day and I am not prepared for it. I remember it wasn't an easy hike when Eileen and I hiked it together and I am physically weaker today. I don't doubt I'll make it but I do wonder about these sneakers.

By September I'll have walked more than a thousand miles on West Cliff Drive in these shoes. I had to buy inserts because there's so little cushion still remaining. But we started together on this journey and I'd like to end together. Then I'll put them away.

To commemorate Eileen's birthday I chanted what would have been her *Haftorah* portion on Saturday. Her sister, Iris, came down to visit and attend the ceremony. Afterward, Iris proposed an early morning walk on Rio Beach. I blanched. The last time I was there was with Eileen on the morning of her first seizure. I didn't think I could do it but Iris promised she would hold my hand the whole time. She argued the beach would be empty at dawn and that it wouldn't hurt.

Liar! Liar! Pants on Fire! By the time Iris got out of bed, concocted a breakfast of roots, stems and berries and settled on her clothing it was nine in the morning. At the beach we took off our shoes and laid down a prayer blanket. Ten minutes into chanting *Om Namah Shivaya*, Iris announced a need for a bathroom break. The nearest toilet was a half mile down the beach. I reached for my shoes but she said she could get there quicker if she jogged by herself. She left and my stomach knotted. I started to sing *Ish Kalah Mah Bood Lay La*, G-d is love, lover and beloved. As I sang several dolphins appeared at the edge of the breaking surf. They swam in circles as I prayed.

When Iris returned, we walked alongside the seashore. She scattered rose petals, gathered from the garden, and the beach became a wedding aisle. I was retaking my marriage vows and the dolphins who kept pace with us were the bridesmaids accompanying my beloved.

These sneakers look like me. There's hardly anything left. Any less and I'd need duct tape to hold them together. But they made it. Hallelujah. I'm not sure, but maybe I made it as well. I leave tomorrow for Yosemite.

SPREADING HER ASHES

Holding a hand painted urn to her breast, Spring came to the house with Eileen's ashes. We put the urn inside a wicker laundry basket and placed it in a corner of a closet. In time her ashes were scattered on a wind swept mountain crest in Nepal, at Lama Foundation in New Mexico, and in White Buffalo Calf Woman Canyon in Arizona. More ash went to Morocco and India. But to me, she asked only that I carry her back to Oregon and Yosemite National Park.

I've grown accustomed to living in confined space and consciousness. I feel safe remaining close to the house and largely determining with whom I share time. The trip to Oregon is everything that I have not done for ten months.

I've driven along the Columbia Gorge many times. I have driven it in snow, torrential rain, black ice and glaring sun, but I do not know how I will bear seeing Latourell Waterfall. I am deeply fearful of the trek and dread the possibility of having to spend a night in a motel room or wait hours in an airport terminal.

Dylan, Eden and three of Eileen's siblings are planning to meet me at a restaurant. At the door of the eatery there is a painting of a giant chicken with a circular hole cut out so people can poke their heads through and pose for photographs. It is peculiar why people would do this. From there we are carpooling to the creek that runs wild a block from Eileen's childhood home

Eileen spoke of it so often that I had a clear image of the creek and the giant rock downstream from the house. Eileen told me many stories about the creek but she never mentioned how to get down to it.

Together we cautiously made a path through blackberries and poison oak, helping each other over the brambles and fallen trees. We made creekside with only a handful of cuts and bruises, but the rock was at least a quarter mile downstream. There was only one way to reach it. I waded in. In most places the creek was six inches deep, unless it was suddenly two feet. Everyone slipped, sloshed and yelped when they stepped into deep holes. This was so much Eileen's style, we all felt she was laughing.

When we arrived at the rock our spirits were high. Iris read a Rumi poem and others shared creek stories. Owen mentioned Padre Pio, which reminded me of a story.

"It began in the dark along West Cliff Drive. I was keeping the angels awake with my cries and Eileen came to soothe me. She asked why I was in distress."

"I miss you and I want to feel you."

"You're being silly. I'm right here. I'm on the wind."

"It's not the same."

"It's not the same. Now I can be everywhere at once. Wherever G-d's breath is felt on earth, I'll be there. It's everything I ever wanted. I can do so much good from here. Please be happy for me."

I finished telling the tale just as a gust of wind came swirling down the creek. It had been a hot still day in the high desert and the wind had come from nowhere. It danced around us, the trees bowing to its rhythm.

Oregon had been for Eileen's family. Yosemite was for me. Friends and family offered to come along, but this was a solo journey. I made reservations to stay in Yosemite for two nights. I'd spread her ashes on the valley floor the first day. On September 15, 2010, thirteen months from the morning she died, I would spread her ashes in the high country of Tuolumne Meadows.

Rosh HaShannah has left me with no time for errands. I leave for Yosemite tomorrow. Today was the only opportunity to shop for something I could use to carry Eileen's ashes. I entered the first store and knew immediately I wasn't emotionally capable of conducting trade. I returned home empty handed.

Back at the house I searched for something meaningful and poetic that I could use to carry her ashes. All I found was a quart sized mason jar. As I rummaged, I noticed Eileen's medicine pouch resting on an altar. It was filled with amulets, tobacco and corn given to her by Grey Antelope, an elder of the Santa Clara Pueblo.

Eileen had sewn the leather pouch. Leather draw strings kept the pouch loosely closed, not so tightly that ash wouldn't simply pour out, but if held upright, could safely be taken on a hike. It might just be big enough to hold all of the ash. The pouch was decorated with bird feathers and a beautifully intact dried crow's foot. I emptied the pouch, placed it before me and asked permission to use it. It took a while before the pouch agreed, but on condition that I be careful in my treatment and promise to return it to its place on the altar. I agreed. I leave at first light.

Ten miles from the park entrance was a rock shop. Past the ubiquitous Yosemite Park key chains and post cards, among bins of petrified rock, fools gold and quartz crystals, I found rose quartz. Some say rose quartz strengthens and heals the heart. I purchased three stones that each had somewhat of a heart shape.

I planned to begin at Mirror Lake, but had to park two miles from the trailhead. I prepared to walk but first had to transfer the ash from the urn to the medicine pouch.

There were two pounds of ash in the urn packed within a heavy duty plastic bag. I tried lifting the bag out of the small mouth of the urn, but it wouldn't come. The ash would have to be poured directly from the urn into the medicine pouch. Not to spill any of the ash required two people, one holding the pouch open, the other pouring. I was alone and my hands shake. As I poured, a cloud of ash filled the rental car, coating my face in grey dust. It was classic "Big Lebowski."

I followed the Merced River. I paralleled Half Dome. I kept Bridal Veil Falls to the west and still I could not find Mirror Lake. With sun setting, I came skidding down a steep slope onto a broad expanse and saw a plaque describing Mirror Lake. The plaque said the lake is seasonal, filled with snow melt until the end of summer, when the lake entirely disappears. I was standing on Mirror Lake.

Haggard, I turned from the non-existent lake to walk among the stones. I knew many of them. At every bend there was a giant stone on which Eileen and I had lain, a boulder we had pressed our hearts against, a granite we had embraced. I scattered ash on all those that I remembered and twice heard calls from stones reminding me of their connection to Eileen and their wish to be dusted. As I went among my brothers, I heard their chatter. I placed the first rose quartz in a crevice beneath a rock where we once crept to stay out of the rain.

I reserved half the ash for the high country and was about to leave the trail when Eileen's spirit came to me in a huff. No time during the scattering had I named what was the intent of returning her ashes to Yosemite. She suggested I give it some thought before starting out the next day.

The trail head to Glen Aulin is across from Tenaya Lake which is fifty switch back miles from the valley floor. I wanted to see the sun rise over the lake and to say my morning prayers surrounded by grandfather and grandmother granite outcrops.

My destination was a lava flow where massive round rocks dot the slope, defying gravity. On our last hike in Yosemite, we had cooled our feet in a tiny pool, shaded by one of the boulders. There I would scatter the last of the ash. There I would place the second rose quartz stone. The third stone I will keep on a mantle.

The trail head began in a new growth forest surrounded on two sides by barren granite outcroppings and smooth, long, steep lava flows. Half a mile down the trail my eyes caught the iridescent sheen of blue jay feathers on the forest floor. A woodland predator had eaten the head, but from the neck down, the bird's body was undisturbed. Death had come during the hot Yosemite summer and the body dried quickly, without mold or insects. I picked it up. In my left hand I held the medicine pouch adorned with a crow's foot and in my right hand I bore a blue jay's body, both its delicate feet dangling down. I will walk as a kabbalistic Tree of Life, carrying Eileen's totem on my feminine left side and my totem on my masculine right. They'll meet in the center, *Tifereth*, a place of beauty. Tifereth, which was Eileen's Hebrew name.

As I walked deeper into the high country I stepped away from myself. I saw the firs and junipers, I smelled the pine needles and I heard the wind, but I wasn't there. I had blurred into the landscape.

At mid-morning I reached the field of round boulders. The stone I sought was perched close to the trail. I sat, ate an orange, and unlaced the medicine pouch draw strings. This time I spoke my purpose.

"Holy Light, I am returning your daughter's ashes. She was a daughter of the Goddess and a sister to the stones. She had faith the stone elders would help bring peace to our troubled world. Now she is a part of you, still holding that vision, and coming to plead humanity's needs. I loved her dearly. I'm glad I was able to bring her home."

A hundred feet above me was a stone, shaped like a recliner. It would be a perfect place to sit and read a book. To anyone who doesn't have a fear of heights, the hundred feet wouldn't have registered as an obstacle, but it set my heart racing. Dang if this wasn't more of Eileen. She was always urging me to reckless behavior. I resolved I would keep my dignity as I ascended. If it came to crawling on my belly, I was turning back.

I arrived as triumphantly as any mountain climber ascending Half Dome. From here I could see into the next valley and directly looking down on me was a Grandmother Stone. I got comfortable and from the daybag brought out a copy of Oriah Mountain Dreamer's book, The Invitation. It'll be the last book I read to Eileen.

A young friend once asked Eileen's opinion of a suitor and Tofah sent her a hand written copy of the poem called "The Invitation". The book grew out of the poem in which the author described the soul mate for whom she yearned. I read aloud but this time Eileen would not fall asleep and tomorrow will not ask me to begin where we left off.

It doesn't interest me to know where you live or how much money you have. I want to know if you can get up, after the night of grief and despair, weary and bruised to the bone and do what needs to be done to feed the children.

It doesn't interest me who you know or how you came to be here. I want to know if you will stand in the center of the fire with me and not shrink back.

It doesn't interest me where or what or with whom you have studied, I want to know what sustains you, from the inside, when all else falls away.

Back at Tenaya I washed in the snow-fed lake. A great sized crow circled over head and several times swooped down landing close to where I sat. It seemed to want me to follow it. Around a bend and across a rivulet the bird led me on. When I caught up to the bird it was standing on the beach. At its feet a crow feather, a gift from my beloved.

GUESTS AT A WEDDING

Eileen did her best to tie up loose ends before she died, but she couldn't stay around another ten months to officiate at Dana and Bernard's wedding. Dana was one of Eileen's students and had requested Eileen officiate at the ceremony. Now she was in a quandary about whom to ask to minister. I offered myself. My fee was a pound of salt water taffy.

The wedding is June 12th, which is my birthday and the twenty-fifth anniversary of the night I embraced Eileen outside The Wax Museum. I'm thrilled to celebrate it this way.

The couple were unsure how to move forward. Bernard is in awe of the beauty that has offered herself to him. She is on a spiritual quest and he is an engineer. Together they can build sacred space.

We began with structure. Where and when? How formal? Who will be in the processional? Will there be bridesmaids and ring bearers? Questions that have answers. Answers that give shape and make tangible the vision. I took notes. Then on to the as- yet unanswerable. What form shall the invocation take? Will there be readings?

They needed time to consider these. I loaned them books describing alternative wedding ceremonies. I gave them homework. "Read the books together. Talk about what inspires you. Have fun. Start privately writing your vows. Don't worry that your vows will not be identical. You are not identical people."

We will meet again in two weeks. They looked relieved as they prepared to leave. I looked up to Eileen. She was smiling.

They have chosen a resort overlooking the bay for the ceremony and reception. It is down the street from where Eileen and I made our first home. We once thought to purchase the resort and transform it into a spiritual center. What strand in the spider web's magic lures me there on June 12th?

I am going to wear the black pin stripe suit I purchased for Eden's wedding two years ago. Back then I was reluctant to spend a thousand dollars for a suit I intended to wear one time, but Eileen was adamant that I be dressed handsomely. I have lost thirty pounds since Eileen died and the suit drapes me well. I tried it on and thought I look like a minister.

At Dana's bidding, along with welcoming the guests, I will invite the spirits of grandparents, elders and especially Tofah Eileen to join in the celebration. I will also invoke the spirits of humor, kindness and love to cobble their dancing shoes, to embroider their bridal sheets and to canopy their home.

They have crafted a lustrous ceremony. Dana and Bernard will pour ten small cups of wine into a single goblet to honor each of the world's major religions. In the blessings of the rings, bride and groom will circle one another seven times, remembering the creation of the world, realizing in their circling the creation of the new world they are about to enter.

Dolphins arrived for the celebration as the groom's father was reading an Apache blessing:

"Now you will feel no rain, for each of you will be shelter to the other. Now you will feel no cold, for each of you will be warmth to the other. Now there is no more loneliness for you, for each of you will be companion to the other."

I signed the marriage certificate and walked quietly from the reception. I walked past the house where my life with Eileen began. I walked down the steep steps to the village, the steps leading to the village ice cream shoppe where we had shared one scoop cones. Out onto the wharf where fishermen mingled with the tourists. I turned around, returned to the party and tasted the wedding cake.

STUFF

"People don't own stuff. Stuff owns people. If you don't believe me, try throwing stuff away and see how hard it is to do."

— George Victor Stataskis

When people die, they leave behind one hundred percent of their stuff. With Eileen it was two hundred percent. It was not okay for her to die and leave me with all this, but she did it anyhow.

She left behind eight couches, five desks, six exterior doors stashed in the attic and enough dinnerware to run a small café. We had nineteen cartons filled with gift shop trinkets and seven milk crates filled with assorted bathroom tile which Eileen acquired for free. For sure there were at least a gazillion flower vases. The flower vases were not Eileen's fault. They were left here after the memorial service.

I returned the nineteen boxes of trinkets to their original owner. A friend was building a patio for a neighbor living on limited income and used the tiles in lieu of concrete. Whenever anyone visited, I insisted they leave with a flower vase. That left me with everything else.

I have a friend whose husband died a year before Eileen who cannot go into her garage because it is crammed with her husband's tools, toys and the kitchen sink. I have another friend who, three years after her husband died, boasts of finally making half of the house her own.

I understand this problem. I consider myself an expert on the subject. I have a Ph.D. in Deep Grief with a Major in Getting Rid of Stuff. I had always been a thoughtful giver of gifts and had faith I could ribbon whatever I offered in poetry and love.

I had a month to arrange the memorial service. I thought of Eileen's large family. Many of them were in pain and needed something they could touch. In the early days of our friendship I had written a poem to Eileen.

When fallen leaves
layer the earth,
and the clear winter sun

awakens the day,
let us then go walking.
We shall make
cotton candy cones
with our breath,
and I shall find a penny
in your deep coat pocket
where our fingers
intertwine.

I began a search of Eileen's clothing and found enough
pennies for everyone in the family. I placed copies of the poem,
the treasured pennies and a piece of Eileen's jewelry, selected with
each person in mind, into draw string, silk bags.

I kept the beaded barrette which was a gift I brought when I
visited Eileen in California twenty-one years ago. I held on to the
earrings and matching necklace I bought for her to wear to my
nephew's wedding. It was expensive and Eileen was delighted I
wanted to spend so much money on her.

I touched and caressed every pair of earrings, necklace, and
pendant. I had memories of almost all of them and my tears
crinkled the wrapping paper, as I sat and tagged each gift with
a person's name. Some of the tears reached my lips, they tasted
sweet and salty. Others dried on my cheeks and I enjoyed the way
they tighten the skin as they dried.

I have a different attitude toward tears than a lot of folks.
I think of them as holy. I don't hide them from sight. I don't
apologize for them. And I don't wipe them from my eyes. I figure
there are a lot of reasons to cry but for persons who are grieving
we mostly cry because we have loved someone and in certain
moments we are remembering that love more tenderly. Tears are
birthed from an open heart and in assembling the gifts my heart
was as big as Big Sur.

The house was in shambles and so was I. I decided I would spend time each day putting the house in order. The few dollars I might earn on Craigslist didn't interest me as much as a chance to entwine sacred and recycling. I set standards. Each day I reduced the amount of my material possessions by at least the size of a salt shaker. Most of the time I reduced by much, much more than a salt shaker, but regardless of how much I reduced one day, I did not accrue credit for future days.

Always seeking its highest good, its maximum benefit to others, I endeavored to find the right person to receive my gifts. If that didn't work, I'd give them to anyone whose hands were empty.

One of the members of a grief group I joined was having trouble sleeping. I gave her packets of Dead Sea Bath Salts to relax her body. Softball bats went to the Little League. The doors in the attic became part of a stage set for a theatrical production. I was given free tickets to the show, but I don't speak Tamil.

Christmas was approaching and it was said of me that I knew how to keep Christmas well. Nevertheless, I was done with the holiday. I gave the Christmas tree stand, lights and tinsel to a group organizing a garage sale to raise money for a gay, lesbian and transgender community center. The five- foot – blow-up Santa rested against a neighbor's chimney and the ornaments presented me with another opportunity to gift Eileen's family.

Our trees were adorned with angels, in cloth, ceramic, glass and wood. The collection included buxom opera divas with angel wings, piglets with angel wings, cats with wings and Andean pan flouters with wings. There were so many wings on our tree, I expected it to fly.

I mailed three dozen ornaments to Eileen's immediate and extended family. I set out the remaining ornaments and invited everyone entering the house to take home a memento. When someone couldn't decide which of two ornaments they preferred, I urged them to take both. I did keep the Santa Claus costume because I never know when a good disguise will come in handy.

Eileen was the ultimate party girl. Twice a week, minimum, for ten years, she held gatherings here at The Garden. I had the evidence to prove it. Two entire kitchen shelves were piled high with napkins, paper plates in every size and shape and mountains of plastic forks, spoons and knives. By the way, there is hardly any use for plastic knives. Don't buy any more of them. If we all agree to stop buying plastic knives and share the ones we have, there are sufficient plastic knives to last a millennium.

A neighbor knocked on the door and asked if I would give her a tour of The Garden because she was looking to hold a fund raiser.

In February the coastal villages of Chile were devastated by an earthquake as well as a tsunami triggered by an 8.8 magnitude shake. The small Chilean community living in the San Francisco Bay area intended to build five communal kitchens for a village that was destroyed. Each kitchen cost three thousand dollars.

This fund raiser would be the first party held at The Garden since the memorial. The first one I would be solely responsible for ensuring things went smoothly. There would be folkloric dancers in Chilean dress, a violin concert and a prepared dinner. I tried remembering how much we charged for day long affairs that included use of the kitchen. I couldn't recall and it didn't really matter because I knew I wasn't going to charge them. The only thing they had to promise was that they would use my napkins, paper plates and plastic forks.

The party was a huge success but there were still way too many picnic supplies. I initiated guerrilla gifting. Guerrilla gifting is when it's done without notice and can't be traced back to its source. On Wednesday mornings I unlocked the shul and made small surreptitious weekly contributions to the supply closet. It was like manna from heaven. No matter how many paper plates they used, there were always more next time.

When doing guerrilla gifting, it can be strategically important to gift-wrap stuff. I managed to distribute five years' worth of Bon Appetite magazines by bundling them in Christmas wrap and leaving them on the doorsteps of unsuspecting friends.

Sometimes it was fortuitous. My neighbor wanted to build a chicken coop. I had a stack of 4x4s and 2x12s hidden behind a shed since the remodeling ten years ago.

Sometimes it was so clearly meant to be passed along. In the attic were our camping gear, sleeping bags and sleeping mats. Eileen would never again use the equipment but how could I give them away? To whom would I give the pad my wife had lain upon?

As I was preparing to drive home from Yosemite after spreading Eileen's ashes, I stopped for two hitch-hikers. It's something I never do. They were twenty year old kids from England on their way to a music festival north of San Francisco. He was a musician and she danced with a hula hoop. They were a disheveled duo without a road map. I offered to give them a ride to Santa Cruz which would be the most feasible route to hitch hike up the coast the next day.

The girl got in beside me. It's a six hour drive and we talked the whole way home. Kathleen told me how they had begun in Mexico, were coming from Burning Man, took acid in Yosemite and might possibly hitch cross country to Vermont. She wasn't sure about Vermont. Her mother's family came from the mountains there, but Mom had married an Englishman and moved across the sea. Kathleen's mom died not so long before Eileen and the American side of the family had turned their back on this sweet child. She told me she hadn't told anyone of her pain until just now and didn't know why she was telling me.

After dinner we looked at their gear. They were going into wet, cold country and they were ill prepared. I gave them fifty dollars to buy parkas and then I noticed. They didn't have sleeping mats and Eileen's wind breaker fit Kathleen perfectly.

Sometimes I simply had to strike when the iron was hot. I was at a Christmas gathering and a guy complimented my slightly off-color tie. I whipped that tie off so fast, you'd think I spent years working as a pole dancer.

When measuring cubic inches lost its luster, I began to weigh the stuff leaving the house. I gave away fourteen pounds of stainless cutlery, two pounds of jigsaw puzzles, nine pounds of Christmas lights and six ounces of an outdated bottle of tumeric.

There were lessons learned. When I couldn't match someone up with what was leaving, I put a pile of it in front of the house on Sunday mornings to lure passersby. I have very good success with this reuse method. In nice weather, I occasionally pulled out a lawn chair, and waited to see what happened to the stuff.

One morning I placed five tennis rackets on the street. I haven't played tennis in twenty years and one of the rackets was possibly my father's who hadn't played in thirty years. I thought about the four Rs. Reminisce, to recall fondly, however falsely, a past that included playing tennis. Skip to Regret: to rue that I no longer play tennis. Short hop now to Remorse: to be pained that I am no longer truly capable of playing tennis and on to the last stop, Regression: to feel like I am less a person because I no longer play tennis. And all I could think about was, "I'm getting five tennis rackets lighter."

Ten minutes later a friend stopped by to visit. I offered her a beach chair and told her I had been watching the tennis rackets. I asked her what she saw. She told me she had been a tennis star as a young girl and she is still holding on to her tennis rackets with reminiscence and regret. We talked a lot that day about tennis rackets. Gurus each and every one of them.

Photographs, the old kind, are the delicate lace worn by memories. I separated them into three stacks. The first pile was the ones of Eileen and me. I kept these. The second pile was photographs of Eileen among her family and friends. I distributed these. The third pile, the largest pile, was of mysterious landscapes and smiling strangers. These became my get- rid- of- today pile.

The most dangerous stuff in the house was paper. Eight and a half by eleven, twenty pound vellum, what could be so dangerous? It's the words. I never know what I will find in the stacks of paper. I sigh with relief when it's a grocery list. I cringe and sometimes crumble when it's a medical report. And I take the hit when it's a picture postcard of The Lake Country where years before Tofah and I sat on a pier as swans swam back and forth beneath our feet. You have to be brave to touch paper and I have no advice to offer. It sucks.

It took courage to sort through paper, but it took my breath away to open Eileen's clothing closet. Inside, there were dozens of long flowing robes she wore in ceremonies, velvet skirts and lacy blouses she wore to go dancing and a parasol for our Easter Sunday parade up the avenue. The closet held the garb of a Goddess devotee and the clearest memories of my beloved. The wedding dress she sewed by hand, the red cowboy boots she wore to receive her Masters Degree, the shawl she wore as she stood before the shrine to Mahatma Gandhi, all competed for room in the closet with the down parka she wore in Nepal, the sleek black gown she wore to the opera and the tennis shoes caked with flakes of paint. I couldn't donate these to Goodwill and I couldn't keep them forever. I waited thirteen months, until *Sukkot*.

The *sukkah* is smaller than the ones we built in the past but there is enough room for The Dakini Band to sit in it and perform while the guests pass through and into the gazebo which will be filled with a give- away of Eileen's dresses, blouses, pocketbooks, combs, shawls and jewelry. For the men who join us, I'll also put out her drums, violin, rattles, paints, two games of Scrabble, table cloths, opera glasses, books and... flower vases.

On Saturday evening I lit the gazebo and *sukkah* with fairy lights and we were suddenly transported to the desert. At the back, the band played *zhikr* while fifty women moved gracefully through the improvised Arabian *Suk*, fingers outstretched for a last moment to touch Eileen, to breathe in her fragrance. Someone would hold up a flowing gown and others would sigh or recall when she wore that dress. And then a person would take the dress and drape it on a woman and say, "It would look so good on you," and other women would echo the thought. And finally the dress was chosen. The Dakini Band played *zhikr*. It was Christmas in the desert.

At 2:30 in the morning, I said good night to Brother Owen and family. I walked them to the car and stopped to look in the gazebo. It was nearly empty. A couple of blouses remained. In my bedroom closet still hung Eileen's red coat with the deep pockets where I once found a penny when our fingers intertwined.

INITIATIONS

I completed my tax return. Lots of average citizens ask for extensions and the widows I've talked to say they have an especially difficult time simply paying monthly bills much less filling out a 1040. But I am committed to walk through this fire and wanted to get my taxes in before the deadline.

Every piece of paper was a stick of burning wood placed on the pyre of our marriage. I touched and retouched every sheet. I recorded each bill, placed a grain of sand in the mandala of love and filed away the memory. Every cancelled check had a story to tell and too many of them told of hospitals. It took forty hours to complete.

Ultimately this leaves me dancing on an edge. There's nothing more I want to accomplish and nothing more I want to be. It feels dangerous.

This morning, Rabia initiated me into Sufi Movement. She meditated on my Sufi name throughout the week seeking a transmission. Before the initiation I shared how little interest I have in living. She said the person who isn't afraid of death has the power to speak the truth. She named me Shamshir. It is a variation on an Arabic word meaning a curved sword.

I told my grief therapist, who is a practicing Buddhist, about my initiation and she thought Shamshir shared qualities with Manjurshree. Manjurshree is a male Bodhisattva wielding a flaming sword in his right hand representing the realization of transcendent wisdom which cuts down ignorance and duality.

I had to have a statue of *Manjurshree*. I attended a *puja* at Land of Medicine Buddha where prayers were being offered for the soul of Eileen. Afterward I visited the gift shop. I took home a hand-painted, gold-plated, four-hundred-dollar statue. Me, who has never before purchased an icon.

I put the statue on a make shift altar. *Manjurshree* glared at me. I placed a crystal in front of it. It continued to frown. I draped a *khata*, the Buddhist prayer shawl, around its base. No change. I tried to engage the statue in conversation. Nothing doing. I placed a small container of Eileen's ashes next to the statue and I heard a still small voice say, "Thank you."

For my birthday I was gifted with an hour of crystal light therapy. Each quartz crystal centers above a different chakra. This instrument was received from John of God in Brazil.

The stones came and spoke. "Your separation from your beloved feels long to you but you will be reunited. To our thinking you are two sand pebbles on the beach, made distant by the last receding wave, soul mates who will be brought back together with the next incoming rush of water. Have faith. It's only an instant away. Jay, try to remember your clanship with the stones. Find your strength. Don't be afraid."

Out of the blackness of the stones emerged ferocious tigers. The white Bengal tiger we had seen at a Florida zoo led the pack. He spoke to me. "You are not being offered clanship. But I felt compassion in your lover's heart when she saw me in captivity and so for a time the tigers will walk alongside you and teach you fearlessness."

We were drinking hot chocolate at a sidewalk café when the shaman said: "I am getting chills up my spine because I suddenly got that one of the reasons I came to Santa Cruz to teach this weekend was to help you."

With a ring of dark Brazilian chocolate around my lips I answered, "I went to the retreat because I was told by spirit to find you."

We sat in the gazebo. I held the last smudge stick Eileen had used for ceremony. A pair of candles from the holy city of Sfat, in the northern Galillee, lit the space.

"Chanting can help, but only if you have done the work. It can't do the work for you. This chant has the power to take you to an open doorway. From there you can glimpse a place beyond this pain. The chant won't shove you out the door, but maybe, just maybe, it might give you a small nudge in that direction. Let's begin."

For twenty minutes we chanted in Hebrew: "Go thru The Gates. Clear the way of the people." It felt like balm.

I described the weight I carried on my back, the weight of Eileen's memory. Again she reminded me that chanting can't resolve the feelings, but if I could give those memories to G-d, I wouldn't forever be looking behind me for Eileen. Was I ready?

We chanted: "My beloved, my hidden treasure. I give you to G-d." I felt Eileen leaving me. I burned to call out: "Please. I am so scared of losing you." And Eileen came to me and said: "Don't fear. Feel me on the wind. I am yours forever."

I showed Hawk the crow feather and the body of the blue jay I found in Yosemite. I asked his take on them.

"The crow is a trickster and easily distracted. A candy wrapper will draw his attention. He will take you where you need to go, but it will be a very round- about journey. The feather is here to warn you not to be distracted from your way."

"And the blue jay?"

"The blue jay is the town crier, the woodland sentry. He sees everything and talks a lot. When the bird sees something out of the ordinary, he shares it with every living creature in his vicinity. When danger enters the forest, it's the blue jay that calls out a warning. I think, taken everything together, this means you were given an initiation."

"You think I'm an American Indian Medicine Man?"

"No, you're still a kid from the Bronx, but you're being told to speak."

Much of what I believed or was taught has turned out untrue. I ask questions journalism students are taught to pose: who, what, when, why and how.

"Who" is whomever. It could be you, the neighbor down the street or a child born on the streets of Bangladesh. None of us choose

our role in the script. We can look for reasons why this person has brain cancer and not the one sitting alongside, but all the explanations in the world never add up.

"What" is whatever. It's a perfectly sunny day and a thunder storm erupts or you think your partner will live forever and then she dies. We simply don't control what happens in our lives.

"When" is always right now because nothing else exists but right now. One hundred percent of what we remember is a delusion. It never happened the way we remember it. Since the future doesn't even exist, one hundred percent of the future is an illusion. Yet the more time we hang out in the delusion and illusion, the more it influences the present moment.

"Why" is the joker in the deck. We can ask "why" until we are blue in the face and we will never get an answer. Take your pick. It's part of a bigger plan, chaos theory, karma or luck of the draw. We'll never know why.

That leaves only one question: "How." How do I want to be with whomever and whatever is happening right now? I'm pretty clear that the only thing I have control over in life is how I respond to it. I see that life is a lesson in impermanence. I am humbled by my inability to choreograph this grand ballet. I don't choose its rhythm or its song. But at least to some extent, I get to choose how I want to dance.

I've learned grief is spoken in a language without words and solace can be found in stillness. I get that there is no comfort drawn from even the best intentioned advice nor is there a better prescription for the bereaved than a strawberry cheese Danish brought by a friend who can sit with us without chatter, not shying from the pain, not rushing to dry our tears.

Finally – I learned it's okay to wobble.

EPILOGUE

An Excerpt from the Memorial Service

The week before Tofah crossed, I was by her side one night and in a vision saw her and *Padmasambhava* sitting on lawn chairs on a valley floor having a conversation. When he noticed me he turned to Tofah and asked who I was. She said I was her good friend and he gave me permission to watch and listen but to be quiet. Then he turned to Tofah and suggested they merge.

Tofah said, "*Padmasambhava*, I so want to merge with you, but I have this problem. I'm also in love with Jesus."

Padmasambhava said, "No problem." Jesus appeared and merged with Padma. Again, *Padmasambhava* asked Tofah to merge with him. And she said, "I so want to merge with you, but I have a problem?"

"What's the problem?"

"I am so in love with the *Shekinah*.

"No problem," he said. The *Shekinah* appeared and merged.

And so on and so on. Finally when all the great beings, guides, prophets and saints had all merged, *Padmasambhava* asked Tofah to merge and she said, "Yes. Now I'm ready."

An Obituary

Dear Friends,

My wife, Tofah Eileen, was once your Homecoming Queen. She crossed into the arms of the Beloved on August 15th at 11:53 a.m. I thought you'd like to know how proud you can be of one of your Queens.

Throughout her life, her reverence for the Divine, which began at your local church, blossomed like a most magnificent red rose. She led monthly Circle of Stones gatherings for women. She became a marriage and family therapist. She was a nationally recognized, nurturing spiritual guide in the Sufi movement. She built a beautiful Sufi Center and led the Dances of Universal Peace throughout the Bay Area.

She was diagnosed with brain cancer at the beginning of June. She refused to undergo a brain biopsy or chemo-therapy, preferring to spend her time in prayer and alternative healing modalities.

Lamas came to play flute at the side of her wheelchair. Rabbis gathered in circle to chant the Islamic Rose Zhikr that Eileen had written. Holy men and holy women were at her side. There were times when literally around the world, Sufis, Catholics, Jews, Buddhists, Hindus, Sikhs, Native Americans, Goddess Worshippers and an entire village in the jungles of Mexico were simultaneously offering prayers for her healing.

Her journey did not include a lot of pain and her passing was a graceful expression of departure. She exhaled and she was gone. As words became more difficult to speak, she chose more carefully. Among the last sentences that she spoke was this: "Don't be afraid to linger with the sublime."

Sincerely,

Jai Lev

About the Author

Jai Lev's first literary attempt, in seventh grade, promptly resulted in his suspension from school for a week. Having assessed the freedom from schoolwork as a result of his writing, Jai Lev embarked on a life long literary career.

He is the author of two books of children's literature, Tales for a Child's Heart and Dreams of Cloud Dancing. Tales was voted the best book read by a third grade class in a Los Angeles school district and Jai Lev was the guest of honor when the students performed the story.

He has been a newspaper columnist for several weeklies and was the guest editor of the Santa Cruz Sentinel for many years.

The Underwood his father used to type countless "letters to the editor" sits on Jai Lev's desk as a reminder that words can take us to the mountain top.

To order signed copies of

A Santa Cruz Love Story

or for a free download of

A Song Journey Through Grief

~ a 23 minute musical odyssey composed during
the eighteen months that followed Tofah's crossing,
contact:

Sunrise Publications

www.jailev.com
3070 Prather Lane
Santa Cruz, CA 95065

www.ingramcontent.com/pod-product-compliance
Lightning Source LLC
Chambersburg PA
CBHW020758250626
47155CB00003B/1137